SLEEPING AROUND

SLEEPING AROUND

Morgan Vega

This is a work of fiction.

Names, characters, places, and incidents either are the product of the author's imagination or are used fictitiously. Any resemblance to actual persons, living or dead, events, or locales is entirely coincidental.

First edition August 2021

Cover art by Morgan Vega

ISBN 978-1-7370595-0-9 (paperback)
ISBN 978-1-7370595-1-6 (hardback)
ISBN 978-1-7370595-2-3 (ebook)
ASIN B0974W6BJF (ebook)

Published by Tearstain Books
www.tearstainbooks.com

Content Warnings

Includes underage drinking; very brief mentions—not depictions—of infertility and police brutality; and lots of sexual innuendos.

Susan and Allison.

I've never been good at making friends. Luckily, I don't need to be.
I already have the best of friends (and bandmates)—my sisters.

And Mom, my first and forever music teacher.
For the violin lessons, at-home practice, and piano accompaniment.
I hope your ears have recovered, though you never once called my
scratchy attempts noise.

Movement One

movement = "principal division or section of a
composition"

Nine months isn't long enough to form an attachment to four walls. I stand in the doorway of my soon-to-be ex-room, the room that saved me from aging out into the streets, yet I'm as bare as my sheetless bed and empty desk.

This room will save a new system kid now. Another room waits for me in Harmony Hall.

A tingle slides down my arms, like when I play Violin for over three hours straight.

I'm almost out.

I grab my packed trash bag—stuffed with minimal clothes, generic-brand toiletries, and faded lavender bedding—pick up Violin, and shut the door. The bag thuds down the stairs behind me, sounding the alarm of my nearing departure.

The other Borns College freshmen must have suitcases and

storage tubs filled with high thread count sheets, cotton-microfiber towels, saxony plush rugs, and other college must-buys from Target I couldn't afford. My college shopping list consisted of five items, in order of importance: a jumbo box of tampons, a value pack of toothbrushes, a five-subject notebook, and the cheapest ballpoint pens I could find. Most of my spending money went to the tampons. No surprise.

My savings went to Violin and not a laptop for school. Reasoning: students can check out laptops from the library, and multiple academic buildings have computer labs. Plus, I have a smartphone. People write manuscripts and screenplays and business proposals on their phones, so I can manage some ten-page papers on mine.

Music majors prioritize their instruments.

Though I bought my Model 400 D Z Strad Violin at a legit music store in town as an early graduation present, I couldn't afford its case—the one with the purple velvet lining that snuggled my violin. Violin cost $1,250, warranty and case not included. My stack of one-, five-, and ten-dollar bills—which I'd saved since I was eleven—dwindled to $85 the second the cash register dinged. My saving grace, the bulky case I found at a pawnshop, has matted gray faux fur and is covered in scratches—a few of which I hid with a giant "wtf" sticker. Violin swims in the extra space. But I could afford it and, hey, it's better than no case at all.

At the bottom of the stairs, I dump the trash bag at the front door and place Violin beside it.

Violin: *No way you're leaving me out here.*

Don't you trust me? I wouldn't dare.

I bought Violin, as opposed to the other fancy violins in the store, for two reasons. Reason #1: It played smoother than the others and smoother than my past rented violins. Reason #2: It spoke to me—and not as in a cliché. As in, its thoughts were—*are* —my thoughts. As in, it's a part of me.

Did it freak me out at first? Of course.

Would I trade Violin for the world? Absolutely not.

Have I told another human this? Hell no.

Violin's my family now. My *only* family. Having its voice— my voice?—comforts me on the hard days. Days like today, when my life is upturning yet again, though for the best of reasons.

I open the entryway closet to a pile of shoes. Some belong to feet that left them behind on their way to permanent homes. The owner of the princess light-up shoes left three months ago.

Part of me wonders why my fosters, Tom and Kathryn Wells, hold on to all these forgotten shoes. The other part of me figures they don't have time to donate them. They're busy enough as it is with their jobs. Tom's Store Manager at Barnes & Noble, and Kathryn's the Director of Corporate Giving at a nonprofit women's clinic downtown. Keeping up with me and the other foster kids is a full-time job in itself. Or maybe they keep the shoes because of their revolving door of foster kids, hoping they find new wearers one day.

I toss the shoes into the pile by the door to make room for my trash bag and Violin in the closet. Can't be too careful in a house full of system kids.

Better?

Violin: *You're so good to me.*

True. But you're better to me.

On my way through the living room to the kitchen, I step onto quick pain.

"Dammit."

A plastic T-Rex roars as if injured on the carpet. I grip my bare foot, and once the sting subsides, I kick the dinosaur toward the bin full of chipped plastic toys. The other foster kids never pick up their shit. They never take out the trash either—the stench of trash reaches my nose before I reach the kitchen.

Without referring to directions on the pancake mix box, I run through my mental list of ingredients and gather the goods on the peninsula.

First and foremost: maple syrup? (No point making pancakes if we don't have syrup.) *Check.*

Milk? *Check.*

Eggs and lots of butter? *Check, check.*

Vanilla extract? *Check.*

Baking spice? *Check.*

Mixing bowl and spoon? *Check and check.*

One of the other foster kids, Steven, shuffles to a stool in baggy pajamas as I stir the milk lake into the dry mixture. He crosses his scrawny arms and rests his head on the laminate countertop. His usual pale cheeks have a touch of pink from playing outside yesterday.

"Who's gonna make Saturday pancakes now?"

No wonder he wakes up at the first clinks and clanks of pans from the kitchen. He started his last year of middle school a week ago, but he looks like he started his first on account of his thin frame. He's still catching up from the pre-foster-care months he went without much food. Plus, the boy burns through calories from unabashed yearning for his mom. What he does eat and doesn't hoard, that is.

Sloppy batter sizzles. I shrug. We both know Kathryn won't carry on my tradition.

"My mom will when they let me go back." His expecting sunken eyes zero in on me for consolation, as I flip the golden-brown pancake onto its goopy side.

What I think: *Well, she can't buy pancake mix without a job, and she can't make pancakes without a kitchen.*

What I say: "You'll be together again. She'll get back on her feet." Which is sure as hell not happening soon.

Steven closes his eyes, and I flip another pancake on the griddle. The sweet, buttery stack soon grows to tower above his head. His shoulders twitch with a quick snore, and a dribble of drool lands on his hand. As I turn off the heat, the front door opens and bangs shut, and he bolts upright.

The shrine of shoes I built to past foster kid's feet clunk, clunk, clunk collapses into the entryway.

Kathryn, back from her daily morning run, huffs as she fills a glass at the sink. Sweat drips down her forehead and dampens her shirt, leaving dark horizontal lines across her stomach and shadows beneath her armpits. Her drenched blonde hair looks as if she stepped out of the shower, but the smell of her BO tells me otherwise.

She doesn't mention the shoes.

Both Kathryn and Tom are more oblivious than parental: Kathryn's spandex tank tops constrict her indifferent heart, and Tom's books get more face time than us foster kids. As far as foster houses go, though, theirs isn't a horrible place to come back to for college-recognized holidays and summer vacation. Perks of extended foster care.

Kathryn gulps down the last of the water. "I meant to make breakfast for you, Coralee." Her voice lacks emotion either from her ten-plus-mile run or insincerity. Maybe both.

"No worries. Can't skip my breakfast routine on my last Saturday here." Steven's shoulders straighten with pancake panic, so I add, "For a while."

He slumps back onto the counter, slightly more relaxed. I roll my eyes and bring the syrup and plates to the table. Without warning, my chest tightens.

Maybe it's not just the pancakes he'll miss when I'm gone. Maybe he'll miss me.

A gruff voice yells, "Shit!" from the living room, as the dinosaur roars again.

Guess I didn't kick that damned toy as far as I thought. And I guess I need to lecture the younger kids about not cursing again. I've given the same lecture to countless foster kids:

> Me: "We don't have the luxury of cursing. We don't have the luxury of messing up, being human. So, stop!" *claps hands for emphasis*
>
> Them: *bottom lips quiver* "That's way harsh, don't you think?"
>
> Me: "I'm not harsh, the system is harsh! Foster parents can get rid of you for a lot less than cursing. And I've learned the hard way so you won't have to."
>
> Them: *eyes well up with tears*
>
> Me: "And you better not forget."
>
> Them: *nod through sobs*
>
> Me: "Good. I'm going to go make us pancakes now." *pat them on head*

I cringe as Kathryn shouts, "Zeke, language!" but she heads upstairs without further comment for a much-needed shower. She and Tom haven't kicked out any foster kids—or not that I know of.

Zeke Gamble, the oldest besides me, slumps onto a stool next to Steven with a notebook tucked to his side. He carries it everywhere, constantly scribbling, but slams it shut whenever anyone's eyes drift its way.

With his deep voice, strong jawline, and now acne-free brown skin, Zeke looks like the star high school senior. Except he won't win homecoming king anytime soon, on account of his reserved—indignant, even—demeanor and multiple detentions. He doesn't seem to have friends either. On the weekends, he locks himself in his room and won't resurface till Monday morning.

Aside from Saturday pancakes, of course.

I like Zeke, though I don't know basic information about him. Not his favorite color or his subject in school, his hobbies, or why he's in foster care.

Foster Kid Rule #1
Don't ask other kids why they're in foster care.

Teachers ask. Classmates ask. Strangers ask. They ask because they don't know the pain in answering. The conversations go like this:

Them: "Why are you in foster care?" *lean close like about to hear a secret*

Me: "Um, my parents didn't want me. Or couldn't take

me. I wouldn't know. I've never met or talked to them. But thanks for the reminder."

Them: *stare with a blank expression*

Only Tom and Kathryn know Zeke's story. Because of Foster Kid Rule #1, I don't ask. His story isn't my business.

Steven, however, made his story my business the day we met, the day I arrived at the Wells' house. I had yet to set down my trash bag before he waltzed inside my new room with an unopened Juicy Juice.

"My mom got laid off, and we lost our house. One of our neighbors reported her. Found out we were living on the street. Here." He handed me the juice box. "This one's fruit punch. My favorite's kiwi strawberry," which he then pulled out of his back pocket and stuck in a straw. "I'm Steven Hart, by the way."

"Coralee Reed." I followed his example and took a sip.

Fruit punch wasn't my favorite either.

I gulped the drink until splutters remained, then offered, "Lifelong system kid."

He didn't respond. The only evidence he heard me was his arms hugging his sides. On the way out, though, he looked over his shoulder with a grin that didn't carry a trace of pity. No one had smiled at me like that in a long time.

Another juice box poked out of his pocket.

Since then, my mission remains to make him smile as often as possible. The easiest way is with food, hence our Saturday pancake tradition.

I carry the pancakes to the long kitchen table, followed by Zeke and Steven, who both find seats nearest to the plate. Tom already sits at the head of the table reading a romance novel with

Camila Garcia, the youngest of us fosters, in her rainbow-heart-patterned pajamas on his lap.

She has tiny feet for being eleven years old. They'd fit in those light-up shoes.

Our entire neighborhood knows Camila's story. Her stepdad got busted for dealing, and the system split up her and her little sister Nicole until after the trail, after their mom can prove a stable home environment. Tom and Kathryn take her for her sibling visit every month, but a month is a long time to be separated from her six-year-old sister. Camila runs away to find Nicole on the other side of town every other month on average, so neighbors on our block stand on 24/7 lookout duty. It takes a village, or in this case, a subdivision. Her sense of direction always impresses me—she's almost reached Nicole's foster house a couple times.

Tom likes for us all to be at the table before we start eating, but the smell of butter and maple proves too strong. We snatch the pancakes, but I save the last two for Kathryn. When she does join us—this time without her sweat—she ruins them by forgoing the maple syrup and spreading organic almond butter on them instead.

Before she takes her first nutty bite, Kathryn says, "The whole band wanted to give you a little something, Coralee." She winks at me and slides an envelope across the table.

Steam from my pancakes warms my face. I tuck the envelop on my lap to open it with a smidgen more privacy and pull out a purple construction paper card with Tom's all-caps handwriting on the front:

WE'LL MISS YOU

Not only did they remember my favorite color, but they wrote notes—even Zeke—and Tom and Kathryn stuffed three hundred dollars inside. I shove the money into my duct tape wallet (Steven made it for me in a Home-Ec class) before they change their minds, but also to distract from the building pressure behind my eyes.

Moments like this, when they do more than what the system demands, my heart begs to give Tom and Kathryn more credit. After all, thanks to them, I'm going to Borns College.

When they found out their new foster kid played the violin, they bought tickets to the Borns String Orchestra's winter concert. I'd been at their house for a week. Tom brought me early to look around campus, a fifteen-minute drive from their house. We could walk from one end of campus to the other in under ten minutes; people held doors open for us to each building we managed to peek inside; and when the auditorium dimmed, the audience fell silent, the director raised his arms, the first-chair violinist raised her violin to her shoulder, and her bow raced across her strings in the most precise yet ethereal solo I've heard performed live.

She played without fault. She demanded attention with each perfect note.

The applause rings in my head nine months later.

"Aren't you gonna read it?" Steven squirms in his chair, unable to contain himself any longer.

What I think: *Not with you staring.*

What I say: "I'll read it when I need it. Like if I'm super nervous before a test or audition or something."

I turn to Tom and Kathryn. "Thank you both. That was really generous."

"Of course." Tom sniffles before dabbing syrup off of

Camila's face with a cloth napkin. She doesn't stop eating, though, and more syrup drips to her chin to replace the last. "You deserve it."

"This and more," Kathryn says. "And you don't have to wait to read the card. You know you can call us, no matter what or what time is. We'll be there."

"I know."

I tuck the card back inside the envelope to avoid her eyes.

Movement Two

bridge = "the part of the stringed instrument that supports the strings"

Momentous events deserve music. The clinks of forks and Tom's abating sniffles compose my atonal going-away song. (Is he teary over me leaving for college or over his book? He never stops crying over a book.)

The "band," as Kathryn likes to refer to our makeshift family-not-family, demolishes the pancakes. As I shove my last bite in my mouth, the doorbell rings.

"Shoot," Kathryn says.

She gulps the rest of her water—to wash down that gritty almond butter?—and shuffles to the door. Her knees don't bend much. Must've been a long-distance run day.

The front door sighs open. I fiddle with the corner of the envelope, and Steven chews in slow motion like he's trying to savor the end of his pancake.

"Come in, come in." A forced strain. "Watch out for the shoes, Drew."

Drew, my most recent caseworker, follows Kathryn to the table. "I hope this is still okay." She smooths her strawberry brown chin-length hair before her toothy beam fixates on me.

"Of course." Kathryn stands behind Tom and gives his shoulders a squeeze.

His eyes lift from his book, and he reenters reality. "Oh, hi, Drew. When did you get here?"

Drew and Kathryn exchange a smirk.

"What's the story about today?" Drew asks.

"You'd love this one." Tom twists in his chair to face her. "Two competing bookstore owners. One moved back to their hometown from the city. The other never left. They graduated high school together, where their rivalry started over an essay contest, and now they're picking up their banter where they left off. I just got to the scene where the power goes out in their zone because of a squirrel on an electric line and—"

"Alright, Tom." Kathryn squeezes his shoulders again. "I'm sure Drew came here for Coralee and not a book recommendation."

"Right. Sorry."

Drew leans over with a conspiratorial grin. "Text me the title," she whispers, before addressing me with her cheerful professional voice. "I can't believe you're moving to college today, Coralee! So exciting. I wanted to see you off and go over your case plan again."

"Sure."

Kathryn and Tom get everyone in gear. They excuse Camila, who skips off for the toy bin. Zeke retreats to his room after stacking the plates, and Steven carries the dishes to the sink. Camila's already playing with that damned dinosaur when I follow Drew into the living room.

Drew sits on the floral loveseat, and I sit opposite her on the dated checker-print couch. Tom and Kathryn rush to sit on either side of me. The couch dips toward the middle.

Tom's been mentioning upgrading their furniture since I got to their house, but Kathryn always says, "There are other things we could spend that money on." She eyes me or one of the other fosters when she says it. I half want to tell her to buy a new couch—we're all suffering with these eyesores.

Drew wiggles her shoulders into a perfect posture and clears her throat. "As you know, Coralee, to remain on extended fo—"

The dinosaur roars. Camila roars along with it.

"To remain on extended foster care and keep your scholarship," Drew continues when the roars die down, "you have to stay in school full-time. You need good grades. You've rocked your last year of high school, despite everything, but college is different. I know I've said it before, but it is."

I nod. "Got it."

What I think: *Doubt it.*

I made A's and B's (and a few C's here and there) throughout high school, despite uprooting to new foster houses and schools again and again. College should be easier—not harder—since I'm not changing foster houses, I'm not changing colleges, I'll know my professors, and I'll follow a set curriculum. No more showing up to classes mid-semester, months behind everyone else.

I mean, has she read my file? College promises more permanency than I've had the past eighteen years.

Still, without decent grades in college, I could lose my scholarship. Become another foster kid statistic, another foster kid that didn't graduate. Lots of us don't graduate from high school or go to college.

Drew wants me to prove the statistic wrong.

"Next order of business. You can come back on the weekends and during breaks from school—"

"Or whenever you want," Kathryn adds.

"Yes," Drew continues, "but it's not guaranteed that you'll have your old room. Another foster child might live here."

Tom leans forward on the couch, and his novel slides forgotten on his lap. "I thought, legally, Coralee needs to have a room with a door."

Since when is Tom concerned with my legal rights?

Drew clasps her hands on top of her black pencil skirt that contrasts with her fair skin. She lifts her chin like we're in a boardroom. I wouldn't blink twice if she had a presentation prepared. "For foster children, yes, but Coralee's on extended foster care. A lot of regulations no longer apply. Or have altered. Plus—"

The dinosaur and Camila roar again.

"Plus, we—"

And another round of roars.

Camila bares her teeth and parades the roaring dinosaur across the coffee table. We bust out laughing, Camila pouts, and she runs off with the dinosaur to her room.

At least no one will trip over it now.

"Plus," the corners of Drew's matte coral lips tremble with a tampered smile, "we now consider Borns College her permanent address."

Tom's bearded face drops, and he thumbs a corner of his book's pages. "Will you check on her while she's at school?" His low voice carries disappointment, as if—I must be wrong—he wishes their house would remain my address.

Despite Borns College being a short drive, I'm living on campus rather than commuting. The system kicked me around like a hacky sack, but now I can kick myself out before my fosters can. The less Tom and Kathryn bother with me, the greater the chance I have of staying with them until I graduate and turn twenty-one. Extended foster care still requires foster parents, much to my disappointment.

"I'll call," Drew says, "but I'll only visit from time to time when she comes back here for breaks. Unfortunately, I won't be visiting her while she's at Borns."

Thank god.

Drew can't visit me at college. If she ever rings Harmony Hall's doorbell, I swear I'll lie to my housemates that she's the niece of the ex-wife of my distant cousin. Through marriage. Twice removed. Whatever.

The chains of foster care, Drew included, won't fit in my trash bag—despite being a jumbo, extra thick contractor trash bag that Tom and Kathryn buy on account of having a messy household full of fosters.

After I'm dismissed (so the adults can talk about me without me), I tackle the stack of sticky plates from breakfast. The dried syrup requires extra soap, and I pour more than enough on the deteriorating sponge. I wash and rinse, and Steven shows up to dry and put away.

We've perfected our Saturday routine.

I'm ready for a new one.

♪♫

Later, after Drew leaves and I take out the trash, I find Tom in his reading closet. A stack of romcom, how-to-write, and Barnes & Noble employee-loaned romance books wait for him to read next on an installed plywood board that serves as a desk.

Tom had an office: my ex-room. Maybe he can have it back, unless he gets landed with another kid. Don't get me wrong, every foster kid should have a placement like Tom and Kathryn's house. But if I deserve three hundred dollars, he deserves a re-upgrade that's less chaotic than a hallway closet of a foster house.

"You ready?"

He turns a page, more invested in some bodice-ripping scene than toting me off to Borns. I clear my throat to no response. I knock on the wall until his faraway eyes meet mine.

"Ready?"

He nods and places a grocery receipt from Food Lion between the pages as a bookmark.

"I'm gonna say bye to the kids real fast. Meet you at the car."

Tom says, "Take your time," and a slight tremolo wobbles his tenor voice.

As I head upstairs, Steven finds me on his way from the kitchen to his room with a granola bar and orange juice bottle in hand. More snacks stockpile in his pockets.

Kathryn and Tom should check under his bed again.

Steven squeezes me around the waist, and my arms envelop his slight frame in return. "Come back soon."

"To make you pancakes?" I half-tease.

He peers up without a hint of a smile, not needing to respond.

At the top of the steps, Steven disappears into his room. Zeke has his door shut, so I yell goodbye rather than knock. My stomach flips at his muffled, "Yeah, good luck."

Oh god, do I need luck?

I breathe in on a count of four and out for a count of eight. *No, I need Harmony Hall.*

Living on campus with other music majors is a blank sheet of music. I compose these next four years, and this semester starts with no foster care reverb.

"Camila?" I push open her door with steadier hands.

The room seems empty.

"Little fish?"

She's not on her bed or at her folding art table covered with construction paper and a hundred crayons.

Shit.

Did she run off again when we weren't looking?

I jerk back a step when that damned dinosaur roars from under her bed, but my shoulders drop when her head pops out.

"What are you doing down there?"

Camila slides the rest of the way out and jumps for me to catch her. "Playing archeologist. I'm looking for bones in a cave." She wiggles in my arms. "Ven aquí!"

I set her down. "Sorry. I can't play. I have to go now."

Her lips tremble, but she presses them together until they turn a pale pink. I drop to my knees in front of her and take her small hands in mine.

"Hey, I'll be back."

She looks down at her bare feet and wiggles her toes. Kathryn painted them with glittery blue nail polish last night. "I'll miss you. Not as much as Nicole, but still."

My eyes blur long enough for me to feel like Tom.

"I'll miss you too." I tuck a black strand of hair behind her ear. "Get Tom to do your fishtail braid, okay? Kathryn's braids always turn out crooked."

Camila stomps her foot. "But yours are the best.

"Tom's will get better with practice." I stand up and ignore the grip on my heart. "Be a good little fish while I'm gone. Don't swim away from home."

Camila gives me one last hug around my thigh. "I'll try not to find you too."

I boop her nose before heading to the downstairs bathroom to dab my eyes and fix my smeared mascara.

I've had hard goodbyes but none this unexpected.

As expected, though, Tom and Kathryn wait outside, and I stand on the cement porch with Violin and my trash-bag-suitcase for a moment before joining them. Thanks to Camila but mostly thanks to their generosity, I've met almost every neighbor that lives on our block. Mr. Rogerson across the street let me borrow his shovel to clear the driveway when we got a fluke snow this past March, and Dr. Richards in the house over invited us over for a barbecue in the backyard with her and her partner a couple months ago. Best macaroni and cheese I've had, and I've tried at least eleven different recipes.

Almost all the houses appear identical to Tom and Kathryn's, aside from the differing side paneling and shutter colors. The houses look more alike today. Most of the mailboxes have crimson and gold balloons tied to them—Borns College's school colors. Tom, Kathryn, and the other foster kids aren't the only ones who welcomed me here.

And now the neighborhood is sending me off.

I've been here nine months. I'm not attached to this place.

I'm not attached to these people.

Kathryn crosses and uncrosses her arms, as I set the trash bag on the paved driveway. She bounces on her feet like she's gearing up for another sprint through the subdivision. She won't make it far in her slippers.

"Are you sure you don't want to put your stuff in a duffle bag?" Kathryn asks. "You know I have plenty."

She has acquired at least seven athletic bags from 5k races and half marathons. Most of them have two pockets for running shoes. An actual zipping bag with multiple compartments would be convenient. Yet when Kathryn first offered, the thought of using anything other than a trash bag made me feel like the splintering horsehairs on a violin bow. I mean, I have only used a trash bag for the past eighteen years of my life.

Then again, a trash bag screams, "I'm a foster kid."

"On second thought, that would be great."

Kathryn's tanned face brightens, and she darts inside the house and back in less than a minute.

She runs faster in slippers than I do in sneakers.

She's not even out of breath when she hands me an enormous worn duffle with a racing number still pinned on the side with safety pins. "Here you go. It's my lucky bag. I've used it every time I've hit a new PR in a race." She must see my confusion because she adds, "Personal record. Or PB for personal best."

Tom holds my pillow and bedsheets as I dump the contents of my trash bag inside. I do some minor arranging to fit my pillow, but the bag zips shut with little effort.

Huh. Wasn't expecting that.

Maybe this duffle is more than lucky. Maybe it's magical, like the jeans in *The Sisterhood of the Traveling Pants*. Like it will fit anything I need it to—which works out, because I need it to hold everything I own.

Kathryn holds her small hips, and the lean muscles in her

arms bulge. "Remember, call if you need anything. Homework included."

I open the door to the backseat before she can catch me in a hug and shove aside junk mail and fast-food trash (not Kathryn's because runners don't eat fast food, apparently) to make room for the duffle. Violin comes with me to the front.

Ready?

Violin: *Hell yes.*

"I'll text and call. Promise." I open the passenger door and smile at Kathryn over my shoulder. "Thanks for letting me borrow your bag."

Before backing out of the driveway, Tom chuckles with a glance at Violin. "I don't have to ask you what you'd save in a fire."

I grip its scratched case tighter and ignore the celebratory balloons as we drive through our street.

Playing the violin has gotten me through all the figurative fires in my life. But I'm done with fires now.

At least, I hope I am.

Movement Three

prelude = "musical introduction to a composition or drama"

Foster House #7 holds the record for my shortest stay: less than two months. Yet another move shouldn't discompose me, but the flutters in my stomach say otherwise as Tom takes the exit for Borns College.

My fingertips press the fingerings of Vaughan Williams's *The Lark Ascending* into my sweaty palms.

"You all right?" Tom eyes my tapping fingers.

I nod and continue through the unheard piece.

Not two months into eighth grade at my new school, my seventh foster guardians, Mr. and Mrs. Murad, decided to move and that I should move first. I went from school straight to my next foster house.

"Mrs. Murad got a job offer in another state," my caseworker at the time, Mr. Hill, said, as I got into the backseat beside my packed trash bag. "They thought it would be easier this way."

Easier for who? I thought.

Only thirteen, and I couldn't muster a single tear over another upheaval. My imagined adoptive home had vanished: a light blue two-story—gone; rose bushes lining the wrap-around porch—gone; a treehouse out back with a tire swing—gone; and parents (musicians, one pianist for accompaniment) with kind eyes that show up for every violin performance—gone.

My hope for adoption—forever gone.

Mr. and Mrs. Murad didn't cry over me, and though Tom has shed a tear or two like a proud dad, Tom and Kathryn will forget me. I'll vanish from their lives at the end of extended foster care.

We turn past a sign for Borns, and Tom runs a hand over his piano-key-colored beard. "My advice? Put yourself out there. Every freshman's nervous too."

He pulls into campus without more unasked advice, but his thumb rubs the steering wheel. A pep-talk forms beneath his squinting eyes. He knows I'm not a pro at fraternizing.

My one friend from high school, my only friend, Maddie, is going to college four states away in Florida. Maddie and I became friends eight months and one week ago. We had advanced P.E. together and bonded over our hatred of weightlifting. Making friends is not one of my strengths. Keeping them is near impossible, when house hopping and changing schools. So far, I've kept Maddie.

Mental note: text Maddie after I settle into my room.

The brick buildings seem larger than when I toured last month. Kathryn insisted I take the official tour, though I'd already enrolled and auditioned for the music program. I made up my mind during that Borns String Orchestra performance—and when I received my scholarship.

Less tuition for undergrad, less student loans for Juilliard.

Out my window, students and their families carry suitcases and bean bags and TVs half the size of Tom's car. They lug memory foam mattress pads along sidewalks lined with maple trees and lampposts with crimson banners of our college crest: an owl perched on a star- and book-filled shield above the year 1853 and the phrase "Incepto Ne Desistam."

No idea what it means. I took two Spanish classes in high school, not Latin.

I jerk around to look at someone carrying their hanged clothes, with a trash bag tied to the hook as a garment protector. Inventive. I almost wish for a familiar trash bag until a car with U-Haul cargo trailer pulls up in front of the dorm. There's a stark contrast between a 4x8 feet trailer and a 30-gallon trash bag. How the hell are they going to fit all that into a dorm room?

Tom hands me the campus map he printed last night. "Tell me when to turn."

The drawings are a near-perfect representation of the buildings, minus the real ivy crawling up the sides. I'm still inspecting the map when I realize we're about to miss our turn.

"Here!"

After a few mishaps I blame on the map's microscopic street names, we pull up to a line of parked cars in front of Harmony Hall. One of my soon-to-be hallmates carries her clarinet up the steps, while her family lags behind with the rest of her belongings. Her white high-top Nikes coordinate with her white jeans and the white lettering of "Borns College" on her crimson t-shirt.

Should I have worn college apparel instead of my baggy

crop top? Is wearing clothes with your school's name plastered across it some kind of college norm I missed? I hug my sides as to not reach over my seat for my duffle bag and search for another shirt. It's not like I have any college apparel, anyway.

Another freshman (who's not wearing anything with "Borns College" on it, thank god) trudges inch by inch, doubled over, legs apart. His stack of music books reaches over his head and blocks his vision. The books wobble. A few freshmen (only one wearing a Borns shirt) rush to grab a few books off the top, call out directions, and hold the door. It's a miracle he gets through without hurting himself—or worse—the music.

Tom smooths the steering wheel again with his thumb. "Let me carry your stuff."

I'm out of the car before he can take off his seatbelt. Foster care can't pollute my first college memory.

"Thanks, but I'm good. I can check myself in and all that."

"You sure?" Tom leans across the passenger seat and tries to change my mind with a comical pout.

No luck.

"I got this." I raise the duffle bag for emphasis. Zeke, Steven, and Camila need parental figures—not me. "Take care of the kids."

"Always. You take care of yourself, Coralee."

"Will do."

I close the car door. I've been taking care of myself my entire life. College won't be any different.

"Coralee?" He waits for me to walk to his open window. "I remember my freshman year of college…" He taps the steering wheel a couple times. "It's worth it to be vulnerable. To give yourself a chance to really love it here, even if things aren't perfect. Sometimes that makes it all the more fun. And you should have fun too, okay?"

He glances towards Violin, and my grip stiffens.

"Okay."

We both know it's a lie.

"All right, end of lecture." He starts putting up his window. "I'm gone."

I wave from the sidewalk, and his reflection in the rearview mirror wipes away a stray tear. A strange ache in my chest draws Violin tighter to my side as the car gets further and further away. Can Tom navigate out of campus without me? Can I navigate college on my own, without him or Kathryn or Drew?

Before the car is out of sight, I turn towards the dorm and follow a student holding a trombone case down the sidewalk.

I can *do this. I'm a college student.*

I'm about to live in a dorm with other people who think practicing hours on end is fun. People who like going to concerts —instrumental ones, not whoever's on the radio. People who don't ask the difference between a violin and a fiddle.

Music majors like me.

$\oint$

Movement Four

violin = "familiar four-stringed bow instrument; the
leading instrument of the orchestra; the highest
pitched member of the violin family" (and also called a
fiddle, but sure as hell not by me)

Before walking up the steps to Harmony Hall, I adjust my
purple-tipped ponytail at the nape of my neck to show off
my treble clef tattoo.

Kathryn helped me dye my hair with Kool-Aid about a
month ago. When I asked if she would help me, I expected her
to laugh and take off on a run, but she grabbed her car keys.
(Kathryn didn't approve of my tattoo, though. Tom drove me to
the tattoo parlor instead. He said he got a tattoo after his
eighteenth birthday too, the quote from *Pride and Prejudice* on the
inside of his arm: "I declare after all there is no enjoyment like
reading!" Though I had just enough cash left from what I didn't
spend on Violin's case, Tom paid for it.)

On the way to the store, Kathryn said, "My mom dyed my hair once. I wanted blonde highlights, and she turned my hair orange. Looked awful. But I learned from her mistakes." She glanced over at me with a grin before turning back to the road. "Now we can make some new ones."

I covered my face with my hands. "Please don't mess up my hair for college."

She shrugged. "It'll grow back."

"But we're not even cutting it!"

She laughed the rest of the drive. I didn't trust she was joking until she mixed the sugary dark purple paste and showed me how to rub it into the ends of my hair. The dye stained my light and her sun-kissed hands magenta for a week, and for that week, we had something in common.

In Harmony Hall, I'll live with people I have lots in common with, Kool-Aid not necessary.

The dorm is like a stage during dress rehearsal, filled with building energy and nervous chatter. I step into a long line of music majors, from freshmen to super seniors, though most upperclassmen opt to live off campus or in the on-campus apartments. They hold instruments from teeny piccolos to monster tubas.

The front door opens behind me, and the summer heat warms my back.

"Hey, is this the line to get our room keys?"

Another violin case with two stickers—an equality sticker and a sticker for The Mason Musical Repair Shop—catches my attention. You can tell a lot about a person from their instrument case: this must be a reasonable human who has worked at some music shop, maybe to pay for advanced lessons?

"I guess."

What does my "wtf" sticker say about me?

"My dad owns the shop," says the guy holding the case, after catching me zoned out on his sticker.

Something about his shaggy dark hair seems familiar, though not the ring in his slender bottom lip. Good thing he's not an oboe player.

"Let me guess," I say. "You work there too."

"Since I was nine." He nods me forward to an opening where a girl wearing a Borns College polo hands out dorm keys. "See you in class, Coralee."

I freeze mid-step, my converse-clad foot hovering midair. I didn't say my name, right? How do we know each other? I turn with a raised eyebrow, the blaring question across my face.

"Dylan, remember?" His thin lips spread into a sly, lopsided smile at my continued confusion. "Dylan Mason? The most talented violinist you've ever met?"

With a rush of returned frustration, I *do* remember. I remember I can't stand his highflying overachieving guts. How did I not recognize that smirk? Then again, he seems at least three inches taller, and his lip ring and biceps (not that I'm looking or anything) are new.

Dylan sat first chair in both all-county and district orchestra my freshman and sophomore years of high school. I sat beside him in second, though I did make first chair our sophomore year for district orchestra. We shared a stand, sheet music, and whispered insults during rehearsals and performances. He even got my number sophomore year, though I don't remember how, and would send me taunting texts. Thankfully, we never went to the same school—until now.

"Most talented?" I scowl, as his smirk stretches into a full-out grin. "You forget I was first chair the last time we saw each other."

He has the audacity to laugh.

Violin: *Forget him. He won't be laughing soon enough.*

With an exaggerated swing of my duffel bag, I approach the table and leave Dylan behind, just as I plan to do when auditions come around for our chair placements in string orchestra.

Student handbooks, stapled paper packets, and campus maps sit on the table next to an upright metal cabinet full of keys. The girl in the polo crosses her arms as I set down my duffle in front of the table, as if she's annoyed that I slowed down the line from my run-in with Dylan.

"I'm Tiffany, she/her pronouns, and I'm your Resident Advisor."

She smooths a stray hair that has come loose from a tight ballerina bun. She stares at a list of names in her hand. I wait for her to say something else, but she sighs with evident annoyance.

"Oh, right," I say. "I'm Coralee Reed. Same pronouns."

The impromptu, "But I go by Corey," rolls out of my mouth.

I do not go by Corey. My last attempt was when I asked Maddie, my best friend of three weeks at the time (whose name is short for Madeline), to call me Corey. Her eyes watered when she said, "We shouldn't both use shortened names," which I translated to, "I want to be the only one in my social circle to use a nickname." She did add that my name is "too pretty to shorten." That lessened the blow. Except a so-called pretty name doesn't tell my story.

Tiffany flashes what can only be a sarcastic smile, then hands me a packet from the table. While she scans her list for my name, I scan the pages titled "Borns College Welcome Week Schedule for First-Year Students." Administration at Borns seems to use the word "week" rather loosely, since classes start on Wednesday. Though, for four days, they're packing in a lot of activities, from an honor code presentation to a dance party.

"Hmm." Tiffany purses her down-turned lips. "I don't see your name."

Heat burns my face as if I'm back outside the dorm in the blazing sun. Did the air conditioner stop working?

"What's your full name again?"

I spell it out.

"Well, you're not on my list. Are you sure you're in the right hall?"

This can't be happening.

The fingerings for some composition, I can't process which, press into my palm in time with my racing heartbeat. "I'm sure. Harmony Hall."

Tiffany offers a sad attempt at compassion with a tight-lipped smile. "Give me a sec."

She taps her phone—with long manicured nails I could never have because of playing the violin—and presses it to her ear. After a few seconds, she introduces herself to someone named Ms. Birr.

"I'm here with…" Tiffany glares until I repeat my name for a third time. "She says she has a room here, but I'm not seeing her on my roster. Can she come by your office?"

Tiffany hangs up a minute later and motions Dylan forward. "That was Ms. Birr, the Director of Residence Life. She's in a meeting now but can help if you stop by in an hour."

Blood rushes to my hands and feet with the urge to run, run, run. Instead, I force myself to stroll past Dylan and the rest of the check-in line. His eyes must follow me, though, because the skin on the back of my neck tingles like it did when my treble clef tattoo was healing. I don't turn around to flick him off. Instead, I raise my chin and set my eyes on the exit. I don't need his mocking right now.

Outside, I walk against the flow of students carrying instruments. They smile, squinting into the sun, as I follow my shadow down the sidewalk.

Violin: *We're going the opposite direction.*

I know. But we'll be back. I just have to work things out with the ResLife Director.

Except I don't have a clue why I wasn't on Tiffany's roster. *Can* I live in Harmony? And if not, where the hell will I live?

I'll have to wait for Ms. Birr to tell me. Per usual, I'm waiting for somebody to tell me where to live.

Movement Five

solo = "alone" and "a composition for a single voice or
instrument"

Killing time in the Borns Bookstore is gonna kill me.

Cash registers ding. Parents grumble while handing over
credit cards, and siblings bicker about who gets the now-empty
room. I shuffle through the mayhem, holding my violin case with
the grip of a practiced violinist.

I force my way through to the English shelf and snatch the
last *First-Year Composition for the Well-Rounded Academic* textbook.
My eyes bulge at the $185.99 sticker price. This one textbook, for
my most dreaded class, will leave nothing for the rest. I've lived
off five-dollar bills. Now I can't make three one-hundred-dollar
bills last.

How the hell am I going to afford my textbooks?

A girl with thick red hair and hiking boots yanks a massive
advanced textbook from the same shelf, which makes my

textbook look like a children's bedtime story.

She catches my gaze and shakes her head in commiseration at my (probably horrified) expression. "Expensive, right? We're going to have to sell pictures of our feet at these prices."

Before I process her words, she's off standing in the check-out line. I put the textbook back on the shelf, since there's no way in hell I can pay that much, and trade it for my phone.

Nineteen more minutes until I can go to the director's office.

Outside, students sit on blankets and throw footballs and play guitars on the grassy lawn, also known as the "quad" per my orientation tour guide. I crumple in front of the last unoccupied tree.

Maybe I should call Tom or Kathryn. Talk to someone to make the wait shorter. I text Maddie instead.

Me:

Maddie! You won't believe my catastrophe of a first day. How are you???

Maddie, a few seconds later:

[...]

She never hits send.

Instead of waiting and hoping and begging for a response, my thumb clicks through my phone and then I'm on Maddie's Instagram. Her most recent picture is with a group of similar-looking girls (long blonde hair, sun-kissed complexions, wearing matching sorority tank tops) on the front steps of an old white house, all holding red solo cups.

Don't look when she posted it. Don't look, don't look.

I look: thirty minutes ago.

Only a week at university, and Maddie has a group of friends. A sorority where she belongs. An astronomical 375 likes on her photo that she posted a half an hour ago, but she can't text me back when I need her.

Even though I'm there for her every. Single. Time. She needs me.

Who went school shopping with her and helped her pack for college? Me. Who got their foster parents to rearrange schedules and drop them off at her house to say goodbye? Me. Who, over the past week, is now accustomed to seeing "…" but never reading a message from their best friend? Me, me, me.

Maddie smiles back at me from the photo.

She's miles away. She should enjoy freshman year, make friends, even if I'm not there. Even if I'm sitting alone by a tree instead of eating lunch with my new Harmony hallmates.

With my eyes closed, I try my back-up plan. I hit the call button and wait for Kathryn's voice, but she doesn't answer. My head thumps against the tree.

"You okay?"

My blurred vision clears on a short curvy girl with mousy brown hair standing in front of me in a high school sweatshirt. My earlier unease about college apparel evaporates.

"Do you need help or something?" Her eyebrows scrunch together with concern. That, or the sun's in her eyes.

My short, "No," doesn't deter her, and she takes a step closer. Her silence begs me to elaborate.

"What I need is a place to live."

She plops down beside me. "How come? You're a freshman too, right? Didn't you get your dorm and room number like months ago?"

"Something got messed up with my paperwork, I guess."

Blades of grass blend into a green watercolor, and I press my palms against my eyes before any teardrops fall onto my violin case. I check the time. Nine minutes until I can meet Ms. Birr.

"My roommate doesn't move in until Tuesday." The girl leans towards me with a smile. "Apparently she's not into orientation."

Why is this girl telling me about her roommate when I'm having a breakdown?

"Okay…"

"I don't know about the rest of the year, but you could stay with me in my dorm room tonight, or at least until you figure it out." Her eyes seem to sparkle, while mine feel as if they're going to bug out of their sockets like some cartoon character.

"You're kidding, right? You don't even know me."

"I don't know my roommate either." Her chin juts out with her laugh. "I'm Emma, by the way. Emma Anderson. Now you know as much about me as my roommate."

"Are you sure, though?" I ask, after I introduce myself as Corey. "I don't wanna put you out."

"Now you're kidding." Emma's smile widens, and a dimple forms in the middle of her chin. "You're my first college friend. I don't mind at all."

I hug my knees to my chest. "Well, I better get going to the Director of Residence Life's office, since I have no idea where it is on campus. But fingers crossed I won't need to take you up on that offer."

"Why don't I go with you? I've got the campus map memorized." Emma stands and holds out her hand. "Then, I'll be there if you need to stay in my room tonight."

Emma pulls me up from the grass. I follow her off the quad,

duffle bag and Violin in tow.

Maybe I'm not so bad at making friends.

Movement Six

cambia = "direction in orchestral scores to change
instruments or tuning"

Unlike the usual brick buildings, the bluestone of Montero
Hall appears stately yet cold.

"Wanna know a fun fact?" Emma asks, as we walk up the
steps under the stone archway. She doesn't wait for me to
respond. "My tour guide said girls used to sneak up to the roof
of this building to suntan. I remember because of the stone. I
would *never*. I burn easy. But can you imagine getting caught?"

I nod in agreement. Not because I care about getting caught
—not that I'd want to get caught—but because my pasty ass
burns easy too. Most of my time is spent indoors with
Violin, anyway.

Inside, Emma and I find Ms. Birr's office number on a room
listing in a glass case. When we reach her closed door on the first-
floor hallway, my sweaty fist stops an inch from the door. Emma

gives me a thumbs up. I knock, and when I hear, "Come in," she follows me inside.

A half-empty bookshelf covers one of the white walls beside a wooden desk. Ms. Birr's undergraduate and graduate degrees hang beside a generic poster about leadership. A single picture sits on the desk facing Ms. Birr, who doesn't look at all like I imagined. She's in her lower forties, if I had to guess, and has a slender nose that amplifies her pointed expression. Her hair is a 50/50 mix of blonde and brown.

Which color did she put on her driver's license?

I'd put purple if I had a license. Do they let you put unnatural colors, though? If not, I'd go with brown.

Emma and I shake Ms. Birr's hand and introduce ourselves, and I say my new name after my full name.

"Have a seat." Ms. Birr waves us to the chairs in front of her desk. "You have a room problem, Coralee?"

She didn't call me Corey. No way she forgot that fast.

"Yeah, I'm supposed to live in Harmony Hall, but one of the resident advisors, Tiffany, said I wasn't—"

"Right, well, you can't live there." Her chair squeaks as she leans back. "That house is for accepted freshmen music majors only."

"But I was accepted."

My fingers pick back up *The Lark Ascending* on my palm. A tingling sensation creeps up my back and unsettles my conviction.

Was I?

Ms. Birr shakes her head with a forced smile. "You were accepted into Borns and declared music as your major, but you weren't accepted into the music department. You should have received a letter notifying you of this. Regardless, you can't live in Harmony Hall."

What I think: *Bull shit.*

What I say: "You're kidding."

"Unfortunately, I'm not. I would venture to guess your second letter was misplaced at home."

Home. Yeah, right.

I checked the mailbox every day until I got my Borns acceptance letter, but then I stopped checking. Meaning Tom has been the sole mail-checker since April. Meaning Tom—who loses mail on a weekly basis in our chaotic foster house—didn't hand over the second letter from Borns, rejecting me from the music program. Rejection letters are considerably smaller than acceptance letters, which are easier for the likes of Tom to misplace. To overlook. To forget that 4 1/2 by 10 3/8 inch envelopes contain my future.

Dammit, Tom.

I assumed (yeah, yeah, I'm an ass) that getting accepted into Borns meant I got accepted into the music program. How the hell would I know it's not the same thing? If I had, I would've never trusted Tom with mail duty.

I wipe my hands on my shorts. *How am I not accepted? Did my audition suck?*

Violin: *I was there, and we did* not *suck.*

My shaky inhale does nothing to ease my lightheadedness. "Okay, that's far from good news, but what's my actual room assignment?"

"I'll double check." Ms. Birr types away at her keyboard for what feels like an eternity, and then she shakes her blonde-brown head. Frowns. Shakes her head again. "To be honest, our system doesn't have you assigned to a room. We've recorded some miscommunication with the music department, which may be why you thought you lived in Harmony Hall. They had more people audition this year than past years, so the department waitlisted more people than usual for the program, since we guarantee a spot in Harmony for accepted Music majors if they so choose. The department included you on their first list of accepted freshmen by accident and retracted you from their second list." A flush of red tints her face. "Which leads me to believe that you may not have received a letter from the music department about your status after all. If you did, it might have been the wrong one."

Sorry, Tom. I take it back.

Ms. Birr frowns at the screen. "Unfortunately, there aren't any available rooms either."

Gray dots cloud the periphery of my vision. "Wha-What do you mean?"

"Like all colleges, we overbook to prepare for students dropping out, so every room on campus is full as of now. It's standard Residence Life practice." Ms. Birr's voice carries an uncomfortable laugh. "I'll have to find you a two-person room that can accommodate a third person, or if you prefer, you can live off campus. Either way, I'll refund you your housing deposit."

Emma touches my arm, but I can't turn my head to smile, to signal I'm okay when I'm not. I might pass out if I do.

"But my scholarship covers my room and board too, not just my tuition. Am I losing that money?"

Ms. Birr blinks at me for a second. "If I'm not able to find you a room, which I assure you I can, you'll receive that portion of your financial aid via a check to cover living costs. However, we will have to update your documentation in our system as a commuter."

"I can't be a commuter."

If I commute, I won't commute from an apartment. I'll commute from Tom and Kathryn's house, and I can't stay there. If I do, I'll stay a foster kid.

Emma's concerned eyes turn from me to Ms. Birr. "I told Corey she could stay with me tonight, since my roommate isn't here yet."

Warmth spreads through my chest at "Corey."

Ms. Birr asks for Emma's last name and dorm while clicking around on her computer. "Perfect. Your room permits three people. Coralee," Okay, she's definitely refusing, "you'll live in Roselawn with Emma and Harper for now, and I'll contact you when a room opens. Until then, I'll inform your RA to bring in a third bed and provide an additional room key."

Shit. This is happening.

This can't be happening.

Emma shifts in her chair. She didn't sign up for this. She must wish she never met me. God, how am I not an accepted music major? How can I live in a dorm that's not Harmony? If I can't live in Harmony, I should live in a room with an empty bed that has my name on it, so to speak. Not a room with people already assigned to each bed. And Harper doesn't know me. A stranger will move into her room before she does.

When Ms. Birr waits as long as she can for a response, she says, "If that's it then…"

I clear my dry throat.

"Are you sure you don't have an empty room or empty bed somewhere, anywhere on campus?"

Ms. Birr crosses her arms. "As I said before, as per standard practice, we're overbooked. I wish I could tell you something different. I really do. But a temporary triple is the best solution, and I'll have another option for you in a few weeks at most. Freshmen constantly change rooms and change schools the first month. A room will open up before you know it."

The office phone rings. Ms. Birr checks the name that flashes on the small screen. "I need to get this, but thanks for coming by. Take one of my business cards on your way out." She picks up the receiver. "Call or email me anytime, Coralee. You both have a nice day now."

What I think: *Screw you.*

What I say: "You too."

Emma grabs far more than one card out of Ms. Birr's business card holder. "Just in case," she whispers, handing me one as we trudge out of the office.

College meant an end to house hopping. It meant an end to the system dumping me on strangers. It meant a start at permanency, at least for the next four years. I planned on living in Harmony all the way through to senior year.

I didn't cry on my birthdays that passed without a party. Or when Mrs. Baker from Foster House #5 said, "Three strikes, you're out," after I forged her signature on my sixth grade report card. Since coming to Borns, my eyes won't stop watering.

I wipe away a tear as Emma and I walk down the hallway. "I'm really sorry. This escalated so far beyond what I thought. Sorry you're stuck with me."

"Don't be, roomie. Ms. Birr should be sorry." Emma's chin dimples with a smile. "I can't imagine what you must be feeling. But silver lining, we both made a friend."

My shoulders relax a bit. "True."

"And we can go to all the hall meetings and activities together now too!"

As we head to Roselawn Hall, someone tumbles out of a

hammock with showmanship onto the grass. A few people on the quad break out into applause, and when they take a bow, Emma giggles along. Though I can't quite match her beaming expression, she earns a smile or two from me—a difficult feat when my future at Borns and ultimate violin career is falling apart.

College has to be better than foster care.

Sooner or later, I'll get into the music program and live in Harmony Hall. In the meantime, I'll manage living in a temporary triple until Ms. Birr calls. Someone has to transfer or drop out or get sick of their roommate. Hopefully Emma and Harper don't get sick of me before then.

Movement Seven

fingering = "directions for use of the fingers in playing instruments" (and something else entirely on Urban Dictionary)

By the time Emma and I hike up the stairs to the third-floor of Roselawn, my crop top sticks to my back. I'm the big, bad, sweaty wolf, huffing and puffing, ready to blow my way into Emma and Harper's dorm down. *Our* room.

I'm less a wolf and more a cockroach invading their living space.

Hell, Harper hasn't set foot on campus yet.

Two colorful paper owls—in honor of the Borns mascot, Hooty the Owl—stick to the door with masking tape. One reads "Emma" and the other reads "Harper." Another reminder I'm not supposed to be here.

"Sorry it's a mess." Emma turns her key, and cardboard boxes and reusable shopping bags welcome us inside. "I went to lunch before unpacking and caught you on my way back."

I remain in the doorway, while she slides the nearest box across the umber-colored tile floor to the sole dresser in the center of the room. A large rectangular mirror hangs above it.

No matter which foster home my caseworkers took me, the system guaranteed a room with a door. Rooms are sacred, maybe the one place someone belongs.

I don't belong here.

Emma frowns and arranges pre-folded t-shirts into a squeaky drawer. "Wanna help me?"

I inch into the room. With Violin and my duffle bag on the empty bed—Harper's bed—I grab a box labeled "knickknacks" in loopy, cursive writing. I wince at the fragile clink from inside and place it on the desk in front of the wide window overlooking a sand volleyball court.

"So how'd you get paired with Harper?" I ask, to lessen the guilt of being in her room when she isn't.

"No idea. We both took that Reslife survey, and they matched us over the summer. But I don't think we have a single thing in common." Emma leans against her dresser. "I found her on Instagram and get this: she does CrossFit and MMA fighting." Her warm laugh bounces off the cream cement walls. "The most I've exercised is running the mile for gym class."

I lift a figurine of a unicorn from the box. "Same. She sounds badass, though."

She pulls plain neutral-colored bras out of a tote bag and nods to the unicorn. "My grandpa gave that to me. I keep it to remind myself of him. Plus, I never really grew out of my unicorn obsession."

Sure enough, a large stuffed animal unicorn sits in the middle of her pink and green comforter.

Emma owns figurines and stuffed animals. Violin's my one sentimental possession, aside from my lifebook that Drew's still holding onto for me. A photo album of elementary to high school picture day photos, orchestra concert programs, mementos from my eleven foster houses. Pictures of me at Foster House #1 and #2, the houses I was too little to remember. Pictures of me as a kid with my treasured purple teddy bear I had since Foster House #3, which Mr. and Mrs. Murad from Foster House #7 forgot to pack in my trash bag for Mr. Hill.

Violin: *Excuse me, I'm more than sentimental. I'm a fine tool—no, a vessel—for music. Life-giving, soul-altering, tear-producing music.*

God, you know what I meant. But pardon my offense.

I lift a mahogany picture frame from the box next. Carved hearts decorate the frame, and there's a gap where the ends to one corner don't quite align. Did someone make this by hand?

"My boyfriend made that for our one-year anniversary slash going to college gift." Emma stops unpacking to admire the photo with me like an old woman recalling long-past lovers and not like an eighteen-year-old with a smartphone to FaceTime her boyfriend. "Owen, my boyfriend, plays football for Notaro University two hours from here, closer to home. He's kinda famous at our high school because of his anticipated athletic career."

"Cool."

I couldn't give less of a shit about football.

Beside Owen's over-six-feet-tall frame, Emma looks even shorter. His dirty blonde hair and collared shirt—with rolled sleeves and sunglasses hanging from the top button—bring countless boys from my high school to mind. Boys that'll say "yes, ma'am" and "amen" and dehumanizing jokes in the same conversation. Posturing, privileged, narcissistic, white cis straight boys are everywhere. Owen's probably not one, though, fingers crossed. Emma seems like a better judge of character than my jaded self.

"He's a sophomore." Emma returns to her drawer of granny panties.

I'm compelled to ask, "How'd you meet?" as a result of digging through her personal items.

"From school. We didn't talk until his family joined my family's church, though. I didn't like him at first." She laughs and swishes her long mousy-brown hair over her shoulder. "But he grew on me."

No kidding.

"What about you?" Emma asks. "You must have a boyfriend. Or girlfriend? Datefriend? You're *so* pretty."

"Um, no."

Guys were interested in high school, but I wasn't interested in some fleeting boyfriend picking me up from Tom and Kathryn's. Wasn't interested in him stepping on plastic dinosaurs and Steven bombarding him with personal questions. Him waiting for me to finish making pancakes on Saturdays before taking me on a date. Him listening to Tom's lectures but fearing Kathryn's surveying glances and toned runner's build more.

Violin > boyfriend. Simple as that.

My phone vibrates on top of my violin case.

"Not that I'm an aspiring nun or anything," I add before I read the text. I wasn't interested in a boyfriend, but I was interested in other less time-consuming things.

Unknown:

Did I scare you away or something? Didn't know I was

so intimidating

Me:
Who is this?

"I mean, I've hooked up here and there, but nothing serious." I nod to the picture now displayed on her desk. "Nothing like you and Owen. I've never had a serious relationship. Or any relationship, really."

Emma tugs on the bottom of her sweatshirt. "What do you mean 'hooked up?'"

"You know, hooked up. More than kissing."

Am I really explaining this term to a *college* freshman right now?

Unknown:
Ouch didn't think you'd actually delete my number

Me:
???

Unknown:
The most talented violinist you've ever met…

Me:
Oh my god. I didn't think you'd keep my number.
Delete it now

Dylan is second chair:
I wouldn't dare! You need all the free violin advice you can get
violin emoji *smiley face emoji*

"Can I admit something?" Emma asks, before I can send a *very* explicit clap-back text.

"Sure."

"Owen and I, sure, we have a serious relationship. But we haven't, we've never…hooked up?"

No way. They've dated for a year and haven't fooled around at least once?

"Whatever makes you happy. I've hooked up with plenty of people but," I nod towards the photo, "no one ever looked at me like that."

Emma flops onto her twin bed. "The most we've done is make out in his parents' driveway. But that was one time. Owen's mom walked out on the porch and scared us." She buries her face in her giant unicorn with a groan. "I was mortified. I couldn't look her in the eye for a month! We haven't made out since."

Her comfort zone could fit in one of her cardboard boxes.

"Okay, hear me out. College is supposed to bring you out of your shell, right? Maybe, I don't know, you should loosen up a bit. Explore who you are sexually, with or without Owen."

"What, *cheat* on him?" Emma jolts into a seated position. "Nope. No way. Absolutely not."

"I meant self-pleasure." Her face reddens, and I hold back a laugh. "But that's a relief."

"Oh my gosh, enough about my love life. I'm pretty sure, with being a Christian and all, it's a big no on all the above." She rolls off the bed and gestures to Violin and my duffle bag without meeting my eyes. "Let's finish unpacking."

Her religion may discourage her from having one, but she brought up her sex life, or rather, *lack* of a sex life.

I unzip my duffle bag. "Okay, but I'm here if you wanna talk more."

♪♫

Once her half of the dorm room looks like a page from a PBteen magazine—complete with a rosette hang-a-round chair, waterfall string lights above her bed, a pack of floral notebooks, a personalized "EDA" (Emma Dawn Anderson) desk mat, and iridescent pencil and pen cup holders—Emma leaves for a residence hall meeting. I don't have my third bed or room key, so the RA can't know I'm here yet or expect me. I stay behind.

I'm sure as hell not missing dinner, though.

When she gets back, Emma pulls me into the hallway and introduces some of our hallmates: Julia, who's on the college lacrosse team; Ana, who somehow joined the college's Disney Club already; and Tracy, Ana's friend from high school, who interrupts Emma to tell me everyone's fun facts.

They decline Emma's dinner invitation—thank god, because a headache throbs in my temples from too much stimulus despite the hour alone—and she says, "Next time."

Emma leads the way to the dining hall, not that I couldn't find it on this small campus by myself. We pass the tree where we met earlier. A reminder that I've already made one friend.

Take that, Maddie.

I check my phone. Dylan, the last person I want texts from, has sent me four texts too many. Meanwhile, my best friend hasn't sent me one.

"I'm working in the library this semester." Emma points to a brick building lined with rose bushes. "Just a couple mornings during the week, scanning books. It's a work-study job."

Drew told me not to pursue a work-study or on-campus job when we first discussed my new case plan for extended foster care. Studying music requires hours and hours and hours of personal practice, outside of classes and lessons. Focusing on music outweighed making some extra cash. But the textbooks for my classes outweigh both.

"Do you know if any positions are still open?"

I cross my fingers behind my back. Years ago, some older foster girl told me that, as long as I cross my fingers, my wishes will come true. It never works, but one day it might.

"Not sure. They had two open positions when I applied over the summer, but I think they filled the other one. I can ask around for you, though."

"Don't bother." I uncross my fingers. Should've known. "I'll look for some other on-campus job. Textbooks are just criminally expensive."

"Right? At least in the bookstore. They're way cheaper online."

I frown. "What about shipping costs, though?"

Emma double takes, as if she's checking whether I'm serious. Is it a stupid question?

To Maddie's frequent horror, I've never made an online purchase. Not on Instagram Shop. Not on Etsy. Not on our local music store's website. Maddie constantly buys shoes, blow dryers, jewelry, bathing suits, and makeup online. Most of what she owns, she bought online. Online shopping may seem normal to everyone else, but shopping from a screen seems bizarre and out of reach when (1) you don't have access to your own money because the state gives it to your foster parents to use for you at their sometimes faulty discretion and (2) you don't have your own laptop.

Thank god for extended foster care, though, because Tom and Kathryn helped me set up my first banking account and credit card a month ago before school.

"Depends on where the book's shipping from." Emma's face brightens in the dusk of campus. "I have a membership with one site for free shipping. You can use it, if you want."

"Really?"

She lifts a slim shoulder with a grin. "Only trying to help my best college friend."

We take the stairs beside a concrete ramp up to the widest, though not the tallest, brick building I've seen so far on campus. Emma yanks open the massive glass door.

"Welcome to the MDH!" I must look confused because she explains, "Main Dining Hall."

The campus map Tom printed didn't have acronyms for buildings. "How do you know so much about Borns?"

"My older cousin, Abigail, graduated from here last year," Emma explains, as we stop at in the hallway at the back of a line into the cafeteria. "Plus, I paid close attention on the campus tour—even, I'm not too ashamed to admit, eavesdropped on conversations—and took notes on my phone. Over-prepared is my default setting."

Most students turn up the decibels of sound in the hallway by squealing at their missed friends, showing their favorite TikToks, and talking way past their inside voices. Some students, though, stare at the floor at 0 dB, probably freshmen or transfers who haven't made a friend yet. If I wasn't with Emma, I'd do the same thing.

An older woman swipes student ID cards at the entrance, and her thin lips curl into a ready smile at each student. When we reach her at the front of the line, I pull my ID out of my duct tape wallet. I stopped by the Card Services office to get my ID during the official tour over the summer. My scholarship includes room and board, which includes unlimited meal swipes at the dining hall and almost unlimited swipes at Borns Brew, *whatever* and *wherever* that is. My tour guide said the college closed it over the summer. Borns might've not given me a permanent room, but they at least have to give me food.

The woman smiles as expected and swipes my card. With a raspy alto voice, she says, "Enjoy your dinner, darlin'."

Conversations buzz as Emma and I maneuver through the crowd to the stations of food. A trio of young women wearing soccer jerseys swarm in front of us to a tray of cookies.

And I thought the bookstore was crowded.

The MDH may remind me of a beehive, but it does *not* smell like honey. A stench of lasagna mixed with body odor hangs in the air. Did Borns's athletes all get out of practice at the same time and come here? As long as the students stink and not the food.

My phone vibrates with a text message, as Emma and I stand in another line but for food we've yet to see.

Kathryn:
You settling in okay? Saw you tried to call.

She missed her chance to care, but I'm glad she didn't answer. Like with the Harmony Hall mix up, I need to handle the rest of college like I'll handle life after college: on my own, outside the system.

I shove my phone into my back shorts pocket and grab a teal plastic plate. I'll text Kathryn back later.

Once we go through the station for what turns out to be

Italian food, Emma and I navigate to an empty booth on the edge of the seating area. We haven't sat for a full minute when Emma drops her fork of steamy goop onto her plate.

"I overestimated this lasagna," she says.

I swallow a stale far-too-salty bite. "How do you mess up garlic bread?"

She pushes her plate aside. "Want to get one of those cookies?"

"Right behind you."

We brave the free-for-all for a second time only to find the tray of cookies empty.

"Don't worry. I have a better idea." She pulls a folded campus map from her back pocket.

Does she carry it wherever she goes?

She *is* over-prepared, and I'm an overachiever. Two peas in a pod. Maybe when Harper gets here, we'll be three peas in a dorm room. Maybe Harmony Hall didn't work out, so this could work out better.

Fingers crossed.

♪

Movement Eight

concertmaster = "the first-chair first violinist of an orchestra, often charged with leading the section, deciding all bowings, translating the wishes of the conductor to the orchestra and vice-versa, listening to auditions, and serving as a representative of the orchestra to its larger community"

The smell of coffee spills into the warm evening air as soon as I open the door to Deeds Hall. Though an academic building, the first floor has a coffee shop and study lounge, according to Abigail, Emma's cousin.

Large script letters spell "Borns Brew" inside on the wall above two bulletin boards covered in push pins and student club event flyers. The semester hasn't started, but students pack almost every chair and booth in the lounge. Brick-sized textbooks and laptops with ten-plus tabs open and JanSport backpacks cover tables and the backs of chairs.

Emma's cell rings as we reach the back of a line. Her face lights up when she sees the screen.

"Owen's calling. Do you mind?" She backs out of the line with an apologetic smile.

What I think: *Don't leave me.*

What I say: "Take your time."

Emma answers her phone with, "Hey, hon," but stops before she reaches the door. "You should check if they're hiring. It won't be a work-study job, but it's something."

"Good thought," I say, but I doubt she hears me.

I play on my phone while I wait in line. College seems like a lot of waiting so far: waiting to get accepted, waiting to move in, waiting for Reslife to assign me a permanent room.

Waiting for food is the least of it.

As I scroll through the Chicago Symphony Orchestra's Instagram account, @chicagosymphony, my phone swishes with another text from Kathryn.

Kathryn to the group chat I have with her and Tom:
How are you? Call us again when you can.

Oh, *now* she wants to talk to me.

Me to Tom and Kathryn:
College is going great and I'm making new friends.
Talk to you before bed. Tell the kids hi.

I continue scrolling through the orchestra's profile to pass the time and take my mind off of Kathryn's erratic support.

After college, I'll go to Juilliard, then I'll one day join the

Chicago Symphony Orchestra (CSO). I'm taking career trajectory notes from Stephanie Jeong, their appointed associate concertmaster. No one understands how much I look up to her.

What sucks is Dylan's right. I should take free violin advice when I'm so far behind. I didn't go to the Suzuki Program Music School before I could say full sentences like Stephanie Jeong. I didn't debut with the CSO at twelve years old like her. I didn't win the Feinberg Competition at that same age. I didn't study at the Betty Haag Academy of Music, wasn't accepted to the Philadelphia's Curtis Institute of Music as the youngest student in history.

I spend too much time fixating on her biography, obsessing over the reasons I'll never measure up, when I don't even measure up to the experiences of my classmates. I bet most of them, Dylan included, went to music camps over the summer, when I've never been to one.

Compared to other foster kids, though, I'm far ahead, with going to college and having foster parents that aren't going to drop me at any second. Still, compared to other violinists, I'm years of fancy schools and fancy teachers and fancy opportunities behind. Hell, I didn't hold a violin until I was eleven years old.

I gnaw on my bottom lip as I scroll through post after post of my other CSO musical idols: Rong-Yan Tang, Gina DiBello, So Young Bae.

I'll never play that well.

But every violinist starts somewhere, right?

Thank god Emma thought to check their menu on the way over because I'm at the front of the line before I know it. The line moved faster than my scrolling.

"What can I get you?"

I shove my phone into my back pocket. "An iced chai latte, a blueberry muffin, and an application to work here, please."

The barista wears a name tag that reads "Manager (enter) Luke, he/him." His bright white smile grows at my directness. A red flush tinges his brown face. Though I wish I were the cause, I'm sure it's more to do with the lamps radiating heat over the baked goods.

"The latte and muffin I can do, but you might want to think twice about the application." Luke grabs a cup and scribbles on the side with a Sharpie. "We have one shift available, and it's absolute hell."

"I'll take what I can get," I say, as I swipe my student ID card through the scanner.

His full lips curve into a grin, and he slides a coffee-stained application and pen towards me. "Fill this out and bring it back up here when you're done. I'll have your order out in a sec."

"Thanks."

A couple minutes later, Luke calls, "Iced chai latte and blueberry muffin!" and I grab my order from the counter. Warmth seeps through the muffin's paper bag, and my iced latte cools my palm. I find an empty high top table near the counter and start filling out the application in between bites. I try not to stain the paper further with sugary blueberries and my buttery fingers. Since the only sustenance I've had today is pancakes and stale garlic bread, the muffin's gone in seconds.

I sign my name at the bottom and click the pen closed, then throw my trash away and head back to the counter.

A gulp of chai sends a chill down my arms, but when Luke nods in my direction, my insides warm. I hand him my application and cross my fingers.

"I'll call tomorrow." He glances at my application and adds, "Coralee—oh, sorry, Corey." He must see the Preferred Name section a pause after the First Name section on the application. "Thanks for your interest." He grabs a bag of paper cups and smiles, and I'm sure my insides are now a hot frothy latte.

I find Emma in line and promise to scout for open booths, though I settle on comfy chairs near the door and save the opposite one with a raised foot. Emma nudges my foot aside a few minutes later, holding a scone. My falling foot forces my back straight. When I don't have my violin on my shoulder, I have the posture of a zombie.

"Hey," Emma says, through a bit of scone, "what classes are you taking?"

I pull up my class schedule on my phone and place it on the round table between us.

Monday/Wednesday/Friday Classes
English: First-Year Composition, 8-8:50 am
Violin One-on-One Lesson, 10-10:50 am
String Orchestra, 1-3 pm

Tuesday/Thursday Classes
Personal Development, 1-2 pm
Psychology, 2-3 pm

"Oh my gosh, First-Year Composition? I'm in that class!" Emma claps her hands together. "Want to get breakfast here before class on Wednesday?"

"Of course," I say, and Emma offers to find my textbooks on the site with free shipping.

Now I'll have class with someone I know besides Dylan. Someone I actually like.

Emma hands back my phone. "I didn't add the First-Year

Composition textbook to your cart. You can just borrow mine. No charge."

"Thank you. More than thank you. That book was really expensive."

"No biggie." She smiles and wipes her fingers with a napkin. "What are friends for?"

I buy all my textbooks: *Becoming an Active Learner*, *The Inner Search for Resiliency*, and *A Peak into the Mind: An Introduction to Psychology* (which is used, in poor condition, and possibly the wrong edition—but a whopping $250 off the normal price). My orchestra class and lessons don't require textbooks but sheet music. With my books on the way and only crumbs left from our sugary pastries, we leave Borns Brew for our dorm.

Since the RA hasn't brought my third bed, I collapse on Harper's. My eyes droop and my feet ache and my body crashes from post first-day adrenaline, but the hard lumpy twin bed rejects me. Like it knows it doesn't belong to me. Rationally, I'm sleeping where I'm supposed to. But my brain loops and loops the second rule of foster care.

Foster Kid Rule #2
Invade another kid's space or touch their shit, prepare for retaliation.

Emma snuggles with her stuffed animal unicorn and calls Owen for the second time this evening, so I call Kathryn again, as promised. I need a good half an hour before falling asleep, anyway. This time, Kathryn answers on the second ring.

"Hey, Coralee. Wait a second while I grab Tom?" Before I can answer, she yells for Tom—with the phone away from her face, thank god.

Tom shouts, "Coming!" but his distant voice sounds clear when he asks, "How's your first day been, kiddo?"

Kathryn has it on speaker so they both can hear.

I force myself through pleasantries then ask, "Do you all remember that kid I've told you about before? The one who beat me out of first chair before I came to live with you both?"

"Sure," Kathryn says. "Donald or something?"

"Dylan, yeah. Well, he's here."

They're silent for a moment before Tom says, "You know someone. That's a good thing, Coralee. Maybe you can learn a thing or two from one another."

His words are too close to Dylan's text about "free violin advice" for my liking.

"Can you actually call me Corey now?" I disregard his statement about consorting with the musical competition.

"Of course, Corey," Tom says, no adjustment time needed. "So, what else? How're you liking your new room? You have a roommate, right? Do you need us to bring you anything, like a microwave? Or maybe you need a rug? Your floor's probably tile. Getting up in the morning will be rough when it's cold. Oh, maybe you need slippers?"

In my pause, Emma speaks more softly and sensually than I want to hear her speak.

"No, no, I'm all set." I roll onto my side and hug my knees to my chest. "But I have something to tell you both. It's not a big deal."

At least not to them.

I tell them about not having a permanent room, about living in a temporary triple. I leave out that I won't live in Harmony Hall at all. If I did, I'd have to tell them the music department hasn't accepted me yet, and I can't say it out loud.

"They're getting you a permanent room soon, though, right?" Kathryn's voice sounds higher than normal, as if she's back from a run and can't catch her breath enough to speak. "What even happened?"

She mumbles to Tom with a harsh tone, but I make out, "This is absolutely ridiculous." She isn't wrong.

"Kathryn," I interrupt, "I'm fine. Don't worry about me. I can handle this. Okay?"

I make them swear over the phone that they'll let me be an adult. They'll let me fix my rooming situation on my own. They'll focus on the kids who actually need them, not me.

"You can need us too, Corey," Tom whispers.

"They need you more."

More silence, except for Emma flirting.

"We've got them," Kathryn says, "and we've got you too."

A minute must pass before I trust myself to speak past the emotional rock lodged in my throat, and all I manage is, "Night."

They wish me goodnight, and after we hang up, I close my eyes and cross my fingers underneath my pillow, wishing that Ms. Birr calls me tomorrow because someone drops out or transfers.

Movement Nine

ribs = "the sides of stringed instruments"

I might set my "Borns College Welcome Week Schedule for First-Year Students" paper on fire before Welcome Week ends just for some excitement. Presentations like "Student Resources on Campus" and "Academic Honor Code" might as well be labeled "Boring Presentation" and "Another Boring Mind-Numbing Presentation."

To make matters worse, today starts with a "Reslife Welcome." Some welcome I received from Ms. Birr, who stands in the middle of the stage.

Emma and I settle into our cranberry-colored cushioned seats in Bewley Hall, where I watched the Borns String Orchestra perform. Harper's still a no-show. I hug myself against the auditorium's chill, while Emma's prepared in her oversized high school sweatshirt. Ms. Birr smiles at all of us as if she's not a messenger of crushed hopes and temporary triple room assignments.

Emma leans over with a small frown. "You okay?"

What I think: *Not really.*

What I whisper: "Yeah."

Ms. Birr introduces herself and tosses her blonde-brown hair over her shoulder. "Welcome to Borns College!" Her high voice fakes excitement, but the nasal quality reveals its forced tone. "For the next thirty minutes, I'm going to talk about residence halls, safety, and residence hall activities. Your residence hall is a community…"

Community? Really?

Maybe the music department deserves my fury, since they're the ones who mixed up the initial communication about me living in Harmony, but they're why I'm here. I'm not here for Reslife or Ms. Birr. Sure, don't shoot the messenger and all that, but sometimes it's easier this way. It's easier to blame the messenger when they're the one standing in front of what you love—or in this case, right on stage.

I would know.

I've had practice blaming caseworkers instead of foster families.

Like when the Fitzgerald family of Foster Home #4 decided after three years I wasn't a good fit, I blamed my caseworker. I screamed and kicked the back of the passenger seat and sobbed the entire drive to the God-awful Baker house. Ms. Trudy, my caseworker, kept driving without a word.

I thought, *Ms. Trudy's taking me away. They'd want me if she'd let me stay.*

"This is your fault," I said, after Trudy settled me into my new room.

Granted, I was ten, but I remember Trudy dabbing her eyes before walking out the Baker's front door. Fingers crossed the image isn't a memory but a guilty delusion.

Of course, I don't blame Ms. Trudy anymore. I never really did. Her round face held nothing but rosy smiles for the majority of time she was my caseworker. I don't blame the Fitzgerald's either. The house before theirs, Foster House #3 with Mr. and Mrs. Williams and their hellion son Trent, did a number on me. I wouldn't have wanted me either, especially because of the biting. (I swear Trent's the one who started the habit.)

Now, I blame myself.

Ms. Birr leaves the stage, as a person in a long front-buttoning dress glides on for a lecture about academic resources. I tune that out too. Well, for the most part. They mention checking out laptops in the library and where we can find the computer labs around campus, including the Borns Writing Center if we need help on our papers.

"That's the end of the morning presentations," the young humanities librarian says, after an hour of watching the kid in front of me scroll through Instagram. Their feed looks nothing like mine, all protein shakes and gym weights instead of violins and practice videos, which bored me as much as the presentation. To each their own, I guess. "Now, we're going to split you all up into small groups. Orientation Leaders?"

Fifteen upperclassmen, telling by their slightly more mature faces and their comfortability with wearing sweatpants, take the stage. Including the gym rat, who grabs the microphone.

"Hey, owlets! I'm Jackson, he/his, and one of the orientation leaders. You've heard it before and you'll hear it again, but welcome to Borns!"

Clapping swells through the hall. Some freshmen and other orientation leaders holler their encouragement. Emma golf claps, but I hold my applause. Jackson seems to bask in the spotlight. I don't want to feed his ego.

"Like our mascot, Borns students are wise…and active at night." He wiggles his eyebrows.

One of the orientation leaders asks, "Who gave him the microphone?" but the rest shake their heads.

"What?" Jackson looks around, his arms up with feigned innocence. "I meant we're up late studying." He breaks into a smile. "You know, pulling some all-nighters."

The freshmen laugh, but one of the orientation leaders pushes Jackson out of the way to take charge of what had become an impromptu and immature stand-up routine. "I'm going to call out my list of freshmen," she says, "and we're meeting at the library steps. Get out your campus maps!"

The lights cut on, and the girl calls Emma's name.

"Good luck." Emma hands me her map before giving me a thumbs up and leaving her seat.

Just my luck, out of all the orientation leaders, Jackson calls my name—right after he calls Dylan's.

As I exit through the center aisle to my group, Emma's map wrinkles in my sweaty hands.

Jackson leaps off the stage and jogs over to our group like some upperclassman superhero-wannabe. I attempt to stand as far from Dylan as possible. Once we're gathered, Jackson leads us out of Bewley Hall and straight for a shady spot on the quad.

Before I take a seat sn the grass, Dylan's familiar voice asks, "Moving to Harmony Hall sometime soon?"

I turn to see his mop of wavy dark-golden-brown curls and lip ring, though I also notice dimples I hadn't before. "I don't think so. Unfortunately." I side eye him. "And fortunately."

Dylan's dimples disappear, and he shoves his painted sky-blue nails into his front pockets before sitting down beside me.

"Too bad. So where are you living instead?"

I run my hand over the recently cut blades of grass, as he takes a hand out of his pocket to pick a buttercup. "Nowhere permanent. Nowhere that matters to you."

His bottom lip pouts with mockery, but his straight eyebrows wrinkle with what I mistake for concern. Or maybe hurt?

He holds the buttercup under my chin. His dark brown eyes meet mine. "Yep, you secretly like me."

"That's supposed to mean I like butter." I push his hand away. "Which I do. But not you."

"Okay, owlets," Jackson says, ending our conversation. "We have thirty minutes before lunch." My stomach voices its opinion on the subject with a growl. My face flushes at the possibility of Dylan hearing, though why should I care what he thinks? "Before then, we're going to play some get-to-know-each-other games. Or, as you all might call them, icebreakers."

God, no. Anything but the human knot.

"So, if everyone could stand up."

Anything but that damn knot.

It's the knot.

My very first week at another new middle school, after moving to Foster House #8, my homeroom went against another homeroom at the human knot for field day. The winning class got another point towards winning the grand prize pizza party, a big deal for a bunch of eighth graders who are constantly hungry from their growth spurts. I didn't know a single person, hadn't yet learned their names, but they were tangled up in my personal space. They referred to me as "New Girl" when they wanted me to raise my hand to let someone under. When they told me to step over someone's arm, my foot didn't clear, and my hand slipped right out of whoever's grip on account of my anxious sweat.

We had to start over because my fall created a chain reaction that brought everyone down. We didn't win the knot. We lost the pizza party by one point, and they didn't let me live it down the rest of the year.

Of course, since he made the effort to sit beside me, Dylan takes my right hand in his left. The tips of his fingers are calloused like mine from playing the violin.

Please, please, please don't notice how sweaty my hand is.

Forced physical contact always makes me break out into a cold sweat. Hugging Camila, not so much, but holding hands with a stranger and my nemesis-violinist? Definitely.

After we twist ourselves into a tight knot, someone out of my line of vision shouts suggestions to unravel ourselves.

Dylan squeezes my hand. "You okay? Your hand's shaking."

Our knot shifts, and I have to turn to keep my arm from bending in the wrong direction. I end up chest-to-chest with Dylan. His diaphragm expands past his ribs to mine with each strawberry-smelling breath.

"Just…" I look up into his too-close dark eyes again, "overwhelmed."

The side of his mouth with the lip ring tugs into a lopsided grin. "Lucky for you, I'm almost as good at human knots as I am at the violin."

He starts injecting directions, and not five minutes later, we untangle ourselves from our pretzel. All thanks to Dylan. He even called everyone by their names, unlike those eighth-grade punks.

Next, we play "Two Truths and a Lie." Turns out Dylan has a twelve-year-old sister (who I somewhat remember from our high school orchestra performances on account of her whimsical fashion choices), threw up on his first rollercoaster ride (which he also credits as his most embarrassing moment since he was in high school and on a date), and does not aspire to be on Broadway. He prefers playing his violin if he's on a stage. No one guesses my lie (that I don't know how to swim) because they can't fathom someone hating the holidays. They would too, if they grew up without their family's traditions and were instead forced to accommodate year after year to new ones. Or entirely new religions.

We play another one too many icebreakers, and then our orientation group disperses for lunch. I speed walk to the cafeteria because (1) I'm hungry and (2) there's not enough space on this small campus to put between me and frat boy Jackson.

"Wait up, buttercup," Dylan calls, jogging to catch up. I scrunch my nose at the surprise nickname and try not to notice his returning dimples. "Wanna eat together?"

"Why the hell would we do that?"

"You know." He smiles, unfazed. "So I can give you some of that free violin advice."

I groan and march towards the doors to the MDH.

"Come on, Corey, I'm kidding." Dylan's floppy hair falls into his eyes. "You can't still be prickly over me getting first chair in orchestra. That was, what, like three, four years ago?"

I halt on the steps and cross my arms, as students pass us arm-in-arm. "So what if I am? You rubbed it in my face. Don't think I forgot how you'd wink at me when the conductor paid you a compliment."

He lets out his teasing laugh that I scold with a scowl.

"I'm sorry for being a big-headed showoff. Can we be friends if I promise, pinky promise and cross my heart, that I'll be on my best behavior from here on out?"

He holds out his pinky, and I roll my eyes.

"Fine." I hook my pinky with his.

My hands are sweaty again.

He crosses his heart with the same pinky, and somehow, my heart turns the color of his hopeful nail polish.

Dylan bumps my hip on our way through the doors. "And I pinky promise I won't rub it in your face when I make first chair."

I nudge him back. "You call that your best behavior?"

His lip ring seems to catch the glow of the overhead lights.

"So can I eat with you?"

"I guess." He may be my rival, but I won't make him eat alone. Plus, I don't mind his dimples. "Just don't call me buttercup again."

"I didn't pinky promise that."

"Ugh."

The growing lunch line drowns out my growling stomach, but Emma doesn't make us wait long. She marches towards us with pink cheeks and tight lips. She glances at Dylan, but she doesn't bother to introduce herself.

"Do you know what they make us do?" Emma glances between us. "Icebreakers. Which, by the way, are *supposed* to help you get to know one another. Tell me how holding hands and knotting together into some sort of awkward human pretzel helps anyone get to know one another." She brings a hand to her forehead like she caught a fever. "I hate that so-called game."

I knew I liked her.

Emma complains about icebreakers from the line into the cafeteria to the line for food, though I sneak in a quick introduction of Dylan before we sit.

"None of them were at least fun?" Dylan asks. "Why don't

you offer your orientation leader some feedback?"

Emma's eyes widen as she sets her plate of chicken parmesan onto our table. "I wouldn't do that. They weren't that bad, anyway."

Dylan shakes his head, his dimples on display, and takes a bite of his salad.

I found out in the food line he's a vegetarian.

No icebreaker needed.

Movement Ten

frog = "slightly raised ridge fastened to the upper end of the neck of instruments of the violin family" that "raises the strings over the fingerboard"

As I walk across the quad the next day, a strain of golden light stretches across the weathered bricks and crawling ivy of the music building. Soft yellow rose bushes line the front and surround a metal sign that announces the building as Shenandoah Hall. My new musical home for the next four years.

Today's a good day—the citrusy sweet petals say so.

I have a meeting with my faculty advisor and their other advisees here in an hour, according to day three of the Welcome Week schedule, so an early practice to loosen up my fingers seemed convenient. And necessary. I haven't practiced in *two whole days*.

Stephanie Jeong doesn't go two days without practicing.

Inside Shenandoah Hall, pictures from past performances

hang on the towering walls. Awards and trophies beam in glass cases. The recently waxed floor shines back my reflection. Further down the hallway, a soprano voice reverberates from a stairwell, and I follow the tinkling notes down to the basement. The first room downstairs is the band room, and inside, a large semi-circle of chairs faces a wooden podium box. Through the hallway, instrument lockers of all shapes line the wall, one of them destined to house my violin.

Oh, the irony. Violin will have a permanent place to live at Borns before I do.

Better you than me.

Violin, nodding with a dip of its case as I pass the lockers: *True. Better me than you.*

I've found the practice rooms when the voice sounds as if I'm sitting front row in a concert hall. The insulated rooms have thick doors with glass in the middle, but the soprano didn't shut the door. She wants the building to hear her.

I choose a room further down the hallway, away from the beautiful yet belting voice, which fades to a faint whistle when my door suctions shut. Not only does it have a sturdy music stand and an upright piano, but the room's loveseat molds to my body as soon as I sit down. I place Violin on the piano bench and take a quick photo for IG to post later (à la Grammy-winning violinist Hilary Hahn's account, @violincase, where she posts about practicing). Then I close my eyes.

With my right hand resting on the upper center of my stomach, my diaphragm expands with a deep breath, three deep breaths, ten deep breaths. Tightness I didn't realize I held in my shoulders loosens each time I circle my head clockwise, then counterclockwise, then clockwise again. I massage my neck on the last rotation. On an inhale, I stand and stretch my fingertips as far to the ceiling as possible, and on an exhale, I drop my arms to my sides.

Most of the time, I'd now move on to jumping jacks, lunges, planks into downward dogs, another yoga pose that I don't know the name of that Kathryn taught me, and end on a child's pose. Exercises to waken my muscles and release any stiffness. People don't realize the physical stamina required to play the violin: we have to keep our lower spine to our neck long, our shoulders back, our feet shoulder length apart with more weight on our left feet, our arms raised, our core strong. Standing for an hour alone can be tiring. Playing an hour with perfect posture can be draining, and without a proper warmup, dangerous.

As long as I get in my head rotations, I'm good. I never miss those. Not after I skimped on them a few years ago and had a cramp-spasm combo in my neck for a week. Like sleeping on my pillow wrong, but ten times worse.

Now that my body's warmed up, it's Violin's turn.

I unlatch its case and remove the cloth draped over its body for protection. I wipe a few dust particles from the fingerboard and tailpiece before setting the cloth aside, then adjust the pad across the chin rest. Professional violinists, the best of the best, don't use shoulder rests, so I'm trying to stop using mine. But I make an exception for today. I slide the grip ends around the sides of my violin until the sturdy foam lines up with the dip of my shoulder. Before tuning Violin with the G, D, A and E keys on the piano, I rosin my bow until the horsehair grips the strings.

I drag my bow over each string, four counts each at around 50 beats per minute. The depth of the lowest string reverberates in my chest, while the clarity of the E string grounds me in my body and connects me to my instrument. I extend and contract my forearm as the bow becomes an extension of my right index finger. I listen and make tiny adjustments—my bow a millimeter closer to my fingerboard, my wrist dropped to smoothen the joining of my arm and hand and bow, my left foot turned out a smidgen more—until my sound is warm and lithe. Until Violin's body becomes a part of my own.

After running through a few basic scales, I play "Etude" and "Allegro" from *Suzuki Violin School Volume One* by memory. Nothing impressive, as most violinists can play those by memory; we learned how to play from that book. For the final touch on my quicker-than-usual warm up, I fish out a folded photocopied page from Roland Vamos' *Exercises for the Violin in Various Combinations of Double-Stops* at the bottom of my violin case. My sheet music for "Pattern 1," played on the D and A strings, has seen better days yet less-skilled practices. The paper might actually shred on its own accord one day, it's so worn from use.

With a final roll of my shoulders, I pull up Bach's *Violin Concerto in A Minor* on my phone, which I saved for free from the website 8notes. I download sheet music from that site all the time. Tom and Kathryn bought me the largest phone possible because they were tired of watching me squint (which didn't do my posture any favors) at my last smaller phone during my practices. I'm just glad I don't have to stop in the middle of a phrase to scroll down the page as often.

I used to own two violin books of sheet music, but they're both long gone at a past foster house somewhere. And I had to return everything I played in school because of copyright. Music on my phone is a safer bet.

After setting my phone on a raised music stand, I rest my bow on the E string and take a breath. The 2/4 time signature counts in my head.

One two. One two. One—

My phone rings.

A picture of Maddie's face removes the sheet music from the screen. I place Violin in its case with a sigh.

Sorry.

Violin: *Yeah, yeah.*

I plop on the loveseat and click the green button to accept the incoming FaceTime call.

Maddie's messy bun gathers on the top of her head in a purple velvet scrunchie. Her black mascara smudges under her eyes, but her smile is as big as ever. "Coralee! Omg, how are you?"

I try not to wince at my name. "I actually go by Corey now." The corners of Maddie's lips downturn, but she offers a one shoulder shrug like it's not a big deal. Like she never told me I couldn't go by a nickname or else I'd copy her.

"But I'm good. Where've you been? I messaged you like two days ago." A car beeps several times, and Maddie laughs with someone behind her, as a sidewalk on the side of a road comes into view. "Where are you right now?"

"I know, I know. Sorry about that." Maddie tucks flyaways behind her ear, and I notice she's missing one of her stud earrings. "I've just had so much going on with my sorority. College is the best, isn't it?"

She laughs along with the high-pitched hollers in the background. "We were at a frat party last night, so we're walking back from brunch downtown. Everyone, say hi!"

Maddie flips the screen so a group of girls with matching messy buns come into view. My forced smile tightens my cheeks.

"Yeah, the best," I say, once she turns her camera back around.

"So, you're making lots of friends?"

"I wouldn't call them friends, but yeah. My sorority sisters are already family. It's like having family away from home." The joy sparking in her eyes dims. She must remember she's talking to me, someone with no family at home or otherwise. "What about you, though?"

"Oh, it's...great." I fiddle with a loose thread on the loveseat, and my chest pangs when I twirl it free. "I've made a ton of friends too."

Emma and (hopefully) Harper may not be my sorority sisters, but I've always been wary of friend groups. I'd prefer a friend or two, anyway. Less people to inevitably let me down, forget about me, leave me for a university states away.

I might've been friends with Dylan in an alternative universe. When I first met him freshman year of high school, waiting in an auditorium for our audition times for all-county orchestra, I thought we'd be friends when I let him borrow a copy of the practice piece. Then he got first chair, and the tormenting started.

A faint knock pulls my attention.

Speak of the dimpled devil.

Dylan waves from the other side of the glass. Today his sunshine-yellow nails match the embroidered frog on his fading black t-shirt. His rolled sleeves highlight his lean angular biceps —I glance back to his cheesy face.

"Who is *that*?" Maddie asks, though I'm no longer looking at my phone. "You're totally blushing right now, Coralee."

My face burns like it's turned bright red.

One sec, I mouth to Dylan while holding up a finger.

"Uh, Maddie," I look back at her mischievous grin, "I gotta go. Can we talk more later?"

"Sure. I want to know about whoever that was." She blows

me her usual theatrical kiss with a giggle. "Bye, babe. Talk soon."

"Bye," I say, but Maddie's face has already disappeared from the screen. "Miss you."

Does Maddie miss me? Or does she not have time to miss me with all her new friends?

Dylan doesn't wait for an invitation before flopping beside me on the couch. Probably because I've been staring at the tiled floor for five seconds too long.

"What's the competition up to?" He bumps my knee with his.

"Just contemplating my strategy to take you down." I shove my phone aside with a grin. "You've seen the last of first chair."

He brushes his hair to the side of his forehead with a laugh. "We'll see."

"Aren't you going to practice and at least try not to make this easy for me?" I ask, when I realize he doesn't have his violin.

"We have to go, buttercup. I finished practicing and came for you. Our meeting is in," Dylan glances at his bare wrist, "five minutes."

"God, I told you not to call me that."

He's right, despite his pretend watch. The meeting with our faculty advisor is upstairs on the third floor, and my endurance is best suited for the first—especially since we're in the basement.

Dylan waits as I pack up. He doesn't say a word when I take a selfish second to tuck the protective cloth around Violin's ribs. Once I click the final latch shut on my violin case, we rush to the third floor.

We're both out of breath when we reach the top of the stairs.

"I like," I take a few gulps of air, "your shirt, by the way."

"Thanks. My little sister's into embroidery. Holly." He laces his hands together on the back of his head with a deep breath. "I let her embroider whatever she wants on my clothes—frogs, unicorns, butterflies, you name it."

"Cute," I say, between more gasps.

Dylan, fully recovered, starts counting the room numbers. He stops when chatter guides us to the loudest classroom at the end of the otherwise silent hallway.

A middle-aged man stands beside the door and shakes our hands on the way in. He introduces himself as Professor Perry— who is not only my faculty advisor, but my violin lesson professor and my strings orchestra conductor. He's also the tallest man I've ever met. His head of thinning ashy-brown hair could hit the ceiling if he so much as hopped. Except he doesn't look like the hopping, skipping, laughing type. From his cleft chin to his straight posture to his firm handshake, I can sum up his first impression in one word: rigid. Maybe he won't be so intimidating after the first week of class or so, since I'll see him almost every day of the week. Fingers crossed.

"Grab a laptop if you need one." Professor Perry gestures inside to a rolling cart in front of a large whiteboard. "Then pull up your class schedule. We'll get started in a minute."

Not the warmest of welcomes, but at least it's better than Ms. Birr's.

Someone calls to Dylan as we grab our laptops, and he nods with a flop of his hair and a dimpled smile. "Hey, Henry!"

We weave through the desks to the back of the classroom near Henry.

Dylan tilts his head over his shoulder towards me. "We went to high school together. He plays the cello. He's also the one who witnessed my most embarrassing moment."

"Oh. Nice…or not so nice?"

Dylan was on a date then. Which makes Henry the date.

A surprising pang curls up in my chest as we take our seats.

Before I can ruminate on my changing emotions and—better yet—before Dylan can introduce me to his rollercoaster date, Professor Perry follows the last advisee inside and stands in the center of the classroom.

He clasps his hands behind his back once everyone's seated. "Good late morning, everyone. As you know, I'm Professor Perry, one of two other violin faculty members here at Borns College. A couple of you here are violinists yourselves," he finds Dylan and me in the back of the room and gives us a curt nod, "but I'll have most, if not all, of you in class at some point."

"As your advisor, we'll meet regularly throughout your time at Borns to ensure you're on track for graduation. Registrar will also notify me if your grades slip or if you're put on academic probation. I want each of you to achieve what you set out to do when applying to college. I will hold you accountable."

Someone mumbles, "Damn."

Professor Perry must not hear because he continues, "Next on your Welcome Week agenda is 'Lunch on the Lawn.' I don't want to stand in your way of cheeseburgers and ice cream for too long, so we'll try to make this process as easy as possible. I plan to be there myself." He plasters an unnatural smile on his face. "Professors have to eat too, you know."

Was that an attempt at a joke?

No one laughs.

Professor Perry clears his throat and tells us in his back-to-business tone to open our laptops if we haven't already. Following his instructions, we log in to MyBC, our college portal at mybc.borns.edu. We'll finalize our class schedules, view our grades, and check campus information on the site.

After he passes out index cards with our instrument locker numbers and combinations, Professor Perry works his way around the room to approve our schedules. He hovers over our screens and dismisses us one by one.

"See ya later," Henry says, walking out. He winks at Dylan.

No one should be allowed to wink that smoothly.

As my stomach knots with what I blame as hunger, Professor Perry stares at my schedule for a minute before leaning closer to the laptop. The corners of his mouth sag. "You're not a full-time student right now. You're missing a class."

Of course.

"Is it too late to add one? I have to be full-time."

"It's still Add/Drop, so no." He squints at my screen for two seconds more. "World History is a required general education course. Add that, and you're good to go."

I sigh in relief. My life's issues are easy for once.

"Go with Professor Marsh, if she has any sections open," Professor Perry says. "My students say she's the easiest, and though I want you to learn while you're here, music should be your top priority if you want to get into the program."

I bite my lip and glance at the other students. Fingers crossed no one heard that.

I could ask him about the confusion with Harmony Hall and my rejection from the music program, but I thank him and add the class. That's a one-on-one conversation for my benefit. Professor Perry moves on to Dylan's schedule.

"Wait for me?" Dylan asks, as I stand to leave.

A smile tugs at my lips. He didn't ask *Henry* to wait.

Why should I care?

I nod, but Dylan's busy rearranging his schedule to add a prerequisite. As I wait for Dylan outside the classroom, my phone vibrates in my back pocket.

Emma:
Meet me on the quad??? *ice cream emoji* *ice cream emoji*
ice cream emoji

Me:
Of course!

Once he's finished with his schedule, Dylan appears at the
doorway. "Do you think they have veggie patties?" He starts
walking before I can answer. "Black bean sweet potato burgers
are my favorite, but I'd go for a portabella mushroom
burger too."

"Probably." I follow him down the stairs, but this time, I'm
not lagging behind. Thanks, gravity. "You can't be the only
vegetarian on campus. You're not that special."

He throws his ruffled head back with a laugh.

After we drop off Violin in its new home, we make our way
out of the music building and onto the quad, which is busier
than move-in day. People spread across the grass and edges of
the sidewalk in groups. Five games of cornhole play at once,
huge blocks of outdoor Jenga topple over, and bolas soar through
the air to land on rungs for ladder ball. Dylan and I stand near a
long table covered with a light-yellow linen, and I get out my
phone to text Emma our exact location. Somehow, despite all the
people and all the noise, she finds me before I hit send.

Emma grabs my arm with a squeal. "Oh my gosh, they
have sprinkles."

Tubs of ice cream, crushed Oreos, chocolate, caramel, and
the mentioned sprinkles wait on the table behind us. There's

another table a few feet away with silver trays and bags of potato buns for burgers, but Emma inches towards the bowl of colorful sugar.

"You want ice cream for lunch?"

"Really?" Emma squeals again when I nod.

Dylan shoves his hands in his pockets. "I'm gonna find my veggie patty." He heads toward the other table before I can ask if he wants to meet up at me and Emma's tree. "Catch you both later."

The quad seems less exciting after Dylan leaves us. Emma doesn't give me much time to brood, though. She drags me to the line for ice cream. We load our Styrofoam bowls until I swear they'll snap, then zigzag through the maze of outdoor games to our tree.

We shove spoonfuls of sprinkle-topped vanilla ice cream (Emma's choice) and chocolate-syrup-topped cookies and cream ice cream (my choice) into our mouths in silence, watching the people who will color the next four years of our lives.

A sharp pain pounds in the front of my skull. I press my temples with the heels of my palms and shut eyes.

"Brain freeze?" Emma asks, breaking our comfortable silence.

I nod.

Emma smiles up at the leafy branches. "Can you believe we only met the other day?"

I shake my head, answering her question and ridding my skull of the last jabs of brain freeze.

"Nope. I can't believe tomorrow's the last day of Welcome Week either. Or that class starts in two days." Chocolate syrup runs down my hand, and I wipe it off on the grass. "Hey, do you think Harper knows I'm living with you all?"

"I'm sure Ms. Birr told her." With a look at my face, Emma gulps down the last bite of her sprinkle cereal, since the almost-eighty-degree weather has melted her ice cream into sugary milk, and grabs her phone. "Okay, okay. Texting her now."

I don't trust Ms. Birr to tell Harper. Not when she hasn't told my RA.

Tomorrow, if my RA *still* hasn't brought my bed or room key, I'm knocking on her door after leaving a choice voicemail for Ms. Birr.

"Sent." Emma's phone clicks as it locks. "Harper did text me the other day that she's moving in tomorrow afternoon. Then we'll have the team all together."

"Last night for our duo."

Her chin sticks out with a wide grin. "You'll still be my favorite roommate."

"You'll still be mine too."

We lean back against our tree, our faces lifted upward to the cloudless blue sky, the same shade as Dylan's nail polish yesterday. Today's my favorite day at Borns so far.

I hope tomorrow's half as good.

Movement Eleven

col legno = "striking the strings with the wood of the
bow instead of the hair"

A booming voice that can't belong to Emma stirs me awake
the next morning. I press the heels of my palms to my eyes
with a yawn before squinting at the pale broad-shouldered girl in
the open doorway.

So Harper decided to show.

Better three days late than not at all.

"I haven't even moved in, and you've kicked me out of my
own room?" Harper looks me up and down with a tight scowl
before turning back to Emma. Her thick biceps seem larger than
they did in her Instagram photos, as she grips the handle of her
red suitcase. "Good thing I came early and didn't wait to show
up this afternoon."

Can I dive back under my covers now?

"You're not kicked out," Emma says, pulling her knees to

her chest at the end of her bed. "And Welcome Week started days ago, so technically you're late."

I grab my phone from the side of the bed: 8:43 a.m. Too early. "What's going on?"

Harper focuses her dark glare on me. "You need to leave, that's what."

Well, damn.

There go my hopes of having a pilates-style workout buddy, since I stay away from gyms now after that P.E. class with Maddie. Weight-lifting? No, thank you.

"Corey doesn't have to go anywhere." Emma's face matches the bright pink hooves on her unicorn. Her bottom lip wobbles like no one has yelled at her in her whole life, not even her parents. "I texted you yesterday. Reslife added her to our room until they find her a permanent room. She's our roommate for the time being."

"Oh, she doesn't have a room? Her problem. Not mine." Harper wrings her hands, the gesture contrasting with her harsh words. "And I see two beds, not three."

Emma throws out her arms, as if she can pass Harper some empathy. "They're bringing another bed!"

"I'm paying to put up with *one* roommate. You're clearly enough as it is."

Harper pushes over her suitcase to smack the tile floor.

No one moves. The suitcase remains on the floor at the foot of my bed—Harper's bed.

My heart descends for the both of us. Harper might be a jerk, but we both aren't having the welcome we expected when we first arrived at Borns. I didn't deserve to find out I'm not living in Harmony Hall the way I did, but she didn't deserve to walk into her new room to find she didn't have a bed either. I know, from house hopping in foster care, how much a bed means when you're supposed to live somewhere new. It's your safe space, your only sense of normal.

Still, Harper could've used her "inside voice," as Kathryn tells Camila when she throws a tantrum over another failed escape attempt. A headache's coming on from all her yelling.

"I'll go," I say, breaking the few seconds of silence. Harper's mouth twists into a satisfied smile, as I wrench my bedsheet off to slide on my Chucks. "But I'm coming back."

Harper crosses her muscular arms but says nothing while I tie my shoelaces.

Emma scooches forward on the bed and hugs her torso. "Want me to come with you?"

"Even better," Harper says.

Emma's eyes widen in Harper's direction.

Violin: *Don't leave me either.*

Harper and Emma shouldn't be alone with each other too long. I didn't win any senior superlatives in high school (Maddie won Best Smile), but if there were college freshmen superlatives, they'd win Most Incompatible Roommates.

I side eye Harper, despite the fact she could damage my face with half her effort.

"No, you both stay here. I'll be back." I sidestep around Harper and her suitcase. "This mess started with me. I should talk to Ms. Birr again—alone."

First Harmony Hall, now this.

Fourth day at college, the day before classes, and I'm practically kicked out for the second time.

Movement Twelve

chin rest = "a wooden device attached to the bottom-front of the violin that separates the chin from direct contact with the violin surface"

As I cross the quad's dewy grass towards Ms. Birr's office building, my thumb hovers over Kathryn's name in the contacts on my phone. She might not make Saturday pancakes, but she shows up when we need her.

Like when Camila peed her pants at school last year. Not only did she bring Camila dry clothes, but Kathryn picked her up early to get a pineapple-mango smoothie from Smoothie Goddess, her favorite smoothie place in town. Or when Zeke had a depressive week near the end of his junior year. Kathryn stayed in his Earth Science classroom until the teacher agreed to give him an extension on some project about the wind. And all the nights she doesn't leave Steven's room until he's asleep, so he doesn't go to bed crying from homesickness for his mom.

Kathryn would show up for me now. But I'd have to tell her I didn't get accepted into the music program, the real catalyst for my temporary room situation. I can't tell her, at least not yet. Not until the music department accepts me.

Instead, I text Maddie to call me when she can and head down the empty first-floor hallway.

Most of the florescent ceiling lights are off inside the building, and my thumping heart and quiet footsteps are the only sounds. No light sneaks out from under any of the doors, and Ms. Birr's office is no different. A whiteboard on her door reads, "OOTO," which I then google to learn that the acronym means "out of the office." Doesn't she realize incoming freshmen, despite our texting abbreviations, aren't working professionals and wouldn't know what that means?

Apparently not.

Thanks to Emma, I saved her office and her cell number in my phone from her business card, but when I call her cell, she doesn't answer. Her message says she's busy with Welcome Week activities and upperclassmen move-in. I leave a voicemail that ends with, "Please call me back as soon as you receive this." My confident words fade in the stillness of the dark hallway.

I should've known today would suck.

Foster Kid Rule #3
Ambivalence prevents let downs.

Slammed doors, packed trash bags, and ex-rooms are often the result of getting too comfortable, too hopeful, too happy. Like yesterday. Yesterday was *too* good of a day.

Today's the resulting let down.

I slump against the wall to sit beside Ms. Birr's door. My

back presses into the cool painted-white cement, and a couple minutes later, my phone vibrates with a text.

Emma:
Hey, our RA just showed up! She asked if I could text you to come back. I think Ms. Birr just called her?

Me:
Thank god. Be right there.

Emma:
Big favor, could you pick me up a coffee from the Brew on the way? I need to stay awake after our terrible wake up call

Me:
thumbs up emoji

Emma:
You're the best *red heart emoji*

If I was the best, we wouldn't be in this situation. I'd be living in Harmony Hall as an accepted music major. Not in a temporary triple.

Too bad there's not a chin rest for life.

I could use it to keep my chin up.

Movement Thirteen

jete = "a bouncing bow stroke that involves two to six ricochets in a row"

Every musician knows that, second to your instrument, the most important tool is your pencil. My third violin instructor, Ms. Sherry, who volunteered at a nonprofit called Music Heals that arranged free one-on-one music lessons for foster kids, scolded me my first lesson for not bringing one. (She believed in a tough love approach to healing.) I've kept a pencil in my violin case ever since.

I annotate my music. A circle to hint, "Don't forget that sharp." A tall, scribbled "V" for an upbow. A bold asterisk: "Stop messing up this part!"

The most common phrase of all conductors is, "Pick up your pencils."

The foster care system has conducted my life so far, and if I'm going to conduct my life in college and after, it's time to pick up my pencil. So I dust off my ass from sitting outside Ms. Birr's door and head for Borns Brew on my way back to my temporary dorm room.

Maybe I'll get Harper a latte too. A consolation sorry-I-slept-in-your-bed peace offering.

Temporary Triple Rule #1
Suck up to the angry roommate.

A morning rush fills almost every seat inside the Brew, but my shoulders relax when I find Luke behind the counter.

"Corey, right?" he asks, as I approach the register. "And you're back so soon. What more could you want?"

His warm eyes turn my brain into a run of sixteenth notes. But underneath, repeating quarter notes remind me of dimples and lip rings.

"Three lattes and a bagel, please."

His eyes flash to the line behind me before he turns to grab three paper cups.

"Don't worry about toasting the bagel," I add. "You're busy enough."

He writes my name in all caps on the side of each paper cup. "I've got time."

"Good. I mean, not about toasting my bagel. You really don't have to." I press my violin fingerings into my palm as he pours milk into a tiny metal pitcher. "But good because I wanted to ask you about the status of my application."

"Oh?"

"I thought..." My voice shakes, so I square my shoulders and try again. "I thought reminding you of my interest in person would demonstrate my dedication."

He passes me my bagel in a brown bag. "You got the job, Corey. I was going to call you this afternoon."

I tighten my grip on the bag to fight the urge to facepalm.

"But we love to see the dedication," Luke says, as another person steps to the counter. "I'll have your lattes right out."

Luke calls my name a few minutes later when my drinks are ready, but he's busy with the line stretching to the door, so I don't bother saying goodbye. I balance one latte against my side with my arm and grip the other two in my hands, along with my bagel bag. Some kind soul holds the door for me on my way out. I roll back my shoulders and keep a quick pace without spilling the lattes.

So much has already gone wrong at Borns, but I have to make my living situation work. I have to smooth things out with Harper. We started on the wrong beat, but the song must go on. Because I have nowhere else to go.

If there's one I know about us musicians, though, we keep picking up our pencils until we get it right.

Movement Fourteen

double stops = "playing on two strings at the same time"

Rounding the corner from the stairs into the hallway, a wooden bed-frame and twin mattress rest against the wall outside our dorm room. The RA stands outside the door holding a folder and a pen, which she clicks on the back of her hand. She stops pulling her bottom lip through her teeth as I approach.

"Coralee?" The corners of her mouth don't reach high enough for a smile. "I'm Maxine, your RA. Are you okay?"

"Corey, actually, and yeah. I'm glad you're here."

Her attempted smile lifts a bit higher. "Me too, Corey. And I'm sorry I didn't bring your bed sooner. Ms. Birr called me a while ago and told me about your temporary triple. I didn't even know you were here."

"I figured. I should've found and told you."

"Eh, not on you. Ready?" Maxine motions to the door,

making her black curls bounce against her chin, and I follow her inside.

Violin: *Oh, thank god. Took you long enough.*

The room looks a lot different from this morning. For starters, posters of Amanda Nunes and Ronda Rousey hang from Harper's side of the room. Not that I knew of these strong women mixed martial artists before now; their names sprawl across the posters in black and bold letters. While a couple ceramic unicorns sit on the top hutch of Emma's desk, two gigantic champion award belts cover the surface of Harper's.

Only Ms. Birr would pair them as roommates.

Emma hugs her knees to her chest on the edge of bed. She lifts her fingers to wave at me with a tight smile, but Harper doesn't acknowledge me or Maxine, even when I put her latte beside her on her (already messy) desk. Her headphones remain over her ears, playing muffled rock music as she stares at the ceiling from her bed—now covered in her black sheets and bedspread. My sheets rest in folded squares beside Emma.

I hand Emma her latte before taking a seat in her desk chair, and her thankful squeal makes up for Harper's silence.

Before sitting down, Maxine hands us each a paper from her folder labeled, "Roommate Agreement and Conflict Resolution." Maxine stands in front of Harper—with more guts than I would've given her credit—until Harper yanks the paper from her hand and grabs the latte.

"I appreciate you all having me in your space today." Maxine flares out her flowy paisley skirt and rests the folder on her lap. "Aside from being your RA, I'm a junior History major and founding member of the Gosh Yarn It knitting club."

This earns her a scoff from Harper and an, "Oh, wow!" from Emma.

"I'm meeting with all roommates on our hall floor to go over roommate agreements, but I wanted to meet with you first after this morning's incident." Maxine clicks her pen twice before continuing. "That's why I adjusted your roommate agreement to include some of our conflict resolution paperwork."

Her grip tightens around her pen as she turns to me. "Again, I wanted to apologize to you, Corey, for the lack of planning on our part." Our chairs seem too close together because of how clear the red rim around her bottom lip is from gnawing on it.

Harper scoffs. "You're seriously apologizing to her?"

Maxine doesn't address Harper until I nod, accepting her apology.

"I know your living situation isn't what you thought it would be, Harper, but Corey and Emma are in the same situation. A few other freshmen across campus are too. None of you planned on living in a temporary triple."

"Right, and the fact we're all forced into this is supposed to make this better?"

"*Temporarily*," Maxine says. "Remember, this isn't permanent. A room should open up soon enough, and after waiting a semester, freshmen can request roommate swaps."

"So you're saying I have to live with these two for a semester before Reslife will let me and some other sorry freshmen swap rooms?"

"Yes."

"But why?" Harper's bed squeaks as she leans forward. "What if I convince some poor sucker to switch? What then?"

Maxine shakes her head and tucks an expressive strand of hair back behind her ear. "Still no freshman roommate swaps until the end of the semester. It's a Reslife rule."

Harper's eyebrows raise as if to say, "You didn't answer

my question."

Maxine's pen clicks a few times before she sighs. "Or else every freshman would request a new roommate every day as people make new friends. Or would request a new room at the first sign of conflict. The college wants students to learn conflict resolution and resiliency skills. I know it's hard, living with people other than your family for the first time."

Not the first time for all of us.

"Let's move on." Maxine takes another paper out of her folder. "I gave each of you a copy of the roommate agreement, but don't fill it out. Just follow along. I'll take notes on mine while we talk, so you can give your copies back to me and write your initials on the completed document. Make sense?"

We nod, and Harper refrains from rolling her eyes this time.

The first page of the document isn't too bad. First, we talk through room cleanliness:

Emma: "A clean room is a clean mind, as they say."

Me: "I don't have that much stuff so…"

Harper: "Don't touch my shit."

Then, our privacy and visitation expectations:

Emma: "My boyfriend will never stay the night, promise. That would be so rude."

Me: "All I care about is sleeping. Undisturbed."

Harper: "Don't touch my shit, and don't talk to

my friends."

Last, we hash out how we feel about sharing our personal belongings:

Emma: "I'm happy to share!"

Me: "Just ask first."

Harper: "Don't touch my shit."

After we discuss each section on the front, Maxine stops scribbling and tells us to flip over our papers to two questions: (1) What's the conflict from your perspective? and (2) What's your ideal yet realistic solution?

"Let's move on to the conflict resolution portion," Maxine says. "Please use 'I' statements and respectful language. Please." She doesn't hide her glance in Harper's direction.

Harper raises her hands in mock innocence to frame the print of Led Zeppelin's *Physical Graffiti* album cover on her shirt.

"I think we established the conflict, so I'd like to jump to the second question. Harper, what would be your solution, other than swapping rooms?"

"My ideal would be to not go to this college." Maxine drops her head to the side in annoyance, so Harper crosses her arms (showcasing her shoulder muscles) and says, "Fine. I guess, if my solution has to be realistic, it's for them to bunk their beds and stay on their side of the room."

For the most part, foster care allowed me my own room, so I've never had a bunk bed. In middle school, my brief friend Taylor started sharing one with her younger sister. Taylor complained for a month straight. She lost having her own room because her mom was having another baby. I remember thinking, if I was her, I'd want to share my room. I'd want my siblings close.

"I've always wanted bunk beds," Emma says.

I return her smile. "Fine by me."

Before she leaves, Maxine has us write our initials beside each section of her completed roommate agreement and sign our full names under our conflict solution. She hands me a room key taped to an index card, and then we move my bed in from the hallway and on top of Emma's to form our new bunk bed. Maxine offers to bring me a desk from the supply room, but I turn down the offer. A desk would make the room more cramped. It would be another eyesore—another reason for Harper to hate me.

Despite this being her ideal set up, Harper's probably counting down the days of this semester to swap rooms. Maybe I should do the same, considering her entrance this morning. But who knows? This semester, having double the roommates, might go better than any of us expect.

We'll have to play our temporary triple by ear, and I'm good at playing by ear.

At least with the violin.

Movement Fifteen

open strings = "the unstopped strings of violins, lutes, etc. shown by the sign O" (which always make me think ORGASM)

Sheridan Hall holds all English, Communications, and History classes—and is the jarring opposite of Shenandoah Hall, the music building, with its bare eggshell walls and scuffed and gray-speckled tiled floors. As Emma and I walk through the second-floor hallway to our shared First-Year Composition and first-ever college class, my phone vibrates again and again with incoming texts in my back pocket.

Kathryn:
Good luck today! Call us later.

Tom:
Be confident and trust your talent. We believe in you!!

Drew:
You got this *thumbs up*

I react to their texts with hearts and inch closer to Emma, towards the edge of the packed hallway. Students sporting messy buns and sweatpants carry large coffees and thin book bags, much different from the bursting book bags of high school. Not to mention much better for spinal health.

We near our classroom, and my stomach feels as if someone dumped all the notes from my sheet music inside. I tap my palm with violin fingerings, this time one of my favorite sonatas by Bach. Shouldn't my chest burst with anticipation? Shouldn't my face hurt from smiling? I've already come farther than most foster kids, but maybe that's why I gnaw on the inside of my cheek. I don't want to let the other foster kids down. Zeke and Steven and Camila have to know that they can go further than people expect.

No pressure.

"Hey, Emma?" Her eyes are round like cymbals. Seems like we both could use a distraction from our nerves. "What's your major?"

She has known my major—declared, that is—from the minute we met, but I don't know hers. I haven't asked. The notes stop scrambling and start sinking. What kind of friend doesn't ask that stuff?

Emma takes a careful sip of her orange spice tea. "I'm undecided."

"Oh." I fiddle with the lid on my coffee as we walk inside our classroom.

Emma organized her folded shirts by color. She studied the campus map and college website until she could give a campus tour. She strategized when to eat at the MDH and when to eat at Borns Brew based on the flow of students. She debated with Owen last night about what year they should get married based on their student loans. Emma, who needs to have her days and weeks and years planned out, hasn't decided on a major.

Her chin quivers. So much for a pleasant distraction from our nerves.

We take a seat in the front at one of the eight rectangular tables in the classroom, along with the other freshmen and transfers who've arrived early to make a good impression on the professor. Except he shows up two minutes late.

"Good morning, class." A thin yet lean man turns the second light switch on, and students squint up from their phones. He adjusts his circular-framed glasses. "I'm Dr. Lavery, but please call me Calvin."

After setting his sporty briefcase down on the front podium, he zips around the room, passing out index-card-sized papers. "We're going to do an in-class writing assignment today. An analytical paper. Please introduce, explain, and analyze this quote."

Emma shoots her hand up, as I sink down into my seat. "Is this for a grade?"

"Nope." Calvin moves around the tables like he runs marathons, reminding me of Kathryn. "This is for me to assess where everyone's writing levels are at."

He places a few copies on our table, and Emma slides one over to me:

A foolish consistency is the hobgoblin of little minds, adored by little statesmen and philosophers and divines. With consistency a great soul has simply nothing to do.

He may as well concern himself with his shadow on the wall. Speak what you think now in hard words, and to-morrow speak what to-morrow thinks in hard words again, though it contradict every thing you say to-day. — 'Ah, so you shall be sure to be misunderstood.' — Is it so bad, then, to be misunderstood? Pythagoras was misunderstood, and Socrates, and Jesus, and Luther, and Copernicus, and Galileo, and Newton, and every pure and wise spirit that ever took flesh. To be great is to be misunderstood. (Ralph Waldo Emerson, *Self-Reliance*)

I reread it a second time, then a third and fourth.

I communicate through Violin, when I connect its bow to its strings. Sound pours off the stage into the audience and communicates more than I ever could with my mouth or with my pen.

Music is my first language. I'm more fluent in it than any other.

"You're dismissed as soon as you finish the assignment." Calvin rests his laptop on the podium instead of a nearby table, so he can type while standing. "Get a laptop from the station at the front if you need one. Make sure to pick up a syllabus from me before you leave."

Emma finishes in under thirty minutes and leaves first. I stay the entire brutal fifty minutes and leave last.

♪♫

The door to Professor Perry's office stands open, revealing globes and maps and pictures from his travels. Multiple diplomas and certificates and awards hang about the walls. In one of the many framed photos, Professor Perry stands with a group of musicians in front of a giant sign made of stone with gold Chinese characters and letters that read, "Xi'an Conservatory of Music." In the photo beside it, Professor Perry shakes hands with world-famous cellist Yo-Yo Ma.

My second-hand nervous laugh alerts Professor Perry of my arrival, and he says, "Come on in, Corey." He follows my gaze. "I studied at the conservatory after getting my Doctor of Musical Arts degree from Temple University in Philadelphia. I actually taught a masterclass there about three years ago now."

"Wow." I stand in the middle of his office, ogling over the filled walls.

Professor Perry visited China as a violinist, and from the looks of his pictures, he's traveled all across the world with his violin. He's that good.

No pressure, but now I have lessons and string orchestra with him.

"Enough about me." Professor Perry extends a hand to the empty chair in front of his desk. "Take a seat, Corey."

I rest Violin against my chair.

"Before we get started," Professor Perry says, his amused expression turning somber, "I wanted to check in with you. Ms. Birr left a message for me a day or so ago and explained how our program emailed two different rosters for Harmony Hall. As I hear it, this caused some challenges with your living arrangements."

I slump, think better of it, and sit up in the chair. He can't know about my poor posture.

"I can assure you, on behalf of every faculty and staff member here in the music department, we are happy to have you." He offers a tight-lipped smile that does nothing to alleviate my burning cheeks or sweaty palms. "We had more students apply this year. Like yourself, they are all dedicated, talented musicians. Unfortunately, we could only admit so many when considering our resources, including space in Harmony Hall. We had room for one freshman violinist, and while we listed you as the tentative recipient, another student's audition surpassed yours."

Oh my god.

Dylan.

He took my spot into Harmony. He's why I'm not accepted.

"However, there's one way you can live in Harmony Hall this year. As director of the music program, I oversee the dorm assignments—along with Director Birr, of course. We have some music majors graduating this December, two of which live in Harmony. You'll audition for chair assignments in string orchestra during midterms. You make first chair, I'll guarantee your acceptance into the music program and a room in Harmony next semester."

"Really?"

He nods and rolls up the cuffs on his gray-striped button down, and I'm not sure if it's a fidgety habit or if he's preparing to play his violin. "I remember your audition for the program vividly. I have no doubt our lessons will catch you up to speed before then."

Catch me up to speed?

My face must give away my disbelief because he explains, "You're a skilled musician, Corey, but we have much technical work to do if you want to make first chair. Which brings me to today's lesson."

We both get out our violins, and he brings his to his shoulder.

"I want you to play son filé—long sustained bow strokes—on each open string." He sets a nearby metronome to a slow drudging beat then demonstrates. "The exercise will refine your ear and master your bow control."

After playing back his instructions, I play each string for what feels like fifty more times before he asks me to add double stops, then dynamic variations, moving from piano to forte and back to piano. Per his instructions, I tweak slight movements on each exercise. I relax my left hand yet widen the space between it and the violin neck. I turn my left foot a centimeter inward. My bow transitions back from the D to G string. I lessen the rock of my bow between strings for a subtler movement. He tells me to listen, listen closer, and make my own adjustments.

I haven't played a single page of sheet music when the lesson comes to an end.

"Great work today, Corey. I emailed you and my other violin students an article right before your lesson from *Strings Magazine*." Professor Perry packs up his violin, and I follow suit. "Everyone comes from a different background with one-on-one lessons, so hopefully this article gives you an idea of my approach —or rather, what I expect from yours. Pay close attention to the quote from Victoria Chiang."

I nod as I click the latches shut to my violin case and avoid meeting his eyes. He had me spend the last fifty minutes playing open strings like I'm pre-*Suzuki Violin School Volume One*. Like I better hit some musical gas pedal if I'm to "catch up to speed" and get into the music department come auditions.

Like Dylan's a better violinist than me.

"See you in a couple hours for orchestra," Professor Perry says.

Thirty minutes later, after grabbing to-go sandwiches with

Emma from Borns Brew, I check my email from my top bunk. Sure enough, Professor Perry sent a link to the article "7 Teachers Offer Insight on a Successful College-Level String-Study Experience," which I skim as I eat my peanut butter and jelly. I read Chiang's quote carefully, though.

> I believe the most successful partnership between student and teacher occurs when the impetus for growth comes from the student. As a teacher, I can then provide guidance, information, ideas, and support. So for the student:
>
> - Develop a vision for your playing. Listen to music, go to concerts, gain a conscious concept of sound, musicianship, and style that you want to create.
> - Have an expectation of what you want to accomplish each day, week, and year, including thoughtful practice and methodical preparation for each lesson.
> - Ask for guidance on things you need help with: frustrations, questions, etc.
> - Believe in yourself and invest 100 percent!
>
> —Victoria Chiang, viola faculty at the Peabody Institute at Johns Hopkins University

This doesn't describe my past teacher-led lessons at all, but the first two bullet points are familiar, if you count watching hours of orchestra performances on YouTube as going to concerts. What's most unfamiliar is the third bullet.

I don't "ask for guidance." I follow instructions.

That's what adults in my life have wanted, and that's how I

got through foster care. If Professor Perry wants me to "ask for guidance," we're both going to end up more frustrated than I am after our first lesson.

♪♫

With five minutes until string orchestra, Professor Perry steps onto the podium. I sink lower in my chair and accidentally kick over Dylan's water bottle. Swish and swish and swish, the metal tumbler rolls towards the podium. Professor Perry's eyebrows pull together at the distraction, and I pop out of my seat to hand the water bottle back to Dylan.

"Thanks." Dylan smiles, and his lip ring shines in the stage lights. "Hey, what are you doing this weekend?"

How dare he ask me about my weekend plans. He's forgotten who he is to me. My rival.

Violin: *Yeah, okay.*

I can't let him forget.

"Nothing that concerns you."

Professor Perry shuffles his sheet music and begins two minutes early. "Good afternoon, everyone. We're going to start today with sight-reading one of our pieces for the end-of-the-semester performance. I trust you have all adequately warmed up." He waits for us to respond. Some of us lie, though not me.
"I will not stop conducting, for any circumstance, until you've sight-read the entire piece on your music stands. I will critique you, and I may refer to the mistakes of individuals. As a performer, sight-reading will become a part of your life, if it has not already. Embrace it now, while you're a student."

I sit up straighter, ready for the challenge. I can almost feel Dylan's taunting grin beside me like old times in all-county and district orchestra. The corners of my mouth lift towards the stage lights as I follow Professor Perry's instructions to raise our instruments. Violin rests on my shoulder.

Let's do this.

Violin: *Dylan doesn't stand a chance.*

Dylan can forget any notion about weekend plans. I'm going to get first chair—I *have* to get first chair.

My bow feels like it's vibrating against my chest as it drags across the strings.

Harmony Hall, here I come.

Movement Sixteen

bariolage = "the quick alternation between a static note and changing notes, which form a melody either above or below the static note," and "usually involves repeated string crossings and is common in Baroque violin music"

Thursday, second day of classes, I have my other three GenEd courses: World History, Personal Development, and Psychology. Though I'd prefer Emma's Art History, World History seems like it won't be too bad—Professor Marsh ends class a half hour early because she can't stop sneezing. (I've never heard someone sneeze so loud. Someone actually falls out of their chair.) My guess, Professor Marsh will shorten and cancel class a lot, if she keeps showing up with white cat hair on her all-black clothes. She said she's allergic but just rescued a new cat.

Personal Development and Psychology, on the other hand, seem worse than I could've imagined. For starters, Harper's in my Personal Development class. She sits right behind me and makes a point of not meeting my eyes or saying thank you when I pass back the syllabus. Worse than Harper, though, Professor Reed assigns our first project: five group exercises at the Borns Recreation Center or three sessions at the Borns Counseling Center. I avoid gyms at all costs. After taking advanced physical education with Maddie senior year, I'm over grimy dumbbells and sticky yoga mats that fifty other people have touched that day. I don't care if people wipe it down after, that's gross. I'll take counseling over the gym, and I've had my fair share of counseling sessions in foster care. Counseling has helped me before, but counseling means talking about my past, and my past includes foster care.

Thoughts of foster care belong in that 30-gallon trash bag I left behind with Tom and Kathryn.

Then there's Psychology, which might be harder than First-Year Composition. Professor Dixon tells us not five minutes into class that a fourth of us will probably drop out. She spends more time lecturing about the brain than going over the syllabus, unlike my other professors. Oh, and Dylan's in that class too. Joy.

On Friday, I do my Wednesday classes all over again, so I spend more time with Violin on my shoulder than a pen in my hand. Not a bad way to end my first week of college.

Now to my first of many 6 p.m. to 11 p.m. Friday shifts at Borns Brew.

As I walk across the quad on my way to work, my phone rings with a call from Drew. I'm not *not* happy to talk to her. I like talking to her—usually. But right now, seeing her name on my screen jolts me from college back to foster care. One second, I'm on the quad, and the next, I'm in the back of her car on my way to Tom and Kathryn's house.

"Just calling to check in!" Drew's chipper voice makes the past remembered me slide down my seat in the car. "How's it going?"

"Good." A warm breeze plays in my purple-tipped flyaways. "On my way to work."

Drew's upbeat tone takes on a shrill edge. "Work? Where are you working? I thought we talked about you focusing on your classes."

Whoops.

I drag my hand over my face. "Yeah, yeah, we did. But then I saw the prices for textbooks. Plus, not having a…"

"Not having a what?"

"Nothing," I say. "And it's an on-campus job. At a coffee shop."

Drew's silent, so I add, "I'm almost to work. I should go."

I can almost see her close her eyes and take a meditative breath.

"I guess as long as you keep your grades up." She sighs. "We'll talk more about this later, though."

No use begging her not to tell Tom and Kathryn. She's probably planning to text them right now.

We hang up the moment I reach Deeds Hall. I tighten my low ponytail and roll my shoulders before opening the glass door. Only a few people study and sip on lattes in the lounge area. I bet the rest of the student body is drinking/pre-gaming with other beverages right about now.

Well, except for Emma.

Drew shouldn't worry. I did a couple part-time jobs during high school in order to pay for Violin. I've never worked in a coffee shop, though I've wanted to since sophomore year when I started drinking a daily morning cup of coffee. Plus, from all my time scrolling through the app, Instagram has romanticized coffee shops.

Luke's attractive face only adds to the appeal.

"Meet our espresso machine," he says, after I put on my required apron that reads "Borns Brew" on the front. I follow him behind the counter to stand in front of the daunting metal monster. "You'll get espresso shots here and steam the milk there."

He reaches under the machine and opens a hidden refrigerator door. "I'll show you how to make a latte to start."

He begins by pouring whole milk into a metal pourer and placing a thermometer inside. Next, he submerges a metal tube attached to the machine into the milk and holds the pourer at an angle before pressing a button. I take a step back as the machine rumbles louder and louder like a roller coaster building to a start, then zooming past us.

Can this thing explode?

The red bar on the thermometer rises. Luke snags a cup and pushes another button, and a shot of espresso drips from the nozzle into the cup. The milk bubbles and steam rises. He pulls out the thermometer, wipes it on a rag, and pours the milk in with the espresso.

After fitting on a coffee cozy and smacking on a lid, he hands me the cup. "Done."

Perfect temperature, frothy milk, sweet espresso. It's probably the best unflavored latte I've had.

"This is good," I say.

"Damn good." Luke hands me the pourer. "Now you try."

Some milk splashes on the counter when I fill the pourer. I set it on the espresso machine and press the button. I forget the thermometer. By the time I set it in the milk, the espresso shot finishes. I grab the milk, and the thermometer tumbles out onto the floor. I pour the milk into the cup and add the cozy and lid.

"Um, here."

I hand Luke the cup, but he hands it back to me. I take a sip and almost spit the latte in his face, it's so bitter.

Luke takes the cup from me and snaps off the lid. "You have about thirty seconds to get the milk into the cup. If you don't, the espresso dies, and it loses its sweetness."

He pours my failed contents into the sink behind us, and I wrap my arms around myself.

"Don't worry about it, Corey," Luke says, turning back around to meet my eyes. His full lips turn up at the corners. "You'll be a professional barista in no time. Harder than it looks, though, right?"

I nod.

Thanks a lot, Instagram.

♪♫

Emma and I's weekend goal: give Harper as much space as possible. If we do that, this temporary triple situation just might work out.

So Emma and I spend Saturday afternoon on the quad. We sit on her thin, pink blanket in front of our tree, Emma reading her Art History textbook while I study my sheet music for string orchestra. With my headphones in each ear, I listen to the pieces and follow along with my part.

Not thirty minutes into studying, and groups of students haul and set up folding tables around the edges of the quad in a giant rectangle.

"I can't believe I forgot," Emma says over my music.

"Today's Student Club Day."

I take out my headphones. "Plan on joining some clubs?"

"Two or three," Emma says. "Maybe the Association of Women in Mathematics, and definitely Campus Crusade for Christ. Don't they call that Cru?"

Her eyes sweep over the halfway-decorated tables, so I know she doesn't expect me to answer. I'm the last person to answer a question about specific religious organizations.

Turns out Borns has more religious and otherwise clubs than I realized.

Behind us, there's the table for the club Witch Way (for Wiccans and witches), decorated with Mason jars labeled "full moon water" and "ethical blue sage" and "acorns." Our RA Maxine lays out knitting needs for her club Gosh Yarn It not too far from our tree. There's Gospel Club, the snowboarding and skiing club Ice Ice Baby, and Owl Productions—the club that plans dance parties and Pumpkin Day (whatever that is), according to their giant banner that requires a stanchion and two people to set it up.

I like pumpkins enough, like the next sensible girl, to ask Emma if she's heard of Pumpkin Day.

"Oh my goodness, yes!" Emma spins back to face me. "My cousin, Abigail, the one who graduated last year, told me all about it. It's A Thing here." She grabs her phone, most likely opening her Notes app for intel. "The tradition started back in the sixties? Or maybe the seventies? Anyway," she sets her phone aside to gesture excitedly with her hands as she talks, "the college doesn't announce the exact day until the night before, but it's always the week before midterms. Think all-things pumpkin, except they do watch *The Birds* outside at night. But during the day there's pumpkin carving and painting on the quad. Local bakeries set up like the student clubs today with pumpkin cheesecake and pumpkin cinnamon rolls and pumpkin bread for sale." She sighs with anticipation, and I know she's another sensible girl. "I'm surprised you haven't heard of it yet. Abigail said one highlight is pumpkin lattes from Borns Brew, with pumpkin whip cream and pumpkin spice sprinkled on top."

"God, that does sound good," I say. "Can we go if I don't have to work? I shouldn't have to since I only work Friday nights."

"Of course! But no more talking about it until after dinner. I'm already hungry thinking about pumpkin cinnamon rolls."

We get back to studying, but I continue to glance between my sheet music and the upperclassmen propping up tri-fold boards, spreading out swag like pens and magnets across their tables, and handing out flyers to passing freshmen. Our mascot, Hooty the Owl, shows up to flap around to each booth.

An hour or so later, when I'm somewhat desensitized to the crowd, Emma tosses her Art History textbook, luckily missing my head. It lands with the cover spread open across the blanket.

I pause the music on my phone. "You okay?"

Emma grumbles as she grabs the next textbook. Her chin wrinkles with frustration.

Before she can see my smile, I turn back to my sheet music. I'm about to hit play when a text notification slides down the top of my screen.

Dylan is second chair:
You know our psych test is like three weeks away, right?

Me:
I'm not studying psychology. And I didn't know you saw me.

Wait, do you see me now?

I search until I spot him at one of the student club tables across the quad. A pink, purple, and blue flag waves above the table, and a giant poster that's taped to the front reads, "Borns Bi Babes." Dylan waves at me before looking down at his phone.

Dylan is second chair:
You were hard to miss.

Me:
I was in the back row…

Dylan is second chair:
And your point is???

I tuck my chin so my cropped purple-edged hair covers my blushing cheeks. I guess I can't blame Dylan that I'm not living in Harmony. Really, it comes down to Professor Perry's poor taste.

Dylan is second chair:
2 classes
Doesn't this school know we can't be around each other?
One of us should transfer it's only fair

Me:
Not it

Dylan is second chair:
Wanna draw straws at dinner tonight?

Me:

I thought we were trying not to see each other?

Dylan is second chair:
Well…

Me:

They do say keep your friends close but keep your enemies closer.

Dylan is second chair:
My thoughts exactly

Emma reads another chapter before joining the chaos of sign-up sheets and small talk before we head to the Main Dining Hall to meet Dylan. He texts he's already at a table, so Emma and I go through the food line.

We load our plates with the food that looks the least unappetizing (mashed potatoes and mixed salad) then look for Dylan. Emma spots him first, so I follow her through the maze of tables and students.

Dylan's not the only one at our table. A few people I recognize from string orchestra sit around him—a sophomore violinist named Victoria, a violist who I don't know, and Henry. Dylan's ex-boyfriend? His friend? His soon-to-be boyfriend again?

Emma and I take the empty seats across from them but beside one another.

"Josiah," the viola player says with a nod, after Dylan introduces me and Emma.

"Henry and I met Josiah before Borns at an orchestra camp last summer," Dylan adds.

I force a smile.

God, I want to go to violin camp. One of the many reasons I'm not "up to speed" with the other violinists.

I turn to Victoria, who sat close to me in our first string orchestra class. "Victoria, right?"

Her blue eyes lift. "You can call me Vicky."

"We were just talking about midterm auditions," Dylan says.

I cross my arms on top of the table. "What's there to talk about? You know I'm getting first chair."

Professor Perry said it could happen, and it will.

Josiah says, "Oooooh," and Emma blinks at me.

"Wanna bet?" Dylan asks with a grin.

"Sure." I raise an eyebrow. "What do I get when I win? Other than glory."

Dylan holds out his hand with a shrug. "TBD. Winner's choice."

I place my hand in his, and I think back to orientation and the human knot. So much has changed since then. I meet his brown eyes and shake.

One thing hasn't changed: he's still the competition.

No matter how cute his dimples are.

Harper made a friend—Julia, the lacrosse player, who I met on move-in day—though how, I will never know. Harper doesn't make the best first impressions, to say the least.

They cram against one another in Harper's bed, in the dark, watching a horror movie, when we come back from dinner. Emma and I heard the chainsaws and terrified screams before opening the door (which now has a paper owl with "Corey" on it, thanks to Maxine). Julia waves with a grimace, her eyes still fixed on the gory scene.

I follow Emma inside, and when Emma turns on her desk lamp, Harper stops the movie.

"Seriously?" Harper jolts up, nearly knocking Julia off the bed. "Can't you and your sidekick find somewhere else to be?"

"Fine by me," Emma says.

What I think: *Kiss my ass.*

What I whisper: "Sorry."

I backtrack out the door. I have to make this temporary triple work. Harper will come around—eventually.

Always with a Plan B, Emma grabs her laptop and a box of Oreos before we head down the hallway to the third-floor lounge. She heaves open the thick door, and hot air spills into the hallway. Three frayed couches fill the room. Wobbly-looking coffee tables sit in front of each. We sit on the couch furthest from the door, prop our feet up on the nearest coffee table, and stay up late binging the first season of *She-Ra and the Princesses of Power* on Emma's laptop.

I tear up a few times. Catra's hurt and resentment over Adora leaving her in the Fright Zone hits too close to my non-existent home. Foster care is a real-life Fright Zone.

When we can't keep our eyes open anymore, we tiptoe back into our room, only to find Harper and Julia have left. Emma flicks on the overhead light, then stomps over to turn on her desk lamp before grabbing her toothbrush.

"Couldn't even text us…" she mumbles, as she continues to stomp out the door.

Later, after I answer Tom and Kathryn's texts about my on-campus job (I knew Drew would tell) and I'm away from prying eyes on my top bunk, I scroll through Dylan's Instagram account, careful not to like any of his pictures. The last couple-like photo Dylan has with Henry is from months ago at prom. Still, there's picture after picture of them together from before then: at the music shop behind the register, after a performance in matching black button downs, with ice cream cones stacked three fists high at a local downtown creamery.

My jealousy eases, not because I'm not still interested in Dylan, but because of how happy he looks with Henry. My track record for making people happy—making people want to be around me, keep me—isn't great, considering I've had eleven different foster homes.

But I'm at college now. Foster care is behind me (ignoring that I'm in extended foster care). And Dylan *did* notice me in Psychology and at Student Club Day.

When did I start noticing him?

Movement Seventeen

**G string = one of the four strings on the violin (and a
sexy type of underwear that Emma definitely does
not own)**

First week and weekend at college, gone. The second week is on fast forward. Emma and I continue to avoid Harper, and Dylan starts sitting beside me in Psychology. We say, "Keep your enemies closer," as an excuse, but he's like the tape on the fingerboard of my first violin. He's grounding, especially in our lecture hall of unfamiliar faces and cramped seats.

Third week, he tries to move his piece of tape (and me) back to the front of the classroom. I refuse. This piece of tape is stuck for good near the back row. Why would I sit where forty pairs of eyes can see me, but I can't see them? He surrenders with a shrug, as Professor Dixon dims the lights.

"Today, we're going to label the parts of the brain. Don't worry, though. We won't get through this in one day." Professor

Dixon hands a stack of paper to the front row. "Let's start with the frontal lobe, which determines your personality."

An arrow points to where the frontal lobe is in the brain on the large projection screen. She explains its function, then clicks to the next slide. I write the words on notebook paper since the front row still has the diagrams. My copy doesn't reach me until a third of the way through class, and by then, I'm already behind. My outline is missing a handful of labels she already went over. The black lines pointing to different squiggly parts of the brain remain empty.

I cross my arms across the folding desk attached to my chair, as my heart pumps with the speed of racing bows in the "Flight of the Bumblebee."

I cannot be a Psychology class dropout.

Dylan scoots his paper towards me, complete with the words I missed. I mouth, "Thanks," and copy his notes as fast as I can. I slump back when I'm all caught up.

He tears off a corner of his paper, writes something, and passes it to me.

Study buddy?

I nod with a relieved smile.

"Now to the amygdala," Professor Dixon continues, unaware of my previous internal panic. "It's the part of your brain that controls your reflexes. You've all heard of the fight-or-flight response—or, now more commonly, the fight-or-flight-or-freeze response—I'm sure. When you're afraid, the amygdala controls your response, and it helps you remember your reaction."

Maybe Camila has an overactive amygdala. Maybe that's

why her flight response prompts her again and again to run through our neighborhood to find her sister Nicole.

As I write more strange-sounding words on the diagram lines, I consider my own brain. I don't want my amygdala to control me like Camila's does. I don't want to be controlled by fear—not when it comes to Violin, not when it comes to living with Harper, not when it comes to a certain boy with a lip ring and a competitive streak.

People underestimate kids—especially foster kids. They underestimate how smart, how strong, how aware they are. Time and time again, my long line of foster parents underestimated my memory. I remembered things they said, from silly things like, "If you behave in the grocery store, you'll get ice cream when we get home" to hurtful things like, "I didn't raise my kid to act that way, so if you're going to live here, neither will you."

The bad memories from past foster houses will forever be the heaviest thing in my mental trash bag.

One memory packed down into a corner is from the first grade, when my teacher Mrs. Rossi read *The Kids' Family Tree Book* in class and gave us a blank family tree diagram to fill out for homework.

I couldn't fill it out. My bio parents made sure I would never know their names with a closed adoption, which obviously didn't pan out.

After school, my tears landed on the round kitchen table in Foster House #3, the Williams family. When Mr. Williams found me and asked me what was wrong, he told me to write "Mr. Williams" above the line for "father" and "Mrs. Williams" above the line for "mother." Trent became another line beside mine under their names.

They were my pretend bio parents for a day, Trent my pretend bio brother, and we haven't spoken since I was seven.

Not that I blame them on account of Trent and I's biting wars. (He probably has scars.) And not that I wish they were my family. Not when they'd take me and Trent to Trent's pick of a fast-food restaurant every Friday after school. I never got to pick. They let him order a fountain drink, but they ordered me water. I never got soda. Sure, I was six and didn't need that shit ton of sugar, but the message sank in: I wasn't as important because I wasn't *really* on their tree.

I should have left that diagram blank.

Sometimes not knowing my parents and my grandparents and my great-grandparents and my great-great-grandparents is like I'm Aang in *Avatar: The Last Airbender*. I've lost my connection to my past lives, to all the avatars before me. I can't talk to them. I can't ask for their help, their wisdom, and sometimes I really wish I could. Other times, I'm glad I don't know. I'm glad I'm not tethered to anyone else's mistakes or failures or warped worldview other than my own. Yet all the time, my fosters—not my bios—fill my mental trash bag.

I can't seem to *dis*connect from them.

So counseling should be a place where I can unpack my bag. Instead, with each step into Counselor Smith's office for my first counseling session, its knot pulls tighter.

"Have a seat, Corey," Counselor Robinson says with a warm, reassuring smile.

I follow his gesture to a cushioned chair across from a table full of sensory toys: a tangle relaxer, a stress ball, putty, a weighted lap pad. He shuts the door and turns on a white noise machine, while an oil diffuser blows calming lavender mist into the air from a windowsill overlooking the quad.

Counselor Robinson takes a seat across from me and scratches the brown skin under his white beard. "As I understand it, you're seeing me because of a class assignment." Behind him on his desk, two toddlers with matching braided pigtails and yellow jumpers grin at me from a framed photo.

I roll my shoulders as if holding Violin and take a breath. "Yes, sir."

He rests his clasped hands on his stomach. "Let's start by telling me about yourself. What are you studying, where are you from, and what's your family like?"

Every counselor I've had starts our first session by asking those same questions, even if they don't know I'm a foster kid. They ask not to unpack but poke my trash bag. See what they're dealing with. See how durable, how flexible, how *full* my trash bag is.

Family seems to fill everyone's trash bags, foster kid or not.

Still, he scribbles on his notepad when I say I don't know my family and that I grew up in foster care. Some trash bags are fuller than others, I guess.

♪♫

My first weekend without Emma starts in a minor key.

Metal slams out of Harper's headphones, as I walk inside our room after my shift at Borns Brew. She stretches across her bed (with her tennis shoes still on, gross) and scrolls on her phone. She doesn't notice me until I'm closing the door.

Where's Emma? I mouth.

Harper stares at me like I have a tuba for a head before

pulling off her headphones.

"Do you know where Emma is?"

Harper rolls her eyes before putting her headphones back on. "Went home."

I kick off my Chucks on my and Emma's side of the room and check my phone. Thank god I have a text from Emma corroborating Harper's story.

Emma:

Went home for the weekend!
Owen has a game *sparkling heart emoji*

So Harper didn't throw Emma out our third-story window. That's a relief.

After I scrub the smell of coffee out of my hair, I crawl into my top bunk, and Harper flips on the tv. She changes channels until she finds some late-night pro wrestling show and cranks the volume until the speakers quake. I hold my pillow over my head to block out grunts, applause, and theatrical banter.

The pillow doesn't help. The bulky, oiled men might as well fight right here in our dorm room.

"Would you mind turning that down?"

Harper presses the volume down on the remote at her nightstand. "Too loud?"

Before I can respond, she presses the volume up, louder than before. She drops the changer back on her nightstand and leans back with her head cradled in her hands. "Go find a quiet dorm room so we don't have to put up with each other all weekend."

I watch Harper watch the wrestlers with my mouth hanging open.

First item to buy after getting my first Borns Brew paycheck: earplugs.

Some students in the library scowl at Emma, as she calls and waves me over to her table next to the reference section. Textbooks, highlighters, and three spiral notebooks are sprawled across the desk. She slides some closer to her side of the table to give me space.

"Oh my gosh, I'm so happy you're here. I've been bored out of my mind studying Art History." Emma holds up a stapled stack of loose-leaf paper with yellow, blue, pink, and green highlighter marked on the pages—probably an elaborate color-coding system. "Got a quiz this week."

"What about your narrative essay for First-Year Composition? How far are you?" I turn on the outdated laptop I checked out at the front desk.

Emma arranges her textbooks into a neat stack. "Finished yesterday. What about you?"

Have I practiced every day for my string orchestra audition (even though midterms are weeks away)? *Check.*

Studied for my Psych exam? *Sorta check.*

Wrote my essay? *No check.*

"Haven't started. I don't know what to write about." I log in with my school credentials and wait for the screen to load. "How was your weekend?"

"The best. I was with Owen all weekend." Emma's cheeks flush, and her chin dimples to hold back a grin. "I went with his family to his football game. What about yours?"

"Um," I open my empty attempt at an essay, "how

you'd expect."

"Harper still a pain?"

I nod. "But from her perspective, I'm the pain that ruined her freshman year."

"Hey," Emma reaches around her laptop to pat my arm. "You can't ruin her entire year just because you live with us. I'm sure if it wasn't you, she'd find something else to be angry about. Me, probably, so thanks. You're doing me a favor."

What I say: "No problem."

What I think: *Pretty sure I'm still the problem.*

I can't help but smile, though. Emma's a good friend. Maybe even a better friend than Maddie, who I decide to text. We haven't talked in days.

Me:

Hey! I miss you. Can you FaceTime?

Instead of reading "..." for the hundredth time, I'm surprised when she texts me back not a minute later.

Maddie:
YES *sparkle emoji*

"Be right back," I say.

Emma nods, and I leave the laptop and my book bag on the table. I call Maddie from a bench outside the library.

Maddie smiles, showing off her bright magenta lipstick. "Hey, girly!"

"You look nice." I tilt my head down to get a better angle of my face. Doesn't work. "How are you?"

"So good." She props her phone on something so she can

curl the rest of her hair. "Me and the sisters are getting ready to go out. Wish you were here!"

"Me too." I wrap my free arm around my middle.

The rose bushes rustle in the late afternoon breeze. I almost wish I had a sweater. Before I know it, the trees on campus will turn orange and brown, and leaves will crunch under my Chucks on my way to class. I can almost smell the cinnamon apple muffins from Borns Brew that Luke told me about.

"How's violin stuff going?" Maddie asks.

"Good. Nerve-wracking." She turns to laugh with someone over her shoulder, so I speak louder over the background noise. "I have to make first chair to get into the music program and Harmony Hall, the dorm I told you about."

"Good job!" Maddie says, turning back. "You always get first chair."

"No, I haven't auditioned—" Maddie giggles again. "Never mind."

Maddie sets her curling iron down to check if she has lipstick on her teeth. "Have you been to any parties yet? And tell me the truth."

"I'm going to one next weekend," I say, though I have no plans to go to any parties.

Maybe I would if I were invited to any.

"Ah!" Maddie claps her hands before picking back up her curling iron. "You have to tell me all about it. Make sure you have a buddy, and don't set down your drink!"

I nod like I care.

"I better finish getting ready." Maddie blows me her signature kiss. "Bye, girly! Love ya!"

Has "love ya" always been a tagline?

"Bye."

For a few minutes before going back inside the library, I sit and watch the roses sway. A few yellow petals fall and twirl to the sidewalk. I can't tell if I've changed, or Maddie has changed, or we've both changed.

Or maybe we haven't. Maybe we were friends out of proximity. High school forced us to bond over our hatred for weightlifting and running the mile. Maybe that's the only bond to friendship we've ever had.

I'm not used to being the one to let others go—I'm used to people letting *me* go. Then again, Maddie might have already let me go, and I missed all the signs. The unanswered texts. The too-busy-for-me schedule. The disinterest in my life.

Which reminds me of how I knew Emma a week before asking her major.

I hug my knees to my chest. Take a deep, rose-smelling breath. Go back inside the library to my table with Emma, vowing to be a better friend than Maddie's been to me.

Movement Eighteen

f-hole = (not what you think—get your mind out of
the gutter) "one of the openings in the face of the
violin, on either side of the strings, that is shaped like
a cursive 'f' but really looks more like an 's'"

My chance to prove myself as a friend comes in the form of a
hall event later on in our fourth week of classes, How Well
Do You Know Your Roommate? Maxine taped flyers on both
sides of the bathroom door and created an over-the-top bulletin
board display with photos of roommates from tv shows and
movies: *New Girl*, *The Golden Girls*, *The Big Bang Theory*, *Pitch
Perfect*, and *The Roommate*.

I haven't seen *The Roommate*. Don't plan to. But I give
Harper a wider berth than usual after I see the bulletin board
Monday morning. The pixelated photo of a girl glaring at her
roommate from the other side of a door makes me shiver. She
looks nothing like muscular dark-haired Harper, but somehow, I

still see her face. So I don't practice Violin as long in the evenings so I'm already in bed when Harper gets in from god knows what she does until after 1am at the earliest every week night. We're only in the room together when we're asleep, and we don't speak or acknowledge each other in Personal Development.

Temporary Triple Rule #2
Don't engage the angry roommate.

Emma and I don't invite her to go with us Thursday evening.

The event is in the first-floor lounge of our dorm. After dinner, we find Maxine and a bunch of our hallmates gathered on the fraying couches and on the scratchy brown carpet. Julia, the lacrosse player and Harper's new friend, smiles at us as we sit down in the back near a foosball table. She's there with her roommate, a girl I recognize, whose name I remember just before Maxine gets started. Ana. Disney Club girl. I met her for a few seconds on my first day, at the same time I met Julia.

"Thanks for coming, everyone." Maxine stands near the far end of the lounge, where a tv hangs overhead. A huge notepad rests on a stand beside her, with markers lined up at the ready. "You've been living with your roommates for over a month now, so we're going to see who knows their roommate best. Winners not only get glory, but they also get this scarf I knitted," no one except for Emma looks enthused when Maxine raises a rolled-up, moss-green ball of yarn above her head, "and a gift certificate for a large, one-topping pizza from the local pizzeria, The Rolling Pizza Stones."

Everyone sits up a little straighter, including me.

If I win, I'd even share with Harper. Who wouldn't be nice

after getting free pizza?

Maxine places two sets of back-to-back folding chairs at the front. "You and your roommate will play against another pair of roommates for round one. Winners will compete against the other winners until there's one pair standing." She grabs four small whiteboards from the corner of the lounge and sets one on each chair, along with a dry erase marker. "I'll call out questions, and you and your roommate will take turns writing your answers on a whiteboard. You'll show each other when time's up. If your answers match, you get a point. I'll keep score on this easel pad."

Maxine calls four people to the chairs, roommates sitting back-to-back. She asks them simple questions like, "How old is your roommate?" (Emma, 19.) "What's your roommate's eye color?" (Emma, blue.) Seems easy enough. I don't feel as confident, though, when Maxine calls me and Emma to the metal chairs next.

At least we're against Julia and Ana. They'd come in second to Emma and Harper's Most Incompatible Roommates superlative.

Emma and I sit with our backs to each other. The metal folding chair is cold beneath my thighs, and the whiteboard doesn't serve as much of a blanket.

"You guess first," I whisper, as Maxine says, "First question."

Maxine opens a spiral-bound notebook that reminds me of middle school when everyone had a different notebook for each subject. "What does your roommate like to do on the weekends?" I write, "Practice my violin" on the whiteboard. When time's up, we hold our whiteboards to Maxine.

"Both groups get a point!" Maxine shouts and turns to add the points to the easel.

"That one was easy," Emma says.

Maxine glances at the next question in her notebook. "Alright, what's your roommate's major?"

I sigh with relief and write "undecided."

Except we don't get the point.

I turn around in my chair to face Emma. "I thought you hadn't picked a major yet?"

Emma grimaces, and the crease in her chin becomes more pronounced. "I forgot to tell you. It just happened. I went to the career center and decided on Communication Studies."

Maybe we should've practiced for this.

After we turn back around, Maxine asks, "What's your roommate's least favorite class?" and we get another point. Emma has a front-row seat to my struggles in First-Year Composition.

"For the record," I say, "I know yours is Art History."

Emma laughs. "True."

"Last question," Maxine says. We're tied with Julia and Ana. If I get this answer right, we're on our way to winning that pizza. And, I guess, the scarf for Emma. "What's your roommate's favorite club or campus activity?"

Easy.

Emma goes to Campus Crusade for Christ meetings every Wednesday evening. After dinner, we split up. She goes to the auditorium in Bewley Hall, and I go to the practice rooms. It's now a normal part of our week.

We turn our whiteboards to Maxine.

"Julia and Ana win!" Maxine shouts, as everyone claps.

I spin around to face Emma, who's already wincing. "Cru?"

"This just happened too. Since I decided on my major, I joined the college newspaper. I had my first meeting earlier today.

I loved it." Emma looks down to wipe "newspaper" off her whiteboard. "And Cru hasn't been…great."

Against all apparent odds of us losing to a lacrosse player and Disney fanatic, Julia and Ana not only beat us, but they're also the last roommates standing. Julie knows the impossible win-it-all question, "Does your roommate have any scars, and if they do, how did they get them?" (Ana has a scar in the middle of her forehead from running into a coffee table at her grandparents' house when she was three.) So much for winning the I'm-a-good-friend pizza.

Emma doesn't seem to care, though. Back in our room, she grabs a Cheez-It box out of the plastic tub under her bed, and we share it while we work on our second assigned papers for First-Year Composition—an expository essay, which I'm writing on the foster care system. They're due next week, and since I won't let Emma help proofread it on account of the content, I can't procrastinate this time.

Cheez-Its aren't pizza, but they serve the purpose: bonding over cheese.

♪♫

Frappuccino shoots through the air and lands on the espresso machine during my Friday shift at Borns Brew. Blended sugary ice sprays across the counter and onto my apron. It slushes to the floor behind the counter. I shield my face from the chunks of ice with my already-wet arm and brace for the continued impact.

"Turn it off! Turn it off!"

Luke's voice jolts me into action. I slam my palm down on the blender's power button. The lid—shiny and clean—taunts me from the other side of the sink.

What a happy end to the week. *Ugh.*

During string orchestra, Dylan invited me to go with him and his friends to a concert. He justified the invitation with, "You can't say I had an unfair advantage when I get first chair." I had to turn him down because of work. So here I am, embarrassing myself in a shower of espresso, milk, and sugar instead of listening to a local chamber group.

Frappuccino splatters Luke's face. He grabs a wet towel with a scowl.

"Sorry." I rub the back of my neck, leaving sticky frappuccino on the last clean spot of my exposed skin. "Forgot the lid."

He attempts to wipe sugary splashes off the counter, but it smears into a congealed puddle. "Don't worry about it. Happens to everyone."

Does it, though?

We clean as much as we can until Luke frowns at the expanding line. "You go take orders. I'll make the rest of the drinks."

I take my place behind the register while Luke readies himself at the espresso machine. I write drink after drink order on cup after cup and hand one after another to him. When the Brew slows back down, I doodle music notes on the back of a napkin. Luke rinses dishes at the sink, looking over his shoulder every now and then, probably checking to make sure I don't light the place on fire or something.

Once he finishes, he chucks the frappuccino-stained towel at the end of the back counter. I set down the Sharpie and exhale. "Don't get too comfortable. The rush will be back when the basketball game ends."

I nod.

"Do you want me to make you something?" Luke asks, as I pull a bag of to-go cups from under the counter. "You like dirty chai lattes, right?"

I blow a strand of hair from my face as I stand. "Sure."

"'Sure,' you want something? Or 'sure,' you'd like a dirty chai?" Luke's eyes twinkle.

I shake my head, and more purple-tipped strands escape from my low ponytail. "Sure to both. But I don't know what a dirty chai is."

His full lips spread into a wide grin. "Let me surprise you."

The espresso machine rumbles while I restock the cups, and Luke hands me my dirty chai not two minutes later.

"Just a regular chai latte with an espresso shot," he explains. "A filthy chai is with two espresso shots. Now you know, in case someone asks for one."

Warm, comforting spices waft from my warm mug, and I lean against the counter. Some of the few people left in the Brew squish together on one of the loveseats and watch a movie on their laptop. Some eat out of to-go containers from a local grilled cheese food truck at one of the high-top tables—along with a remade frappuccino.

"Sorry again about before," I say. "My brain's been a mess this week."

Rather than make a second latte, Luke pours himself a cup of coffee. "How so?"

I shrug. "Just freshman year stuff. Roommate problems and stressful classes. Like my professor reminded us yesterday that we already have a Psychology exam next week, and I just submitted a paper for First-Year Composition that I *know* I bombed." I sip my latte and close my eyes for a second. "Do professors do that on purpose? Assign the most stressful work around the same time?"

"Definitely. It's a whole conspiracy." Luke stirs a splash of half and half into his cup. His full lips curve into a grin. "All the professors meet before the semester to sync up their exam days and paper due dates. Turns out, they plan our failure."

"Ha," I deadpan. "I'm not ready to even think about midterms. Was your freshman year tough, or do I just have the worst luck?"

"To be honest, my freshman year was great. Which is surprising cause I'm a first-gen student, and I had no idea what to expect. My friends helped me out, though. One's an orientation leader now. He can be an ass, but I got through because of him. But last year, my sophomore year, not so much." He takes a swig of coffee. "Ex-girlfriend troubles. But tell me about your roommate stuff."

Ex-girlfriend? What happened?

"Long story."

"Come on." He switches his coffee to his other hand and touches my arm. His fingers warm my skin. "We're not busy. We've got time."

I shove my hands into the front pockets of my apron. Luke bends his head down to catch my gaze, and his charming smile almost tempts me to splatter my worries around the Brew like I did that frappuccino.

"It's nothing." The chai spices work their comforting magic. "I'll make it work, one way or another."

I don't bother crossing my fingers behind my back.

♪♫

After my shift, I'm ready to wash off the frappuccino sticking to my skin and clumping my hair, but I have to delay my shower because Emma cowers outside our room in a pink towel.

"Thank goodness," she says.

Water drips down her legs onto the tile.

"What the hell?" I jog over to her while getting out my room key. "What are you doing out here?"

"Harper came back when I was in the shower." Emma grips her towel tighter around her chest, and a burst of laughter comes from the other side of our shut door over fast dance-pop music. She glares at the door. "And she must've brought a party with her. She locked the door, and I didn't want to make a scene, and I figured you'd get off soon. So I waited." She shifts and her plastic flip-flops squeak. "Could you grab some clothes for me?"

"Yeah." I reach for the door handle but stop. "Aren't you usually in bed by now?"

Too bad Emma's sleep schedule (preferably before 11pm, 12pm at the very latest) wasn't one of our questions for our roommate hall event.

Emma's face flushes to match her towel. "Oh, um, Owen's around. I just got back a little bit ago from hanging out."

Hanging out or making out?

I hide my smile from Emma as I turn the knob.

I open the door to chaos.

Ten or more of Harper's friends, none of which I've met, dance in the open area of our cramped room. None are Julia, either. (She and Harper had a falling out a week ago that Harper indirectly told me and Emma while cussing Julia out over the phone. Something about ditching her at a party for a "loser" guy. Her words.) They sit on the edge of Harper's bed—and they sit on the edge of Emma's.

Climbing up to the top bunk can be a pain, but after tonight, I'll never complain.

No one cares that I've opened the door. Harper catches my eye but doesn't say a word. Not, "Do you need the room now?" or "Are you going to bed? I can move the party."

I push through the tight bodies to the dresser to grab Emma's clothes. There's a row of Jell-O shots on top, and I gulp one down for my troubles and smack my lips. Sour watermelon.

Back in the hallway, I pass Emma a polka dot nightdress and tan underwear. "How did Harper convince people to be her friend?"

"Maybe she's only mean to us," Emma says.

My back slumps against the shut door. "We can't live like this."

Our room isn't an escape or a sanctuary. It's a stage. We're either performing for Harper to ease the tension or hurrying off because it's another group's time to perform.

Emma yawns through another round of laughter. "What choice do we have?"

"I'm going to talk to Maxine. Maybe she can speed things along."

Emma goes to change in the bathroom, and I find Maxine's room two turns down the hallway of our floor. Luckily, she's on dorm duty, so her door is wide open. She's knitting on top of a violet bean bag in the middle of the room. Another green knitted scarf winds down from her hands and along the floor and circles around to her desk.

Maybe that's why she didn't rescue Emma. Or write up Harper. She's supposed to walk around the dorm every hour on her dorm duty nights, but she probably lost track of time knitting.

I knock, and she almost drops her knitting needles.

"Sorry." I take a step back. "Didn't mean to scare you."

"No, no, come in." Maxine rests the yarn on the floor.

"That's the longest scarf I've ever seen." I sit on a chair angled towards the door, as if Maxine placed it in that prime location to catch unhappy residents drifting through the hallway.

How many freshmen, sitting in this same chair, has she listened to already this semester? Today? How many have demanded room swaps?

"It's a blanket, actually," Maxine says, twiddling her thumbs now that her knitting needles are gone. "How's classes going?"

"Fine," I shrug. "Harder than I thought."

A folded, knitted blanket rests at the end of one of the two beds. Not hard to figure out which bed is Maxine's. There's a Fleetwood Mac poster and an acrylic painting of a lavender field above it on the concrete wall.

Maxine ties back her black curls at the base of her neck with a fraying lime-green ribbon. "What about your roommates?"

"That's why I wanted to talk to you." I squeeze my palms together on my lap. The callouses on the tips of my left fingers scratch against the back of my right hand. They're thicker than they were at the start of the semester. "I *really* need a new room. Emma too. Do you know if anything has opened yet?"

"Give it another two weeks or so." Maxine hugs her knees to her chest, and her unpainted toes dig into the beanbag. "But Ms. Birr said she'll let me know as soon as anything opens up."

"What about if I swap? Or Harper?"

Maxine shakes her head, and a curl loosens from the ribbon. "Swaps aren't permitted until the end of the semester."

"I know." I scoot forward on the chair. "Can't there be an exception, though? Please?"

Maxine's thumbs do double-time as they circle each other. "I'll have to write a report to my AC. They'll sign off and pass it on to the director."

"Thanks." I stand and force a smile. "That's all I ask."

I don't realize Maxine says, "Don't get your hopes up," until I'm almost back to our party room. I mistook the words for my inner voice, since I tell myself that so much.

♪♫

Dylan is second chair:
Wanna study for next week's psych test Sunday?

Me:
Yeah for sure
I'll be in the library all day with Emma, meet us there whenever

Dylan is second chair:
Too bad you don't live in Harmony
We could study in each other's rooms all the time if you did

If he only knew he's the reason I don't live there.

Me:
You don't know how much I wish I did

Movement Nineteen

pizzicato = "pinched or plucked with the finger" and
"for bowed instruments, pluck the strings"

In First-Year Composition on Monday, Calvin announces that
he'll give us five points of extra credit on our expository papers
if we visit the Borns Writing Center before the end of the week.
Thank god because, though I don't want anyone to read my
writing, my paper could use all the extra points it can get. I
reread it over the weekend and caught over ten typos that, cross
my heart, weren't there when I submitted it. Next time, I'll pick a
topic I won't mind Emma proofreading.

After string orchestra, I head to the Writing Center on the
top floor of Sheridan Hall, the same building as my First-Year
Composition and World History classes. Computers line both
sides of three long tables in the room. Two of the five tutors have
students already, and they whisper while hovering around the
same computer. I step forward, and a familiar-looking tutor on

the furthest row waves me over with a freckled arm in the air. A folded paper name card reads, "Rylee, she/her" to the side of her keyboard.

Rylee tightens her thick red hair in a ponytail. "Need a tutor?"

She pulls an empty chair closer, and I take a seat.

"Fill this out first." She grabs a paper from a stack behind her computer. "I'll make you a copy afterwards."

After I slide the completed form back to her, she rolls her chair aside, and I pull up my essay.

Rylee drags her chair back over by the heels of her hiking boots when I scoot out the way. "'Foster Care Is Broken but Not Me.' Strong essay title."

Hiking boots? Oh my god, I met her on my first day at Borns in the bookstore. No point bringing up our two-second meeting from weeks ago, though. She left the foot-photo impression, not me.

Rylee skims my essay, and a few minutes later, she clicks on the yellow highlight button. "You have a strong opening and good points, but let's work on your structure. This is your thesis statement." She drags the mouse to highlight the sentence. "Your body paragraphs stray from this later on in the essay. So, let's rework the flow of the topics you introduce."

I rest my chin on my hand as Rylee speeds through my body paragraphs and highlights each topic sentence. "You're really good at this."

"I should be." Rylee scrolls through my paper, and my eyes dart across the screen, trying to keep up. "I've been working here for over a semester. I worked in Borns Brew my first semester of freshman year and started here the next."

"Hey, I work in Borns Brew."

Rylee stops scrolling and spins her chair around to face me. "You might know my ex, then. Luke?"

Is she the *ex? The one Luke told me about?*

"Yeah, um, he's my boss."

"Cool. We worked together my freshmen year, his sophomore year. I quit when we broke up."

So she is *the ex.*

She leans with an elbow against the table, my essay forgotten. "Do you like working with him?"

"Sure."

Rylee stares at me. Does she want me to elaborate? There's not much to say, other than he makes a way better latte than me.

I pull my closed lips against my teeth in an attempt at a smile. Except it's probably my "awkward smile," dubbed by Maddie, because Rylee turns back to the computer screen. The tension only builds the more she scrolls through my paper, the more she drags her bottom lip through her teeth. Did I say something wrong about Luke? Or did I not say the right thing about him? Does she think I like him? God, Maddie's right. I'm so awkward. Rylee peers at me but turns back to the screen before I meet her eyes.

That's when I realize. She's reading my essay. About foster care. And she feels sorry for me.

I swivel my hips to move my chair back and forth as a distraction from the pitying glances.

Why did I come here? Extra credit isn't worth this.

♪♫

For the first time all semester, Harper talks to me in Personal Development.

Not by choice, though. Professor Reed pairs us up for an in-class reflection writing activity.

Professor Reed's flowy, knee-length pants swish together as she walks to the front of the room. "Write your partner's responses on your own paper and swap at the end."

"Fuck me," Harper mumbles, as I turn around in my chair to face her.

The classroom chatter builds. Harper keeps her arms crossed on her desk and her eyes on her paper.

Looks like I'm leading the conversation.

I read the first question: "So, 'what's something you're excited about at Borns?'"

She responds in a low, monotone voice. "The weekends."

I write Harper's answer on my paper, as a group three desks away chat about some upcoming football game. "Well, I'm excited about my string orchestra concert at the end of the semester."

She writes my response without comment and bangs her pen down on the desk as my cue to continue.

I tuck my purple flyaways behind my ear to cover up my flinch. "Okay, 'what's your biggest challenge at Borns so far?' Other than me, apparently."

"Don't be so self-important."

She uncrosses her arms and looks around at the rest of the groups. They're animated—unlike us—and everyone seems to answer the prompts with wide smiles, as if their first-year college plans don't consist of triple rooms and forced roommates.

Harper sighs. "Being at Borns in general is a challenge for me. I didn't want to go here. This wasn't even my Plan B school. More like Plan F."

"What happened?" I toy with my pen under the desk. "You

don't have to answer that, obviously."

"I guess you deserve some explanation." Harper smirks, but the snark in her tone doesn't reach her eyes. "I had scholarships to my first-pick schools for MMA fighting." Her biceps bulge for emphasis as she recrosses her arms. "Long story short, I injured my spine in my last match of the season and lost all my scholarships. The doctors say I'll never compete again."

"Damn."

"Yeah, it fucking sucks." She turns an inch towards the wall, with her back to the rest of the room. "Don't feel too bad for me. I still don't want you living in my room."

"Why, though?" I hold out my hands like she can place a reasonable answer in my palms. "And you don't act like you want Emma living there either, even though it's her room too. How could you not like Emma?"

"You're both like my Plan Z roommates." She draws a squiggly tornado at the top of her paper—my paper—before adding, "No offense."

"Um, yeah, I take offense." Some people a few desks over stop mid-laughter to look at me, so I lower my voice. "Why do people even say that?"

Harper rolls her eyes. "I just mean that I had in my head what my first roommate would be like. Neither you or Emma are what I pictured. I wanted someone more social and less," she frowns while squinting at me, "musical."

"Less *musical?*"

When did "musical" become an unappealing quality?

"And less unicorn-rainbow-flower-child turned disciple," Harper continues, like I said nothing. "Someone to get trashed with at football games and party with till 3 a.m. on the weekends. Someone that won't ditch me." She draws another tornado, this time on the bottom of the paper. "Y'all are a couple of wet fucking blankets."

I scribble an attempt at a treble clef on my/her paper and take a breath. "Well, damn."

She rolls her eyes yet again. "Don't be sensitive. You know it's true. You and Emma both are so—"

"What I *know*," I say, cutting her off, "is that you're not the only one who feels like college isn't what it's supposed to be. And you seem more sensitive than either of us."

"And I have actual fucking problems." Harper's hands clench into fists as she tucks them under her crossed arms. "So sorry not sorry."

I almost laugh.

Sometimes I wish people could paint with a canvas and brush how they paint me in their minds. Would they paint my chin lifted, not because it's a habit from my violin posture, but because they think I'm shallow? Because they think I'm self-absorbed? Would they paint me small and off in the distance, not because connecting with people takes me time after growing up in foster care, but because they think I'm not worth getting to know? That I'm not good enough? The paintings would all be true and untrue. Even my own.

Harper, though, couldn't have painted me *more* wrong.

So what if she didn't get into the school she wanted? I bet she has a family…a family who loves her. And with enough money to cover her medical bills. If I needed surgery tomorrow, I don't know how or where I'd get the money. I'm pretty sure major surgeries aren't included in extended foster care.

Who wants to compete over who has it worse, anyway?

Not me. She can win.

"Just so you know," I draw some eighth notes around the

corners, hoping to slow my pounding heart, "Reslife and the music department messed up my room assignment. That's why you're stuck with me. Because I'm not living where I was supposed to."

Harper's strong jaw flexes, but she continues staring at the far wall of the classroom. "I guess we both didn't get what we wanted."

"Guess not." I turn back around, though none of the other groups have finished yet, and slap her music-note-covered paper on the desk. I pick up my tornado-doodled one and go back to my desk.

With each new foster home, with each new foster parent, I'd have to manage the crisis control on how they already painted me in their heads. I'd make my bed every morning and say, "Thank you," at every meal and help with the laundry without being asked until the painting had brighter colors, smoother brushstrokes. Until the painting would be one they'd keep rather than wrap shipping paper around to send through the mail to some other sorry family.

I thought I'd gotten good at painting restoration.

When it comes to Harper, I guess not.

My and Harper's forced conversation in Personal Development only adds to the tension in our room, which becomes almost intolerable when Emma leaves again for the weekend. Harper hangs out non-stop with her friends in our room until early hours in the morning. Never acknowledging me, but talking and laughing louder than her inside voice. (God, I sound like Kathryn, but how haven't we received a noise complaint?) I stay later and later in the practice rooms, even staying till 3am Saturday night.

At least Harper's giving me a reason to spend more time with Violin.

My new sleeping pattern—or rather, my new hardly sleeping pattern—is why Emma has to shake me awake Sunday morning when she gets back.

"What time is it?" I groan, a few seconds into her tugging on my shoulder.

"Nine," Emma whispers.

I roll over so my face squishes into my pillow. "Too early," I say, though I'm sure it's incoherent to Emma.

"Corey, wake up." She shakes me again. "There's a boy. In my bed."

Her eyes dart between me and the bottom bunk as I sit up. *What the hell?*

Harper's nowhere in sight. She left me alone, vulnerable, with a stranger sleeping below me for god knows how long.

"He's in my sheets and everything." Emma sticks her tongue out like she's about to hurl.

I rub my eyes. "Let's go before he wakes up."

We grab our book bags and sneak out the door of our own room.

"Now I have to wash my sheets again," Emma says. "I washed them right before I left."

We head to the MDH for breakfast, then to the library to study like we do every Sunday. Except today's not a normal Sunday. Harper crossed a line, and I tell Emma as much after I check out a laptop and sit at our usual table.

"I know, I know." Emma pulls her Art History textbook from her book bag. "But I *don't* know what to do. I'm legit scared of her."

"Same. Things are tense."

Because of me.

Sure, Harper admitted she dislikes Emma as a roommate nearly as much as she dislikes me. Yet our temporary triple/bunk bed situation has turned what might've been a civil living environment for Emma and Harper into an uncivil one. Because I didn't beat Dylan during auditions for the music department.

"I talked to Maxine," I say, "but maybe I should talk to our AC or Ms. Birr. No way I'm getting through midterms—or my audition—like this. I'm not sleeping enough. And after this, I'm sleeping with one eye open."

Emma nods. "That might be good. Talking to our AC, I mean. I like Maxine, and I'm sure she cares, but she only has so much power." Her chin and forehead wrinkle as she tilts her head to the side. "What's that saying? The squeaky wheel gets the grease? You need to be the squeaky wheel."

The thought of marching to the AC or Ms. Birr and saying everything I've already said to Maxine over again makes me want to curl up under our library table.

I tuck a purple flyaway behind my ear with a sigh. "Maybe I'll squeak after midterms."

"Gosh," Emma says, "I can't believe midterms are in two weeks."

I can't believe they are either—not when I had my first psych test last week on the human brain that I'd bet my next Borns Brew paycheck I failed, despite me and Dylan's study session.

"I feel like we just moved in." Emma's round cheeks lift with a warm smile. "Except I feel like I've known you forever."

My shoulders melt. I'm a puddle on the beige loop carpet.

What I think: *Oh my god, I feel the same way. Since we first met, really.*

What I say: "How the newspaper going, by the way?"

"Great. Amazing. I've found my calling," Emma says. "I'm so relieved too because my parents had been bugging me about choosing a major every time we talked."

And they talk a lot. Way more than Kathryn, Tom, and me. Emma talks to her mom when her mom's on her lunch break at work, even if it's for a minute. And her parents call her every other day or so after dinner, right before she talks to Owen.

"So what do you write about?" I ask.

"I'm a Campus Writer, so anything that happens on campus." Emma pushes her textbook to the side. "Remember how you asked about Pumpkin Day? It's some day this week, and whichever day it happens, I have to be ready to cover it."

My lips pull back in a tight smile. "Still hanging out together, though, right?"

"Of course!" Emma says. I slump against my chair too soon because she adds, "Except I'll have to do interviews and rush off every now and again. Oh, and take pictures if our photographer can't go. But she said she should be able to, it just depends on what day the administration's surprising us…"

She trails off on account of her mental to-do list.

"Wow." So she doesn't notice my inward panic, I ask, "Are you thinking about quitting Cru, that Christian club?"

"Yes. Maybe." Her eyes refocus on the table. "I feel really guilty for wanting to, though."

Somebody sneezes at the next table over, giving my history professor a run for her money, but Emma doesn't flinch.

"So why don't you like it?" I ask. "You never told me after that hall event."

"A thousand reasons. But the first time I wanted to quit was a few weeks ago, when they split 'boys' and 'girls' into two groups. We talked about modesty and 'family values,' and the boys talked about lust." Emma looks at the table, and her chin creases as she bites down on her bottom lip. "And by 'family values,' they meant chastity and heterosexuality."

"That's so messed up." I try to keep my voice steady—we're in the library, after all—but the words deserve to explode out of my throat and into the quiet. My arms tingle with anger, so I tuck them under my thighs. "They know there are more than two genders, right? And that they're feeding into patriarchal bullshit and teaching hate?"

"Some do," Emma says. "Most don't. I'm ashamed to admit it, but even a couple years ago, I wouldn't have realized how harmful that is. I just grew up in that mindset. My parents, my church family." She purses her lips together until the crease fades from her chin. "My cousin, Abigail, the one who went here, she's been working on me. Sharing Instagram posts with me. She grew up like me, and she said it wasn't until later in college she realized how harmful everything is that they taught us. She said she didn't want me to be stuck in that mindset all through college like her. It took a long time, but last year, things started to make sense."

Emma crosses her arms on the table and looks up at the overhead light. "Now I'm scared to get out, to admit to them and myself that I'm not a Christian like they're a Christian. Or I'm not a Christian at all, I don't know. Either way, if I was to say any of this to the people at home that I care about, they'd straight to my face say I'm going to hell."

My chest is heavy with secondhand pain.

"Do *you* think that?" I ask. "That you're going to hell?"

Tears well in the corner of Emma's eyes, but she blinks

them back. "Yeah, I do. Owen and I started doing more than kissing. Not all the way. But stuff that counts. I guess it all counts to them."

"Well, I don't think you're going to hell. I don't really believe in hell, but even if I did, a normal part of humanity—sexuality, no matter what that looks like—isn't something to condemn. Expressing your sexuality isn't evil, as long as everyone is a consenting adult."

"I guess." She looks over to the information desk, then back at me. "Thanks, Corey."

I shrug. "There's nothing to thank. I wish someone would've told you that before now."

We fall into silence, and while I outline a short reading response for Personal Development, Emma stares at the same page in her Art History textbook for at least ten minutes.

She isn't reading. She's probably contemplating her eternal salvation—or damnation.

Growing up in foster care is trauma, but the fear and self-rejection in Emma's eyes sure looks like trauma too.

Movement Twenty

dirge = "a vocal or instrumental composition designed to be performed at a funeral or in commemoration of the dead."

When Ms. Birr emails me Tuesday night, I can't tap the notification on my phone fast enough. My heart takes on a new happier rhythm.

I don't have to be the squeaky wheel after all.

This is it. Permanent room, here I come.

Except Ms. Birr addressed the email to the entire student body. And the subject line is "It's Pumpkin Day Eve!" and not "You're finally getting a permanent room!"

I flop back down and toss my phone aside. My heart slows to a dirge, commemorating my passing hope.

Emma, on the other hand, squeals in her bottom bunk. "Oh my gosh, did you see?"

I groan in response.

If Harper was here and not out partying mid-week, I'm positive she'd tell her to, "Shut the fuck up," like she has countless times before. One of the many reasons why Emma and I decided not to confront her about the stranger-danger (ugh, I sound like Kathryn again) sleeping in Emma's bed. She'd probably tell us the same response, f-bomb included.

Another reason, which I didn't tell Emma, is *I* was the stranger-danger when Harper moved in. *I* was the one sleeping in her bed. Though, sure, the circumstances aren't quite the same, the guilt keeps me silent nonetheless.

Emma jumps out of bed, and I turn on my side to face her, not bothering to sit up. Her head bobs up and down like a bobble toy. Except I can't see anything below her chin. She must bounce on her tiptoes with excitement.

"Tomorrow's classes are canceled," Emma reads aloud from her laptop, "to celebrate the annual Pumpkin Day celebration at Borns College."

She sets her laptop on her desk so she can jump around the room. "My first actual assignment for the paper!"

A swell of conflicting emotions tangle in my stomach. "We can walk there together, right? Even if you have newspaper duties?"

"Of course, silly." Emma starts packing a canvas tote bag. She grabs her fuchsia pencil case, a large notebook plus a palm-sized one, and a sleek recording device. Why she can't use her phone to record her interviews, I have no idea. "I'll meet back up with you after every interview. Or you can tag along. You can just stand a distance away while I'm conducting the interviews."

I sigh at the reassurance—then jolt into a sitting position at the blast of my ringtone, "House of Bach" by Ezinma (who I've followed on Instagram, @ezinma, ever since I downloaded the app). My phone's on vibrate nine times out of ten.

"Corey!" Tom shouts when I answer. I wince and hold the phone away from my ear. "We called to tell you the good news."

"Good news?"

"Steven moved out," Kathryn says, her tone less like she's passing on good news. Like she knows me better than I do because I don't expect my stomach to drop. Or maybe this is bittersweet for her too. "He's with his mom. He's out of foster care."

I blink up at the ceiling. I try to make my voice light and fail. "Wow. That's, um, wonderful."

"He told us to tell you not to get too excited. He expects you to visit and still make him pancakes," Tom says.

I roll my eyes with a smile as a tear slides down my cheek. "Typical."

I wipe away the evidence that a good thing—Steven reuniting with his mom, his mom getting back on her feet, them living together somewhere safe—doesn't make me jump for joy.

"So, is another foster kid moving in?"

Pause. Then, "Hopefully," Kathryn says.

Tom jumps in. "We'll let you know. Things are still up in the air."

I press my lips against my questions. "Okay."

They're not telling me something. Maybe the system's making it hard to take in another foster? Which would be deplorable. So many foster parents are walking trash bags, but not Tom and Kathryn. System kids need temporary guardians like them.

"Well, have a good night, Corey." Kathryn's voice is soft, empathetic, like she's conflicted over Steven too. "We miss you."

"I miss you both too," I say, before I catch myself.

Tom and Kathryn are silent on the line, and then I hear Tom sniffle.

I close my eyes. "Night."

"Sweet dreams," Tom croaks out.

I smile as I hang up, then face the concrete wall on my side.

No classes tomorrow. Steven's back with his mom.

Emma hums "Walking on Sunshine," while she rummages through her desk drawers. I should crank the music on my phone and dance along with her. Instead, my pillowcase absorbs a few escaping tears.

♪♫

College never smelled so good.

With every step from our dorm to the quad, whiffs of cinnamon and nutmeg become more and more poignant until the cool afternoon air smells like pumpkin pie.

It is Pumpkin Day, after all.

Tables line the quad in a giant rectangle, like on Student Club Day, except adults in overalls and plaid flannels stand beside them instead of overzealous upperclassmen. Instead of t-shirts and pens and other cheap swag, checkered tablecloths and plates of food cover the tables. Emma and I turn in a circle and squint through the October sun to take it all in.

"I thought Abigail was being over the top when she told me about Pumpkin Day." Emma adjusts the strap of the tote bag on her shoulder. "Now I think she didn't do it justice."

I nod. *Steven would love this.*

My stomach drops, remembering how he begged me to make pumpkin pancakes—*colorful* pumpkin pancakes—last Halloween. He got the idea from a boy in his class, whose mom made them special every year with an assortment of purple, orange, and green food dye.

Now he can make them with his mom.

"Happy Pumpkin Day, Owls!" a familiar voice shouts from the center of the quad. Ms. Birr stands on a tiny stage with a microphone in hand. "Pick up your food vouchers at the check-in table," she points to a table near the stage with already a line of students, "and don't forget to stop by Borns Brew for a pumpkin latte. Now, give it up for your fellow Owls in the band Textbook Fighters!"

The five members of Textbook Fighters hop up onto the stage and plug in their instruments. The lead singer and guitarist with a blunt bob takes Ms. Birr's place in front of the microphone stand, singing, "I put a spell on you..." The keyboardist plays a chord, the bass player and drummer join in, and soon the quad thrums with bewitchment.

I must hum along because Emma asks about the song.

"Seriously?" I stop to look at her on our way to the check-in line. "It's from *Hocus Pocus*. Please tell me you've watched *Hocus Pocus*."

Emma's lips bunch to one side of her face. "Isn't that the movie with the witches?"

"Yeah, the Sanderson sisters."

"My parents didn't let me watch it." Emma walks again. "Witchcraft is the devil and all that. They didn't like Halloween much either, besides dressing me up as pumpkins and princesses. I've never really seen a scary movie."

"Damn," I say, as we step to the back of the line. "It's a kid movie, not a horror film. One of my favorite Halloween movies, actually. Along with *Twitches* and *The Corpse Bride*. Oh, and *Coraline*." I shake my head. "The number of times I've wished my name was Coraline instead of Coralee."

"Haven't watched any of them."

God, it's moments like this I realize how sheltered she is.

We take another step forward in line.

"Okay, tonight, we're watching *The Birds*. That's the movie Abigail said they play every year on Pumpkin Day, right? Then we're watching as many Halloween movies we can all month long." I hold out my pinky. "Deal?"

Emma stares at my hand like this is a Big Moment, which seems ridiculous but makes sense, considering her parents deemed *Hocus Pocus* a horror film.

"Deal." She wraps her pinky around mine.

After we check in and pick up our five food vouchers, I talk Emma into getting a pumpkin cinnamon roll with me before she starts her newspaper duties. We each hand over one of our food vouchers to a middle-aged woman in a long floral dress. Emma's hesitance turns to gratitude with her first bite. Even the icing has a pumpkin flavor.

"Holy, holy, holy," Emma says through a mouth full. "This is divine."

I moan in agreement. "Practically orgasmic."

Emma's face turns her favorite bright pink.

Once we finish our rolls, I follow Emma to an open table to interview a man in a weathered Borns College ball cap with bags of pumpkin-flavored popcorn. They're all tied with orange ribbons. I stand far enough to not be a distraction but close enough to hear "Mr. Ralph" explain his process of melting caramel in a pot for two hours, adding pumpkin flavor, and gently mixing it with the gourmet popcorn.

Emma asks question after question, as Ms. Birr and Owl Production members in matching club t-shirts set up games in the center of the quad.

How does an interview about popcorn go on this long?

When Mr. Ralph and I make eye contact for the third time, Emma ends the interview.

"I know I said you could tag along," Emma says, leaving Mr. Ralph to pass out the popcorn bags, "but maybe I can text you when I'm done?"

I look at my Chucks before meeting Emma's eyes. "Sure. Sorry."

"No, I'm sorry. I don't want you to go, really, but I need to interview Ms. Birr next. I know she's a sore spot. It's better this way for the both of us."

I nod in defeat. "Meet up later?"

"I'll text you," Emma says.

She heads to the center of the quad, where Ms. Birr oversees students setting up special cornhole boards. Even the boards are on theme. They have painted pumpkins on the front, with orange and dark green bean bags to match.

Also on theme, I'm on my own, while every other student at Pumpkin Day seems to be with a group of friends. They walk up to tables for pumpkin scones. They take pictures together in a wooden, face-in-the-hole board of three pumpkins (with cutouts in the center) in a hay wagon. At least I'm here, unlike Harper, who said, "Pumpkins are for basic, boring girls" and decided to watch reruns of *The Ultimate Fighter*.

I would've been happy to never know that show existed.

If liking pumpkins makes me basic, then I'm happy to be basic. She can just sit by herself and maybe contemplate her internalized misogyny.

I scroll through Instagram to look busy, and a couple reels of Mia Asano (@miaasanomusic) playing her violin like a bass and then without a bow distract me for a moment—until a photo of Maddie and nine of her matching sorority sisters appears on my feed. I shove my phone into my jeans pocket and walk around the tables to blend into the movement. Not too close, though, so the vendors don't call me over to sample their baked goods. And not too close to the middle, where Owl Productions has set up pumpkin-related activities on the grass. I trade another food voucher for a pumpkin biscuit with pumpkin butter and pumpkin honey, so my hands stay busy.

Why didn't anyone tell me you could flavor honey?

My neck prickles as if eyes follow me. Honey runs down my hands, and I try to eat the biscuit faster. Walk faster. A group of friends cut in front of me, laughing, headed for a pumpkin ice cream cart. Did they notice I'm alone?

Get it together. No one's watching you. No one's judging you.

I'm about to make a break for my room—hell if Harper's there—when I hear my name. Dylan's in the middle of the quad with a group of friends, crowded around a tarp and carving pumpkins. He wears an ombre tie-dyed shirt that fades from pink to purple to blue. Both Josiah and Vicky, neither of whom I've talked to in weeks despite being in string orchestra together, match Dylan, along with two other people I don't recognize. Minus Henry, who's wearing a regular blue polo.

My face warms. Whether from the unusually hot autumn sun or Dylan spending more time with his ex, I'm not sure.

Dylan waves me over, and I stuff the last bite of biscuit in my face before joining them.

"Wanna carve a pumpkin with us?" Dylan asks, mid-carve on his own.

I glance at his friends. Vicky smiles back, but everyone's wrapped up in their carving. "Sure, I guess. I've never carved a pumpkin before."

Dylan freezes. He looks at me how I must've looked at Emma for not having watched *Hocus Pocus*.

"All right." Dylan stands, abandoning his pumpkin and taking my sticky hand. He looks down but doesn't let go. "Honey biscuit?"

I nod, too mortified to respond.

"Oh, and you know Josiah, Vicky, and Henry, of course." Dylan doesn't drop my hand, even though it's covered in honey. Even though Henry can't seem to look at his pumpkin and not our hands. "And this is Liz and Bianca. Liz and Bianca, Corey." He turns back to me, and with his free hand, waves it over his tie-dye shirt. "We're all in the Borns Bi Babes club together."

"Nice to—"

"Not me," Henry interrupts. "I'm not bi. I'm gay."

I may imagine it, but Dylan's hand loosens in mine like he's contemplating letting it go.

"Nice to meet you too, Corey," Liz says with a pointed glare at Henry.

Dylan leads me away to an open trailer attached to a truck with a "Farm Use" license plate. His grip on my hand gets tighter with every step we're further away from, I assume, Henry. The trailer is full of pumpkins.

Dylan squeezes my hand before letting go. "Take your pick."

"Does it matter?"

God, of course it doesn't. It's a pumpkin, not a violin.

"Not really," Dylan says. "I think the medium-sized ones are easier to carve. Not too thick, but not too small to work around with a plastic Born-issued carving tool." His head falls to one side with a smirk. "It's almost like Borns doesn't trust us with knives."

"Well, they shouldn't trust you." I grab a pale orange/almost white pumpkin from the edge of the trailer. "I've seen you with a violin bow. Too jerky."

He tries to keep a straight face but fails. His smirk extends to a wide grin. "I thought we were going to play nice."

I shrug with a smirk of my own.

Dylan nods to my pumpkin as we find a spot in the grass a few feet away from the others. "Nice pick. Ghost pumpkin." I must look at it skeptically because he laughs and adds, "It's not haunted. It's called that because of the color."

"Oh. Right," I say. "Now what?"

He gathers his supplies—a jagged tool made of thick plastic and an edged tool that looks like a mini shovel—and places them beside me in the grass. "Cut a big circle around the stem. After that, scoop out the pumpkin brains."

"Gross." I grimace, which only makes Dylan laugh. "Well," I wait for him to stop laughing, "maybe once I scoop my pumpkin's brains out, I can give them to you. You know, since you don't have any."

Dylan dramatically brings a hand to his heart. "Ouch."

"Yeah, that was harsher than I thought it'd be. I know you're really smart."

He shrugs with a grin. "Like old times."

A repeating question creates a tremolo in my mind until I can't hold it back.

"Why did we start picking on each other, anyway?" I blurt, louder than I mean to. I stop hacking the top of my pumpkin to watch Dylan fiddle his lip ring with his very pink, very graceful tongue. "I've tried to remember when and how this," I motion between us with the plastic tool, "started but I can't. Do you?"

He runs his fingers through the grass like it's hair and avoids my eyes. "I started it. On purpose."

On purpose?

I wait for him to elaborate, but he doesn't. "Why? Come on, I need details."

When he doesn't respond, I saw into my pumpkin.

All this time, we could've been friends. We could've texted about our auditions for Borns. Gone on the campus tour together. Met up after I switched foster houses and left his school district to practice together. He ruined that. On *purpose*.

My muscles from playing the violin are paying off. Carving a pumpkin is harder than it looks.

"Somehow," Dylan says after minutes, "everyone in all-county orchestra our freshmen year knew you were in foster care."

My hand stills. I keep my eyes on my pumpkin.

I didn't know *Dylan* knew I was in foster care.

"Some of the other violinists were talking shit, saying ignorant stuff. Saying you either beat them because the judges felt bad for you, or you beat them because the judges were scared of you." He shakes his head at the memory, and his ruffled hair falls in front of his eyes.

I bite my lip.

Pity hurts, but fear hurts more. Neither's new, though.

Another memory resurfaces in my mental trash bag. Sixth grade, new foster house, and I was invited to a girl in my homeroom's birthday party. A pity invite. Except her mom watched me the entire three hours, even as I walked down the hallway to the bathroom. As I ate my piece of Dairy Queen ice cream cake. I'd seen the same disdain in that mom's watchful eyes before in my foster parents, my teachers. They pre-defined me in one word: troubled.

And so what if I was? A grown ass adult should've behaved with empathy, compassion, not contempt. At least for a few hours to my face.

"It was like they pegged you as someone they could pick on," Dylan continues. "And an easy target." He flicks his hair out of his eyes with a jerk of his long neck. "Actually, no, that's not exactly right. They saw you as a threat too. Which sounds contradictory, but it isn't."

"I know." I smile despite myself. "But you made first chair, not me."

"Yeah, but I'm friendly, and you're…"

"Not," I finish.

His laugh sends the warmth on my skin into the pit of my stomach. "You're rather off-putting when you want to be."

"I'll take that as a compliment."

I meet Dylan's dark eyes, but they no longer hold his familiar twinkle.

"I didn't want what they were saying to get back to you." Dylan drops my gaze. Runs his clean hand, his left hand with calloused fingertips, through his floppy hair. "I thought if I started this rivalry with you, they'd see you as the tough person I knew you were and leave you alone."

A few seconds pass. "And?" I ask.

"And it worked." His smirk returns, and I'm surprised at my sudden urge to kiss the raised corner of his mouth. "You didn't take my shit, and they took the hint. You wouldn't take theirs either." A twinkle. "And it was a hell of fun."

The band Textbook Fighters plays "Monster Mash." Vicky laughs at something Josiah carves into his pumpkin. Groups of friends walk around and walk up to tables of pumpkin-flavored food. I don't look away from Dylan.

"I can't believe you never told me that."

I'm surprised he hears my whisper above the gleeful sounds of Pumpkin Day.

Dylan's voice is soft, despite his words. "And I can't believe you made a joke about me not having brains."

I wince. "Sorry."

Dylan leans back on his hands with a wide grin. "Don't be, buttercup."

Sunlight gathers on his strong nose and wild hair, and a new urge to sit on his lap makes me look down at my pumpkin.

"You keep me on my toes, Coralee," he says, his voice still low.

My real name never sounded so good.

♪♫

Later that night, Emma goes back with me to the quad as promised to watch *The Birds* outside on a projector. A chill pricks the air, making the evening feel like fall when the day hadn't. We dress in layers, some of which I borrow from Emma, and bring two of her pink fuzzy blankets in case we have to sit on the grass. We don't, though. Thanks to Emma's ten-minute-early rule, we claim two of the dozen or so Owl Production folding chairs set up in front of the giant screen.

Bowls of candy cover a lone table left from Pumpkin Day. Emma tells me to go ahead, that she'll save our seats, probably because she feels bad for ditching me all afternoon. We didn't meet back up until dinner, which we spent in our room after grabbing pumpkin lattes from Borns Brew. Both of our stomachs were stuffed with pumpkin-flavored carbs from the cinnamon rolls and scones and pie.

"You sure?" I ask.

Emma snuggles into her folding chair and wraps one of the blankets around her. "Just grab me a Kit Kat bar or something? Please, oh please?"

I jokingly sigh. "Ugh, what an inconvenience."

Emma doesn't smile back because she's already calling Owen. "Hey, babe," she says, as I turn around.

Students claim all the folding chairs by the time I'm at the front of the candy line. Groups of people sit on blankets—some even on textbooks—around the screen, waiting for the movie to start. Groups of friends. Not one friend. I look back at Emma, who's still talking on the phone, before grabbing a Styrofoam bowl.

I need more friends.

Emma almost didn't come tonight, despite our pinky promise, and she didn't spend any time with me at Pumpkin Day. Instead, I spent the day with my rival instead of my friend, though Dylan didn't act like my rival.

Does Dylan count as a friend?

No. Maybe?

More.

Either I'm cold, or the memory of him saying my name sends a shiver down my arms as I put two Kit Kat bars in my bowl. Owl Productions went all-out on the candy supply. They have every kind of chocolate bar Emma could've asked for: Hershey's, Snickers, 3 Musketeers. Butterfinger. Reese's Peanut Butter Cups.

I grab as many as will fit without dropping on the way back to my chair.

Except I drop them anyway, when someone in line touches my arm as I walk by.

"Shit, sorry." The tutor from the Writing Center, Rylee, reaches down and places the chocolate back in my bowl. "My fault."

A muscular guy with buzzed blonde hair stops talking to a girl with perfect ringlets falling down to her mid-back. "Way to go."

"Hi," the girl says with a bright white smile. Her voice is two octaves higher than mine.

Rylee rolls her eyes, reminding me of Harper, before turning back to me. "I was going to ask if I knew you. Now I know I do. Corey, right?"

"Good memory. And thanks." I gesture with my refilled bowl.

Rylee introduces me to her friends, Shane and Brooklyn. Though I don't remember seeing her, Brooklyn says she's seen me around in Shenandoah, the music building. She's a voice major. Soprano. Hence the high, filter-sounding voice. Shane and I's paths have not crossed, seeing he's an Exercise Science major and plays for the Borns football team.

"Been to a game this season?" Shane asks, as they/we take a step forward in line.

"Nope. Haven't been to a single one." Shane's face contorts from a smug curl of his lips to a devastated frown. "But I'm a freshman. I don't have anyone that would go with me."

Not that I would go if I did.

"Oh. My. God." Brooklyn grabs my arm, and I almost spill the bowl of chocolate for the second time. "Come with us sometime! Well, go with Rylee to watch me and Shane. I'm a cheerleader."

I look between them. "Really?"

"Of course! You're a freshman, we're sophomores."

Brooklyn squeezes my arm for emphasis. I debate whether to set down my bowl. Might as well, with so many close calls. "We can show you the ropes."

"Speaking of which," Rylee says, "have you heard about Dalefield Caverns?"

The more I shake my head, "No," the more they smile.

Emma hasn't mentioned it. Maybe she can ask Abigail?

Rylee passes me her phone. "Type in your number. You're coming with us to the game *and* the caverns"

"Yay!" Brooklyn claps her hands. "Just you wait."

Wait for what exactly?

My stomach churns, but in a good way. Like it does in the hush right before a performance, when the conductor raises their baton. I might not know what I'm getting myself into, but a name like Dalefield Caverns has to be good.

Rylee saves my number, and by the time she texts me so I have hers, they've/we've reached the candy table.

"Nice meeting you," Brooklyn calls after me, as I walk back with my bowl surprisingly still intact. "See you soon!"

When I sit in my lawn chair, Emma doesn't seem to notice my extended absence. Probably on account of talking to Owen.

"You're the best," Emma says, as I pass her way more chocolate bars than she asked for.

"No problem." I unwrap my own Reese's and nibble on the edge. "Did Abigail tell you about some caverns? Dalefield Caverns, I think?"

Emma purses her lips, deepening the dimple in her chin. "Only not to go. It's a party. Freshmen really aren't invited. Unless you're an athlete."

I ignore the question in her eyes. "Oh, gotcha."

Sophomores invited me to a party.

Me. A freshman.

A notification pops up on my phone. Rylee invited me to a party *and* followed me on IG. A smile threatens to ruin my nonchalant attitude in front of Emma.

I'm on my way to having less problems, less time wandering the quad alone, and more friends than I did this morning. Three *sophomore* friends.

Thank god for Pumpkin Day.

Movement Twenty-One

**positions = "the position of your left hand on the violin"
(and also an Ariana Grande song about sex)**

In string orchestra the next day, Professor Perry makes the announcement I've been waiting for since he said I had a chance of living in Harmony Hall: auditions are next week. No surprise, though. I circled and highlighted the word "auditions" on our syllabus the first day of class.

I've had lots of auditions, but none has mattered this much. This audition determines if I'm accepted into the music program and if I can move into Harmony Hall.

I *have* to make first chair. I *deserve* first chair.

If I don't, if I don't play perfectly, I might as well change my major. Drop out. Move back in with Tom and Kathryn (that'll be the day). Kiss Juilliard and the CSO goodbye.

The other violinists don't stand a chance, though. Dylan doesn't stand a change. He lucked out on auditions. Professor

Perry admitted he almost gave me the one freshman violinist spot in Harmony that Dylan got. He's a talented violinist, sure, and super cute. But he's the competition.

He's going down.

Now until my audition, I'm living in the practice rooms. No distractions. No Emma, no Dylan, no new sophomore friends— and no upperclassmen parties. Just me and Violin.

Soon, I'll be out of our temporary triple and in a room at Harmony. A two-person room. A room without Harper, thank god.

After class, though, my plan goes to shit because Dylan's waiting for me beside my locker with his wild hair, in a black muscle tank top embroidered with constellations.

I point to the white and silver stars before opening my locker. "Your sister's handiwork?"

"Yeah," he says. "This one took Holly an entire weekend to finish. She even did the zodiac constellations. This one is for Pisces, my sign." He points to a snake-looking constellation. "Your birthday's in August, right? Are you a Leo?"

"No." He must've figured as much, telling by his frown. My stomach flips over the fact that he remembers my birthday month. "Virgo."

"Ah." He smiles like that makes a lot more sense.

I wouldn't know. Astrology isn't my thing.

"This one's yours," he says, running his long fingers over a group of stars that remind me of a long-legged beetle. I nod like it's the coolest beetle I've ever seen.

"So, anyway…"

He runs his fingers through his hair. Looks at his magenta Vans (which would definitely earn a compliment from Emma). He still doesn't continue after I shut my locker and twirl the lock.

"Anyway," I prompt.

He shoves his hands in the front of his mid-thigh denim shorts. "Can we talk?"

It's definitely too cold for shorts. The evening chill has lingered all day.

"Aren't we already?" I ask.

He looks up, his head still dropped, with a sheepish grin and flushed cheeks. "I had a lot of fun yesterday. Carving pumpkins."

"Yeah, me too." My face warms at the memory of him smiling into the sun, holding my hand. "Even if my carved treble clef turned more into an ampersand."

His smirk pulls at the corner of his mouth with the lip piercing. "You'd think you could draw one since you look at treble clefs every day on your sheet music. Unless you don't practice, which is fine by me and my first chair. Don't you have a tattoo of one too?"

I bite my bottom lip to hold back a smile at knowing he's looked at my neck. Since when do I get h-o-double-t hott over such small things?

"At least you didn't draw one for your tattoo artist and end up with an ampersand on your neck."

I cross my arms and lean into the lockers. "Ha. Funny."

When he looks back at me, an intensity in his dark eyes replaces his teasing grin. "Yesterday felt different. Between us. Or, not different, but new. Well, not new either." He can't stop running his hands through his hair. "You know what I mean, though?"

I look down at my Chucks. "Yeah. I know what you mean."

"I like you, Corey. Really, really like you." He shoves his hands back in his pockets, probably to keep them from running through his hair for the tenth time. They'll just find his hair again. "But I don't want to lead you on or send you mixed signals."

Oh.

This is a breakup before the breakup. An establishing of our nothing before we can be a something.

I bite my lip to keep it from wobbling.

Don't tear up. Don't tear up.

"So," I clear my throat to keep the shaky emotion from my voice, "you're not into me?"

"No, I am. It's just…" He groans. "Complicated."

Could there be a more textbook excuse?

A scuff on the top of my right shoe becomes fascinating.

Got any room in there?

Violin: *Get your own locker.*

"If you're into me," I say, finally finding words, "how is it complicated?"

"It just is."

He could've taken me to a practice room behind a soundproof door, instead of rejecting me in the hallway basement for everyone to hear. For everyone to know he's still in love with Henry. Did Dylan hold my hand yesterday to make him jealous? No wonder their group had an undercurrent of tension.

"Okay, so, now what?" I ask. "You're saying you're into me, but you want to stay friends?"

"No, not that." He takes a step closer. "I'm saying I like you, I always have, and maybe we could be more than friends. But I want to be upfront with you. I don't want any labels. Of any kind. But I wanna spend time with you. One on one."

"Like on a date?"

"God, no."

"Well, ex*cuse* me."

He draws his hand over his face. His slender, violin-playing fingers taunt me. "Hang out. I want to hang out. No dating, no labels, hanging out." His mouth scrunches to one side of his face. "This isn't going how I'd practiced."

"You practiced this?"

"Yeah."

Despite how shitty this conversation has gone, a smile tugs on my lips. "Well, hopefully you practice for your audition like you did for this. Cause you'll tank it."

He puckers his lips with fake annoyance. "Are we good? You know I really, really like you, but no labels?"

"I'm confused…but we're good. And I like you too."

"Really?" he asks.

"Really," I say.

"Can I kiss you on the cheek?"

I nod, and he leans in. He smells like dryer sheets and his shampooed hair smells like evergreen trees. His lips brush my round, smiling cheek and send a vibration through my body.

He's the bow and I'm the string.

I'm never washing this cheek again.

All I can think about during my counseling session on Thursday is that I only have one more required session after this. Especially when I exhaust all the topics I prepared to talk about in the first seven minutes.

Counselor Robinson has his own prepared topics, though.

"You haven't talked much about your foster parents." His eyebrows wrinkle with concern, but his mouth remains in a straight line. "Tell me about them. Tom and Kathryn, right?"

"Yeah."

"Do you like them?" he asks.

"They're nice enough. Probably the second-best family I've lived with." A flick of dust drifts down to the tan carpet. "Well, I guess they're the best. They haven't kicked me out."

His leather chair squeaks, as he leans back and waits for me to continue. When I don't, he asks, "Do they support you in other ways?"

"They text and call." I rub the center of my palm with my thumb. "They do the right things, but something's still missing. At the end of the day, I don't really matter to them."

"Why do you say that?"

"Because." I shrug one shoulder with a flippant shake of my head. "That's the way it goes. That's the way it always is with foster parents."

Counselor Robinson pauses, then laces his fingers over his stomach. "Maybe it doesn't have to go that way this time. What happened to the other foster family, the one you considered the best?"

"Mr. And Mrs. Fitzgerald. They were my fourth foster house." I squeeze my palms together so I don't run through violin fingerings. "They almost adopted me." I look out the window to the quad, where people throw a football back and forth and back and forth. "Didn't work out, obviously."

"Do you want it to work out with Kathryn and Tom?"
Someone on the quad rushes in to intercept a pass and slams the football to the ground.

"It doesn't matter," I say. "I'm on extended foster care. When I turn twenty-one, all ties are cut."

"But do you want to cut ties?"

No one's asked me that before.

I should say yes. I told him something's missing in my relationship with them. But without Violin, I only have me. Me, right now, not the future world-renowned-violinist me. Whether I like it or not, I'm an eighteen-year-old nobody without a driver's license, and Tom and Kathryn are the only people I have to fall back on. Cutting ties means I'm on my own for good.

For the first time since coming to college, the thought of ditching all-things foster care—Kathryn and Tom included—makes a bubble of nausea rise through my throat.

"I don't know."

Counselor Robinson frowns. He waits for me to elaborate, but there's nothing else to say. When I look back out the window, the group playing football is gone.

♪♫

My phone vibrates Friday evening with an unexpected text from (a possibly drunk) Rylee. I lick the sticky strawberry jelly off my fingers. Since Emma left to see Owen instead of eating dinner with me in the MDH, I grabbed a pb&j and headed straight for the practice rooms. No time to waste when my audition's next week.

Rylee:
Let's go to a partyyyyy

                                                            Me:
                      Can't tonight. I have an audition next week

Rylee:
Booo

We wanna hang out soon

I guess "we" means her, Brooklyn, and Shane. My new sophomore friends.

I'm so cool.

I wash my hands in the small basement bathroom before finding Violin in its locker.

Ready for next week?

Violin sighs with a whoosh from the locker to my side. *Come on, I'm always ready. Are you?*

I think so.

Violin: *You think? Or you know?*

I know. Or, I will after we practice.

Three hours later, when I'm back in our dorm, I'm alone with Harper. Harper and her three friends—none of which I've met or seen around campus. They've dragged out Emma's now-empty tub of snacks and left the lid in the middle of the room. Cheez-Its, Wheat Thins, fruit snacks, containers of applesauce, and granola bars cover Harper's bed.

I'm not the only one who decided not to eat in the MDH.

My voice shakes as I close the door. "What's going on?"

"Corey," Harper says my name like it's sour candy, "meet my friends Ryan, Bailey, and Matt."

Ryan—who has a buzz cut so short that he only has a fourth of a centimeter left of hair—doesn't stop eating some of Emma's fruit snacks to acknowledge me, but Bailey throws up a peace sign to contradict her scowl and Matt offers a nonchalant nod.

I stand in the doorway, too scared of strangers to walk further into my own room. "Do you all go here?"

"Fuck no," Matt says. "We met at the 24/7 gym."

No wonder he's friends with Harper, who smiles and shoves

her hand back into the box of Cheez-Its. She knows that's the real prize.

"That's Emma's food."

Harper rolls her eyes. "And?"

My legs shake. I'm of no sound body or mind, given my stress over my audition, to stand up to Harper when she has a full belly and some tough-looking goons. But I ask, "Are you going to pay her back?" anyway.

Harper makes a phlegmy scoff in the back of her throat. "I'm sure prim privileged-ass Emma can manage."

Her friends don't laugh or say a word, but they stuff their hands in the boxes and bags of snacks. They eat Emma's food even after I've brushed my teeth and gotten into bed. Except now they turn on some fighting show, yell at the screen, all of which I hear through my cheap earplugs.

Me, at 12:09am to Emma:
Just want to let you know that I'm lying here awake because Harper has some sketchy friends
They raided your entire snack tub. Promise I tried, but they're SCARY *devil emoji*

After the tenth round of cheers and boos, I roll to face the wall and check the time on my phone: 12:37am.

I forgo my pillow in order to place it over my head.

The next time I check my phone, it's 1:07am.

I can't not sleep all weekend. Not when my audition is next week. Not when I need to practice like my life depends on it.

Because it does. My future depends on this audition.

I gnaw on the inside of my cheek. I'm out of options.

Me:

Sorry to text so late but can one of you pick me up tomorrow morning?

Tom, thirty seconds later:

Sure thing. 10 okay?

And you can always text us, no matter the time.

Me:

Sounds good

And thanks

When did my room at my foster house become safer than my dorm room? I press my pillow harder onto my head to drown out Harper, who shouts at one of the wrestlers.

I'm not supposed to run to my fosters.

I'm supposed to run away from them.

Movement Twenty-Two

rest = "silence, pause"

To my surprise, Zeke picks me up the next morning in Tom's sedan.

"What's going on?"

I climb into the passenger's seat, throwing my borrowed duffle bag over my shoulder into the back. Violin rests against my legs in the front.

"Code Yellow Camila," Zeke says. My heart drops. "She wasn't in the house when we woke up this morning."

"Tom and Kathryn weren't watching her, were they?"

My fingerings for *Water Music* press into my palm.

"They do the best they can, Coralee. Corey." His hands tighten around the steering wheel. "Besides, she always turns up or comes back."

I bounce my legs against the passenger seat.

Please be home, please be home, please be home.

This wouldn't have happened if I'd been there. Probably.

"I've been meaning to tell you…" Zeke looks past his shoulder as if to check I'm listening, but of course he has my attention. He never tells me anything. "If you need someone to teach you how to drive, your *younger* fake brother can help."

"Um, no."

There goes the sappy moment I've been waiting for, where he confides in me. Yet again, he's being obnoxious. Still, the mention of "brother" makes me smile.

Zeke turns into the subdivision as the sun stretches into the pink-lemonade sky. Our neighbors' houses blur by in my passenger side window. I've never known homesickness, like Steven when he missed his mom, but the familiarity sends warmth through my chest.

Is this what it feels like to come home?

The flashing red and blue lights in front of the house replace the sensation with ice.

I automatically hit the lock button on the door. Zeke freezes as the police officer gets in their car. We stay put for a few seconds, even after the cop car is out of sight. I lock eyes with Zeke before getting out.

"Okay?" I ask.

He jerks his head in a petrified nod.

Police are a hazard of growing up in foster care. Camila, though, involves them more than the normal system kid with her breakouts. I never liked the arrogant demeanor of most officers, but I never feared them. I don't have to, as a young white woman. But I fear them now—not for my sake, but for Zeke's.

The first time the police brought Camila back, they came into the house, and Zeke retreated into a shell of himself. Sweat clung to his hairline, and his arm shook at his sides. He didn't move. Didn't speak. Kathryn held him for at least ten minutes after they left.

"I'm sorry, I got you, I'm so sorry," she said, over and over. "I won't let them inside next time, not until you're in your room. I'm sorry, Zeke."

She didn't let go until he stopped shaking.

A week later, I asked him about it. I hate that I asked him. He told me in as few words as possible about The Talk he had as a kid with his parents. The conversation *every* Black kid has.

For weeks after that, my search history on my phone consisted of phrases like "police brutality," "what is the prison–industrial complex," and "how to support Black Lives Matter." Hell, I google stuff now. There's still so much I don't know.

But I know to lock the car doors now.

A pile of shoes topples as I open the front door. A whiff of vanilla draws my attention to the scratched cherry coffee table in the living room, where a large candle that Tom bought Kathryn last year on Mother's Day glows in the center. Tom sits on the couch—which is more hideous and plaid than the last time I saw it—with Kathryn on one side and Camila on the other.

Camila, small and sobbing, tucks her head between her knees.

I sigh. *She's home.*

Thank god.

"I want. To see. My sister." Camila wipes her nose with her sleeve. "¡Maldita sea!"

Tom pats her head. "No cursing in this house."

His rule sounds more like a suggestion.

"I don't care about this house. I want to be with Nicole!"

Kathryn reaches around Tom to squeeze Camila's shoulder. She looks ready for a run, with a high ponytail and her double-knotted running shoes. "I know, sweetheart, but you'll see Nicole this week on your visit."

After a few more curses in Spanish and English, Kathryn stands and points to the stairs. "Go upstairs to your room. Running away is unacceptable. And Tom said no cursing."

Camila stomps out of the living room, not bothering to look in my direction.

"Little fish?"

Her pouty bottom lip trembles. She runs to hug me around the waist, and her arms wrap higher than the last time. Weeks and weeks ago, when I moved out for college. She says, "I miss you," before marching to her room and slamming the door.

Tom drops his head in his hands, and his shoulders shake with silent sobs.

"She'll get through this," Kathryn whispers.

It's hard on everyone when Camila runs away. But something seems different. Camila's so...angry. Desperate.

Tom and Kathryn would foster Nicole too if they could. They've tried. But the foster care system is beyond broken. I've tried to make sense of it, but it *doesn't* make sense.

I was hoping Nicole could take Steven's place.

Guess not.

♪♫

I'm practicing and in the middle of a piece Sunday afternoon when I hear Kathryn knock on my door and ask, "Can I come in?"

Violin: *Now? We're not at a stopping point.*
It's fine. It's been like four hours.

I set Violin in its case on my bed. "Sure."

Almost three months ago, I couldn't muster a tear over leaving this room with thoughts of Harmony Hall. Today, I could cry with thanks for a bed I don't have to climb up to get to and for a space without a certain muscular, angry roommate.

My door swings open, and instead of standing in the doorway like usual, Kathryn strides over to me. Her eyes shine as she holds my shoulders. "Corey, that was beautiful. You sound… incredible. Like a professional."

"Thanks."

"I'm proud of you, you know?" Kathryn blinks back tears before they can spill over. "Tom too. We don't take any credit, but it's true."

"Thanks," I repeat.

If they took some credit, I wouldn't fault them. They've never told me to stop practicing because of the "noise," like some of my past fosters.

"Also," Kathryn hesitates with a guilty smile, "Drew's here."

I groan. "You texted her, didn't you."

Part of me's eager to see her familiar face, but the other part knows I'm walking into a lecture, especially after I got a campus job without consulting her first.

Kathryn puts her hands up. "When do you want me to take you back?"

"After dinner is fine. If that's okay."

"Of course." Kathryn gives my shoulders a last squeeze. "Drew's waiting in the living room."

I follow Kathryn downstairs and find Drew on the second most hideous piece of furniture, the floral loveseat. Today, she's wearing a dark green blazer with a brass statement necklace. Does she always have to overcompensate for her age with professional attire and accessories? I get it. I really do. But I'm in my pajamas, and it's almost dinnertime.

Drew jumps up when she sees me and pulls me into a hug. "Corey, it's so good to see you."

She asks how I am for what feels like a thousand times before she seems to believe I'm fine. After eating Saturday pancakes (without Steven, which somehow made the maple syrup not taste as sweet), coloring at the kitchen table with Camila, and sleeping in my own bed, I am fine.

Fine for now.

Drew adjusts her blazer before sitting down and giving the college-is-different-from-high-school spiel—yet this time, I believe her. My classes are harder than I thought, and my stomach flips every time I think about midterms and my audition this week. And god help me if she ever finds out I didn't get accepted into the music program. Or that I'm not living in Harmony Hall. The outcome of my entire year—and the next three years, really—rides on playing Violin for fifteen minutes in order to escape my temporary triple and a roommate that hates my guts.

God, no wonder I'm stressed.

Drew grills me for half an hour instead of the typical forty-five minutes, probably because I sweat through my t-shirt. When Tom calls everyone for dinner, I change into a tank top and take the empty seat beside Drew. Steven's usual seat is empty in front of me.

Tom made my favorite: black bean enchiladas with salsa verde and Monterey Jack cheese sprinkled on top. He and Kathryn must be going all out to make me feel at, well, home because Kathryn does the dishes and sends me upstairs for a few more minutes of practice time.

"I'm glad school is going well," Kathryn says later in the car, after I've practiced as much as my permanently dented fingertips can handle. "Do you have any concerts coming up?"

I squirm in my seat. The last fosters I invited to a concert—the Wright family of Foster House #9—didn't show. Everyone waved to their parents as we walked onstage. I couldn't find a familiar face. After the concert, I waited on the cold marble floor right inside the high school for almost an hour. I was a freshman, stranded at a new school, with no friends to ask for a ride. Now, I'm a freshman again (and I still don't have a driver's license, though that's besides the point). I don't need another letdown.

"At the end of the semester," I say, but I change the topic without pause. "What's going on with Camila?"

Kathryn sighs and turns off the already-low easy listening radio station. "She can't run away again. Or she might go to another home."

"What?" I turn sideways in my seat to face her. "You can't let that happen."

Kathryn's grip tightens around the wheel. "Stop, Corey." She rubs her tired eyes and sits for a few seconds at the first stop sign. Dark circles I hadn't noticed before hover under each like reverse storm clouds. "Tom and I are doing our best. We're trying to work something out with the caseworker, and we're doing everything we can."

I turn around again in my seat, away from her, to stare out the window.

Kathryn reaches over and pats my knee. "You're an adult, but we're the grownups. You're allowed to worry about yourself and have fun this year. Let us worry about Camila and Nicole."

Camila *and* Nicole?

"They're going to be okay. Both of them." Her assured voice calms a thousand dissonant notes in my head. "I promise to do anything and everything in my power."

What I think *and* what I say: "I believe you."

We drive for several minutes in silence.

"Let's talk about you," Kathryn says, no longer comfortable. "I remember my college days. Partying and going to 24/7 diners, road trips to my friends' houses." She pauses, and when she continues, her voice softens. "I know you're rather serious, but you must be having a wild time, huh?" She smiles and raises her eyebrows, prompting me to fill in the details.

What the hell can I say? There's not a single aspect of college that's going perfectly or even remotely right. So nothing worth telling.

"Come on." She jiggles my knee. "I told you about Camila, so tell me about you. What's up?"

My mouth twitches upward. She knows how to get me to talk. "Fine. College is fine." I roll my eyes to mask my smile and scoot forward in my seat. "One of my roommates doesn't like me. My classes are…a lot. And I need to make first chair for string orchestra."

"You 'need' to?" Kathryn turns on her blinker and doesn't wait for my response. She must think I'm being overdramatic. "Is that why you came home this weekend?"

"I kinda wanted to get away from Harper, my roommate."

Kathryn purses her lips, her telltale sign of an impending lecture.

"We love having you back," she says, with too much space between each word, "and distance is good. Sometimes. Other times, you need to stay and work it out."

I cross my arms and force a scoff back down my throat. Foster care hasn't taught me to stay. It taught me to pack my trash bag (or, more recently, a duffle bag).

"You can't leave at the first signs of conflict," Kathryn adds.

I sink into my seat.

She thinks *I'm* the problem? I'm just giving Harper what she wants, and for the first time, what I want.

The foster care system, my foster parents, my caseworkers have all had control over my life and where I sleep—not me. People have always pushed *me* away, but I've never been able to push *them* away. Not even when I wanted to.

If I had any semblance of control, I would've left Warren and Nancy Glick from hellish Foster House #10, the foster house before Tom and Kathryn, long before I did. They might've been my second to shortest stay, but those five months were five months too long. They paid a neighbor boy to meticulously manicure their lawn instead of their daughter or me, we ate off of fine china every night, and they said things like "No wonder no one wants you" when I forgot to put my napkin on my lap. "Elbows off the table." "Smile or go to your room." I stayed in my floral-wallpaper room more and played my school-loaned violin less.

Drew, who was my new caseworker then, sat with me one of my last days there on the power-washed wooden steps in front of the house.

"You're not yourself, Coralee," Drew said.

I stared at a fuzzy caterpillar crawling across the cement walkway and just said, "Okay."

We drive in silence for a few minutes before Kathryn says, "We're here for you, Corey."

"Okay."

I don't know what else to say.

I'm a walking, forgotten, hollowed violin. A forever concave expanse in my chest wants her to fill it, but it's been empty for so long. Too long.

She seems to understand my hesitation. She responds with a tight-lipped smile.

Unlike Tom, Kathryn doesn't need my help with directions when she turns into campus.

"I know roommates can be tough," Kathryn says, as she pulls into a parking spot close to my dorm. "We're all complicated. We all bring our unseen pasts with us, so relationships take time. And I'm sure you'll get first chair. You work so hard, and you're so talented."

I'm not so sure. Dylan has beat me out of first chair before. He beat me out of Harmony before.

I open the car door.

"Hey." Kathryn touches my arm, so I'll meet her eyes. "No matter what chair you get, Tom and I are proud of you. You're Corey the person before Corey the violinist to us."

I give her a side hug.

Somewhere along the way, what I do became who I am. Probably the moment playing the violin, and playing it well, became my one ticket for getting out of foster care and finding success outside of the system.

Too bad I *am* what I do. Too bad people throw me away if I'm not perfect. Too bad I'm not good enough if I'm not the best at the violin.

That's just how the world works.

Movement Twenty-Three

ricochet = "a bouncing bow stroke in which the bow
is dropped or thrown on the string and allowed to
rebound and bounce again, several times

My pillow jerks out from underneath my head. My head bops on the hard mattress. My neck spasms from the close to whiplash.

"What the hell?" I rub the sleep from my eyes.

Since Harper wasn't in the room last night, I went straight to bed the second I got back to campus. Emma wasn't back yet either. I'd meant to go back to the practice rooms for a bit more practice and to put Violin in its locker, but I needed the sleep. Plus, my fingers still hurt.

I'm 100% awake now, though.

Harper tosses my belongings out into the hallway like she plays shot put for our college track team. She chucks my duffle bag out next, and it slides to meet Violin and the pillow she snatched from under my head.

My mouth disengages from my brain. My body too. I've never screamed so much for no one to hear me.

"S-stop!" Emma stumbles out of bed, as Harper throws my Chucks into the hallway next. "What are you doing?"

Harper turns towards me instead, ignoring Emma. "You're never sleeping here again."

My mouth remains snapped shut like a locked instrument case, but somehow my body reconnects because I climb down from my bunk. Everything I own, minus my bedsheets, is strewn outside in the hallway.

Sure, foster parents have kicked me out before, but they've never *thrown out* my shit.

I face Harper and finally manage, "Why?"

She has had every chance to toss me from the room. Why now, when we're half-way through the semester, on the first day of midterms?

"You snitched. Then Emma snitched." Harper's face reddens while Emma's pales. "Our RA wrote me up, all thanks to you. Over stupid snacks."

I almost laugh at the absurdity. She's throwing a tantrum over Maxine "writing her up" (still no idea what that means) because she ate all of Emma's food with her friends without Emma's permission. I almost laugh—until I glimpse Violin turned upside down in the hallway.

My hand slaps over my mouth.

Violin.

I step around Harper into the hallway.

My legs are vibrating strings. My brain is a crashing, wobbling gong. I sink to my knees beside Violin's unmoving body.

I unlatch Violin's too-large case.

My heart smacks the floor.

A choking sob escapes my throat.

"No. No, no, no." I shake my head. "Violin!"

Violin:

Please come back. Please don't leave. We audition this week!

Violin:

Dead. Violin is dead. Its neck is snapped, and only its strings connect it to its body.

"Corey?" Emma's a blur of pink pajamas.

I wipe my tears on the back of my shaking clammy hands.

Emma's eyes drop from mine down to my violin. "Oh, no." She covers her mouth and speaks through the gaps of her fingers. "Is it broken?"

I nod into my palms, unable to look at Violin's dead body. "I don't know what I'm going to do."

Slam!

Emma jumps and spins around. Our door knob clicks.

"Did she——?" Emma's voice catches. She tries to open the door.

Harper just locked us both out of our room.

Emma drops beside me and pulls me into a side hug. "We'll figure this out together, Corey. Promise."

I must be underwater because my muffled sobs sound thousands of feet above me. Water might fill my lungs because I'm not sure if I'm breathing. I'm sinking lower, lower, lower into Emma's arms. She holds me for what could be seconds, days, months.

I'm underwater, and I don't know how to swim.

Maxine jogs through the hallway with her master key to our door. She says, "I'll handle this," but I'm too far gone to respond or care. Because Violin is dead, and I'm drowning.

♪♫

Emma goes with me to return Violin to its locker, its once home and now burial site, after we stuff my belongings into my duffle bag. She decides we should go to the MDH for toast to get something in our stomachs.

I only agree because a wake is the logical next step.

Like at most funerals, or so I hear, neither of us eats. We're too emotional for toast. I'm too distraught, devastated, heartbroken—and Emma's too morally conflicted. She frowns and emails my professors that I have a fever and won't make it to class today. It doesn't feel like a lie. I've never felt more nauseous, and when I think about my audition on Thursday, I break out into a cold sweat. I stare down at my toast, which is as dry as my nonexistent musical career without Violin.

Someone's hand waves in front of my face. "Earth to Corey."

Turning to focus on Rylee is like changing the station from classical to pop without warning. All I can manage is to lift my hand from the sticky cafeteria table in acknowledgement.

"She's in shock," Emma says.

Rylee tilts her head, and because she's sitting so close beside me, her red hair tickles my arm. "All right…"

"I'm Emma. Corey's roommate." Emma reaches across me to shake Rylee's hand and adds, "It's her violin."

Rylee laughs at Emma's formality. "What happened to her violin?"

I come up for air.

"My roommate," I say.

Rylee drops Emma's hand. She scowls at her questioningly.

"Not Emma, my other roommate." The mental image of

Emma, who's still wearing pink pajamas, throwing my violin doesn't even make me smile. "She threw it into the hallway."

"Wow," Rylee says, like this is a lot to process.

Temporary Triple Rule #3
Get away from the angry roommate while you still can.

I let my head fall into my hands. "I can't live there anymore, Emma."

"I know." Her voice is quiet. Sad. "I get it. I wish you could, though."

My toast takes up my vision again until Emma breaks our silence.

"Can I ask you a question?"

"Sure," Rylee says, "I can answer two."

"Why do you have an empty milk jug?"

"Oh." Rylee shrugs, as I twist towards her. An empty gallon of milk is indeed under the table, on her lap. "To sneak out milk."

"Why?" Emma asks.

"Okay, that's three. So I can eat breakfast in my room with no one seeing my bedhead." Rylee leans forward and rests an elbow on the jug. "Speaking of my room, I live in a single. I also have a camping air mattress that's pretty comfortable."

Is she suggesting I sleep outside?

"You can crash with me, on the floor, if you want."

Emma and I both ask, "Really?" at the same time.

"Sure," Rylee says, like this isn't a big deal. "I know how hard roommate problems can be, and my friends crash with me all the time."

Does she feel sorry for me?

Oh well if she does.

"That would be great," I say. "But only for a couple days. Just until I badger Reslife into getting me a new room."

If I sleep on an air mattress, they'll for sure make an exception for a room swap.

"Cool. Since you already have your stuff," Rylee nods to my duffle bag and backpack taking up half the table, "you can come back with me after I get my milk."

Rylee leans closer, and the jug crunches under her elbow. "I'll let you get a head start. Sometimes I have to bolt if the dining staff catches me."

♪♫

After an over-the-top tearful hug from Emma, I wait for Rylee outside the MDH. Luckily, she doesn't get caught sneaking out milk. She carries my book bag and her full gallon, and I carry my stuffed-to-the-brim duffle bag to her single in Valley Hall.

My left hand feels strange not carrying Violin.

I've never been inside Valley Hall, but it looks a lot like Roselawn. Except for wider hallways and more pristine-looking furnishings. Silver lining: no more hiking up three flights of stairs.

Rylee flings the door open to her first-floor room. "Come on in."

I follow her inside, past a bathroom with the tiniest shower I've yet to see at college. "I really can't thank you enough for this."

Rylee leans against her twin bed to kick off her boots. "Seriously, it's no problem. I feel like everyone's always crashing here."

Band posters line the walls: Lord Huron, Tame Impala, alt-J. They're all new to me, on account I mostly listen to classical music. In the corner of her room, a string of lights shines on pictures taped to the white-painted cinderblock wall. A picture of three naked asses running towards a lake catches my eye. One person with red hair, one with perfect ringlets, and one with massive muscles. Rylee, Brooklyn, and Shane. They're in most of the pictures, minus a bunch that are ripped in half.

Must be from a nasty breakup.

Was it Luke?

"We've been best friends since high school. Me, Brooklyn, and Shane. Lucked out we all went here." Rylee grabs the air mattress from under her bed. "Guess what's this weekend?"

"I don't know. A party?"

"Not a party. *The* party." She blows a few times into the mattress, and her face turns red. "Dalefield Caverns. You're coming, right?"

"Um, sure." I turn back to her wall of photos to hide my grin.

Me. A freshman going to an upperclassmen party with sophomores.

I've come a long way from transient friends like Maddie. We haven't talked in weeks, but it feels like months.

"Cool. I mean, of course you are," Rylee says. "There's a football game Saturday before the party too. You should come with."

"Okay."

Maybe football won't be so boring if I'm with Rylee.

"That a girl," Rylee says, then takes a deep breath and resumes blowing. A few minutes later, she presses on the air mattress to test if it's full enough. She gives me a thumbs up.

"All set. And by the way," she falls back onto her twin bed, "I texted Brooklyn about you staying here. Why you're staying here. She told me to tell you she had a friend that graduated last year that played the French horn, and something happened to it and blah, blah, blah, but they rented one from the school." She attempts to take off her thick, white socks with her toes. "I bet you could rent a violin too."

Oh my god. Why didn't I think of that?

I rented my first-ever violin in seventh grade. Well, Mr. Phillips of Foster House #6 did. He coughed up $85 to rent one from my middle school for orchestra class.

"I was a violinist in a past life," he said. "You should be a violinist in your present one."

Thanks to Mr. Phillips and Lindsey Stirling's YouTube channel, I fell in love with the violin. For the first time, at thirteen years old, I had a future outside the system. No matter where the system sent me, I had three constants: a rented violin, my musical talent, and, of course, a trash bag.

"Thanks, Rylee." Maddie must possess my body because I blow her a kiss before picking up my book bag. "You're a lifesaver."

Violin may be deceased, but maybe my future doesn't have to be.

Movement Twenty-Four

rosin, resin = "the substance applied to bows of
stringed instruments to increase traction"

A stained glass lamp glows inside the Senior Administrative
Assistant's office in Shenandoah Hall. I knock on the open
door, and Debby (according to her name placard on the wall),
waves me in with a warm smile that further rounds her cheeks.

"May I help you, dear?" Debbie removes her lilac glasses
from the end of her nose, and the attached beaded fashion cord
jingles as it falls to her billowy tan blouse.

Plants cover the shelves that line the back wall. Cactuses and
petunias. Plants cover the floor. Spider plants and English ivy. In
one corner of her room by the window, a schefflera tree stretches
up to the light. A bright orange watering can sits beside it.

My shoulders slump at the reminder of Foster House #4.

Mr. and Mrs. Fitzgerald loved plants. They taught me to
pull weeds and water when the soil felt dry to the touch. One

summer they surprised me with a sunflower hideout, a circular hedge out back beside the shed.

People gave flowers to people they loved, and I hoped they loved me.

The sunflowers died at the slightest chill in the air.

"Yes, my—" I clear my throat. "I wanted to check with you about borrowing a violin."

She grabs a folder from inside a wide drawer at the side of her desk, then pulls out a form that she instructs me to fill out. "You're extremely lucky. We have one last available violin," she says, after I hand back the paper. "Do you want to use its locker too?"

"Please."

"Just so you're aware," Debbie says, writing with a blue pen on the form before grabbing a sticky note, "we'll charge forty-five dollars for your instrument rental to your student account at the end of the semester."

My grin drops into a frown, but I accept the note with the locker number and combination with thanks.

She waves me off. "Have a good day, dear. Don't be a stranger."

In the basement, I find my rental, and as I turn the dial on its lock, Dylan leans against the next locker over with his violin in hand. His dimples shine with curiosity, but he just says, "Hi."

I lift the borrowed violin without a response, and he must notice the giant "Property of Borns College" sticker on the front of its case.

"That's not your violin."

I shake my head in confirmation. "Mine's broken. I'm renting this one from the department."

Before I can slam the locker door, Dylan rests his hand on

mine. The callouses on his fingertips somehow lift me from the dark sea of my brain. "Can I see yours?"

I shrug and get Violin from its grave.

Dylan sets his violin against the wall before accepting Violin, and a familiar sticker on his case shines in the overhead light: The Mason Musical Repair Shop.

"I don't want you to give your hopes up," Dylan says, as he inspects Violin's snapped neck, "but I might be able to fix this."

"You would do that? For how much?"

I'd sell my soul to cover repairs, since minimum wage at Borns Brew won't cut it.

Dylan closes Violin's case and rests it beside his. "Not a thing. It'll be good practice for me. I want to take over my dad's shop one day."

Though "practice" doesn't sound reassuring, my arms wrap around his neck. "I can't thank you enough."

He hugs me around the waist and spins me around, and I laugh for the first time today.

"I'm not sure if I can fix it," he says, placing me back down, "but I'll try."

I look up into his deep brown eyes. "That's all I ask."

For a moment, just a moment, his lips lean towards mine. I brush my warm cheek where he kissed it the other day with the back of my hand. How would his soft lips feel on mine?

He pulls back before I can find out.

♪♫

I prefer sleeping on Rylee's air mattress to the top bunk in my ex-temporary-triple.

Not because it's more comfortable, but because I don't have

to sleep with one eye open on Harper. How is Emma sleeping at all? I'd move to the top bunk if I were her. Harder to reach. Harder to toss into the hallway.

Yet sleeping in Rylee's room brings its own set of cons. For starters, my shoulders and neck ache after two nights, and practicing on the borrowed violin is hard enough without sore muscles and a kink in my neck. Preparing for my audition would be ten times easier with Violin. I miss the familiar curve of its body and its warm song, unlike the borrowed violin. Its body digs into my stiff shoulder, and its bow has a layer of rosin that makes it scratch rather than glide across its strings.

Professor Perry said I need to adjust to my violin, not it to me, but the other violinists are working from a higher baseline with their newer and superior violins. Thanks to Harper, my baseline's way below the rest. But if I get first chair—*when* I get first chair—I can get off this air mattress and sleep in Harmony Hall, where I belonged from the start.

Another con: Brooklyn comes over most nights and talks with Rylee after I'm in bed.

Better than loud wrestling matches, though.

Of all the nights, Brooklyn sits with Rylee on her twin bed, talking off and on for the past hour with textbooks open, while I (attempt to) concentrate on my sheet music for tomorrow's audition.

Some of us study better than others.

At least I'm not outside.

I wiggle to get comfortable, and the air mattress makes squeaky-fart sounds when Brooklyn's phone dings.

"Ugh. My sister messaged me and my parents." Brooklyn shoves her phone in front of Rylee's textbook. "She got promoted at her lame job. What a bitch."

Brooklyn's doe eyes will me to affirm her annoyance, but I'm not about corroborating that anyone, let alone a stranger, is a bitch. Instead, with all my grace and class, I blurt, "What's with the ripped pictures?"

My real question: Were they pictures of Luke?

While, yes, I'm desperate for a subject change, curiosity has gnawed on my mind non-stop. Precious brain power that I should direct toward my audition.

Brooklyn tosses her phone aside and rolls onto her stomach. "Oh, those are from Rylee's ex. Luke. They went to a lot of cool weird places together. Like the graves of dead authors." She tosses her long hair over her shoulder. "English majors."

Rylee peers at the ripped photos but doesn't respond. She frowns with one side of her mouth.

Brooklyn doesn't notice Rylee's tense shoulders. "They dated for, like, what? A year? A year and a half?"

"Shit, Brooklyn, yes." Rylee glares and scoots to the edge of her bed. "Enough."

Brooklyn smooths her ringlets. "Sorry, thought you'd be over it by now."

She sounds anything but sorry.

The skin over Rylee's high cheekbones darkens past the red of her hair.

Before I witness Brooklyn's murder, my phone vibrates the entire mattress.

Tom:

GOOD LUCK TOMORROW!!! *confetti emoji*
We're so proud of you. I know you'll do well. You always do.
You are a *star emoji* *star emoji* *star emoji*

Tom with his emojis.

Kathryn:
Text us how it goes. Or call us!
Also, Camila and Zeke say good luck. I'm sure Steven would too
if he were here.

Thinking of Steven twists my gut, which is already full of
violin-shaped butterflies.

Me:
Thanks. I'll let you know *fingers crossed emoji*

Hours later, after Brooklyn has left, I fall asleep with my
fingers crossed under my pillow.
I don't need luck, though.
Dylan does.

From the moment I wake up Wednesday morning, a ping-
pong ball of anxiety bounces back and forth inside my stomach.
First bounce: *I have to be first chair.*
Second bounce: *I have to prove that I belong at Borns.*
Third and fourth and continuing bounces: *Or how else can I
expect to belong at Juilliard? Or at the Chicago Symphony Orchestra?*
Before approaching Professor Perry's office, my phone
vibrates with a text.

Dylan is second chair:
Good luck today

No sarcasm

Me:
Ha, I know. And thanks.

I turn off my phone and wipe my sweaty palms on my jeans. My heart beats at an allegro tempo in my ears, though I signed up to have my audition after my lesson. I should save my nerves until then.

"Come on in," Professor Perry says.

He must notice me lingering in the hallway.

I shuffle inside and get out my rented violin. My grip tightens on the bow. My throat dries as I approach the music stand.

Professor Perry doesn't get out his own violin but rests his hands on top of his desk. "Would you like to start or end with your audition?"

My head jerks to face him. "Start." I clear my throat to steady my voice. "If that's okay."

Professor Perry pulls what's probably the audition rubric from a folder. "Your decision."

Is he implying I made the wrong one?

"Please play your D major scale," he says, reading the paper. "Two octaves."

The D major scale may be one of the hardest scales to play on the violin. The scale requires multiple shifts with the left hand to play C# and F#. Of course that's the scale Professor Perry drew from his folder for me.

Not that I can't play it.

With a deep breath, I bring the borrowed violin to my shoulder and raise its bow to the strings. The notes flow up and up and down and down. The tone's harsher than Violin's, but I don't miss a single one.

Professor Perry scribbles on the rubric and, though I can't read his upside down writing from a couple feet away, my eyes lock on the red ink. A quake of nausea slides up my throat.

He sets down the pen. "Now play the pickup in measure 54 to measure 65 from the sheet music that's face-down on your stand."

I flip over the music with shaky hands.

Though the selection is from *Concerto in A Minor, Movement Three* from Vivaldi—one of our string orchestra pieces—I glance over the measures and check the dynamic. It begins with pianissimo and ends on fortissimo, requiring a range of emotion. A handful of sharps hide in the measures like planted bombs.

My fingers curve and hover over the strings. I take another breath, lift my shoulders, turn my left foot a fraction of a centimeter, and play. My bow kisses each string for pianissimo, as my fingers race through the sixteenth notes, then presses against the strings as I build to fortissimo. I don't miss a sharp. My tone doesn't sound half as harsh as it did when I first picked up the borrowed violin.

"Congratulations," Professor Perry says when I finish. "Your technical skills are much, much improved. In a short time and on a rented violin, no doubt. You should be proud."

I gulp down a swell of emotion. I don't trust myself to speak.

As Professor Perry makes additional notes with his red pen, I cross my fingers while holding my bow. I squeeze them tighter together with each repeat of my mantra.

I'm first chair. I'm first chair. I'm first chair.

We're past this, but I text Dylan after my lesson anyway.

Me:
Get ready for second chair

$\oint$

Movement Twenty-Five

intervals = "the distance between two notes"

The odor of hot dogs and sunscreen clings to the Saturday afternoon air. The bleachers bake in the sun, despite the October chill. My thighs stick to the metal. Chirping, overheated birds in the trees beyond the football field rival the piccolos in the pep band.

Rylee:
Where are you?

Me:
In front of the cheerleaders
I'll look for you

With my hand covering my eyes, I search for Rylee while the scoreboard counts down the first quarter of the football game.

I should've brought sheet music or something to study, but I didn't expect to sit alone this whole time. Right before heading into the stands, Rylee ditched me after she got a text. She said, "Be right back."

Fifteen minutes ago.

Rylee plops down beside me. Her hair perches in a curly ponytail on the top of her head, showing off a reddish-purple hickey on her neck.

"How's Shane doing out there?" She yanks aviator sunglasses from her shirt collar and adjusts them on her already-burning nose.

"Um." A corner of my mouth drops.

What's Shane's jersey number?

Rylee sighs and taps on someone's shoulder. Her swollen, red eyes turn to me for the first time. "He made a touchdown. Which apparently you missed."

You missed it too…

Everyone did stand and cheer earlier.

As if on cue, our side stands and cheers again, and I stand to air out my legs.

"You do see the major ass Shane is kicking, right?" Rylee crosses her freckled arms over her chest.

I nod. One of the piccolos sounds sharp. Is it wrong to care more about the pep band than the football team?

"Working for Luke must be shitty," Rylee says out of nowhere, once we sit back down.

"Not really." My sweat glues me to the bleachers. She knows I like him as a boss. "Why?"

She counts his infractions on her fingers: "He's sullen. He overreacts. And nothing anyone does is right." She drops her hand and uncrosses her arms to lean over her thin legs with a frown. "Nothing I did was right."

"Oh."

"Don't get me wrong. I love him, and I want him back. But he really hurt me."

"What did he do?" I ask, though I'm not surprised when she tells me not to worry about it. I'm surprised she told me this much, after looking daggers at Brooklyn the other night for talking about her ripped photos.

Rylee reclines on the bleacher behind her, as Brooklyn and the rest of the cheerleaders make their way to the center of the football field.

Luke screwed her over somehow. A question repeats in my mind as if written on sheet music.

What did he do to her?

♪

From the way she's frowning at her cellphone, Emma might be rethinking her decision to come with me to Dalefield Caverns. She stared at it all through dinner. The only reason she agreed to go and not take Abigail's advice was because I convinced her to celebrate my audition going so well.

Poor Dylan. No way his audition was better.

"Excited for our first party?" I ask, leading the way through the first floor of Valley Hall.

Emma doesn't look up from her phone. "Not anymore."

"Ouch." I stop before we turn down the hallway to Rylee's room.

"It's not you." Confliction tangles in her wrinkled forehead and dimpled chin. "It's Owen. He doesn't think this party is Jesus-approved."

"In his defense, it's probably not."

Emma's phone rings three times before she ignores the call. She stares at the floor, unable to meet my eyes.

"I don't think I should go," she says.

"Your choice. I support you either way, but freshman year only happens once."

"Thanks, Corey." Emma pulls me into a hug. "Breakfast tomorrow?"

"Make it brunch, and I'm in."

Emma turns before she can see my frown.

My gut tenses to follow her, to go to the safety of Borns Brew, but I need to take my own advice. I'll only be a freshman (hopefully) once. And when I talk to Maddie again, if she ever thinks to text me back, I have to say I've gone to at least one party.

Rylee swings open the door when I knock and looks over my shoulder. "Where's your friend?"

"She bailed."

"Eh," she says, "never mind her."

Rylee grabs a small crossbody from behind the door and throws it on her bare shoulder. Her strapless tank top and low-waisted, black slacks make me feel underdressed in my jeans. Does she know it's like fifty degrees outside?

"Let's go. Brooklyn and Shane are waiting at my car."

Sure enough, two shadows linger beside Rylee's Honda Civic in the parking lot behind the dorm. Shane leans against the car with his arms crossed, wearing a one-sided smirk and tight football t-shirt that cuts into his biceps. His shirt makes me feel better about my clothes. The smirk doesn't. However, Rylee's outfit looks like daywear compared to Brooklyn's purple minidress. Her hair falls to her back in her signature spiral ringlets.

Brooklyn's silver bangles clink together as she waves. "Rylee!"

"About time." Shane pushes off the car.

"Remember this is Corey's first college party, so be on your best behavior." Rylee glares at Shane before he clambers into the back seat.

"Corey, you take shotgun," Brooklyn says with a wink.

When we're all inside, Rylee turns up the music. "Get comfortable. It's a forty-five-minute drive."

Not two minutes in, and Shane and Brooklyn's cologne and perfume clash in my nose. They dance in the back seat (without their seatbelts on, which Kathryn would give a ten-minute lecture for) and pass a flask back and forth.

"Damn, check out Luke's Snapchat," Shane says to Brooklyn over the music.

"Wait, let me see!" Rylee reaches a hand toward the back seat, and the car swerves.

Please don't let me die tonight.

Brooklyn sends a draft of flowery perfume to the front with a flick of her hair. "Don't be desperate, Rylee."

"So he's there?" Rylee asks.

"As if you didn't already know that," Brooklyn says.

Rylee's white skin flushes, but at least her eyes are now fixed on the road.

I wish Emma were here. I wish she was driving.

We take sharp turn after sharp turn onto back road after back road. We're way, way off campus.

When I can't take one more turn onto yet another gravel road, Rylee says, "We're here," and pulls into a long driveway with a metal fence on each side. A weathered sign reads

"Welcome to Dalefield Caverns."

Rylee parks a distance away from the other cars. Before we get out, she points to the grand estate on the hill, nestled in a semicircle of pine trees. "The building's near some underground caverns, hence the name."

We walk through the dewy grass to the wraparound porch, decorated with yellow streamers and littered with red solo cups. White paint peels to reveal its jagged boards. Vines grow up the blue-gray stones of the building, and weeds overtake the front flower garden. Shouts and booze-buzzed laughter mixes with the muffled hip-hop music from inside.

At least this Borns College tradition is mid-October and not on Halloween. This place looks like the filming location for *The Haunting of Bly Manor*.

Brooklyn nudges my arm in front of the massive door and hands me a baby blue flask. "Drink some."

I take a swig, but Rylee tips up the end. My sip becomes a gulp. I cough and pass it back to Brooklyn, who passes it to Shane. They take swigs, while I drank half the flask.

The back of my throat burns. *What the hell did I drink?*

Shane opens the door, and a wave of music shakes my organs. "Time to get belligerent!"

Behind the throngs of people filling the expansive entryway and foyer, black and white photos line the walls. The body heat can't compete with the damp chill lingering in the stones.

We push through the crowd to get to the main area, where the ceiling reaches towards the clouds. An expansive fireplace stretches to cover the back wall. Unlit, ornate candelabras hang every three feet, and their spider-leg-looking arms cast eerie shadows from the string lights draped above them. Shane leaves us in the middle of the dance floor to get drinks, though my head already feels fuzzy and my body loose.

Soon, I'm swaying my hips back and forth in time with the music, watching Brooklyn and Rylee dance. The sticky, humid air replaces the chill from the stones. My crop top clings to my back with sweat. Shane hands me and Brooklyn another drink, and the sweet contents coat the back of my throat in a rush. I barely taste the alcohol in my cup and take another gulp, and not a minute seems to pass when another drink arrives in my hand before I can miss the last. I notice Rylee's hand remains empty, though. She's not drinking, thank god. My ride home is sober and secure.

I chug my next drink.

"There's Luke over there. Let's go talk to him." Rylee pushes me through the crowd to a group of people at the edge of the room.

Why does she need me to talk to Luke?

The room blurs, I blink, and I'm in front of Luke. My hand flops in an uncoordinated wave. "Hey."

Luke glances around at his group, then rubs the back of his neck with a sigh. "Corey. Rylee. I didn't know you were friends."

"Yeah, we're roommates." Rylee steps around me to touch his arm with the hand not still wrapped around my wrist. "Corey wanted to come over. I didn't know you worked together! Anyway, it's so good to see you."

I frown, probably with an unintended but tipsy touch of drama. "Yes, you did. I told you he's my boss a thousand times.

Rylee's hand squeezes around my wrist.

"Can we not do this again?" Luke takes a step back and turns to me. "I'll see you around the Brew."

"Cool," Rylee says, with fire in her tone.

I grimace and wave goodbye before Rylee drags me away.

She marches back to Shane and Brooklyn, grabs the cup out of Shane's hand, and downs it in one gulp. She reaches for Brooklyn's.

"Stop, you're our DD!" I try to intercept the cup.

"Forget it." She downs the drink, then grabs my hand and slams her room key into it. "Get your stuff out of my room. Way to have my back."

Brooklyn looks at Shane with Tim-Burton-style wide eyes.

"Just great," I say.

Rylee ignores me and commands Shane to get her another drink.

Even though the alcohol is kicking in, my brain connects the dots. Why a group of popular sophomores would waste time with me, a freshman. She knew from the day in the Writing Center that I work at Borns Brew with Luke. Did she befriend me for an excuse to get close to him again?

I should've known better.

With a roll of my shoulders, I push through the crowd out the way I came. The bottoms of my Chucks stick to the wooden floor with each step from spilled beer.

Outside, I sit on the edge of the steps, out of the way of latecomers, and call Emma. She answers on the second ring.

"I'm so so so sorry to ask you this, but can you pick me up?"

"Are you okay?" Emma asks instead.

"Yeah." I rest my elbows on my knees, as a group heads up the steps into the party. "I'll pay you gas money."

"Just text me the address."

"I don't…know the address," I admit.

Even through the thickening fog of alcohol, I can sense her frustration through the phone. "It's okay, Corey. I'll look up the address." She's on her way before we hang up.

The longer I wait for Emma, the more the world tilts and the less I care about Rylee. Her room key digs into my jean pocket, and for a second, my stomach drops at the thought of not having somewhere to sleep tonight. But the dark trees sway. A new song with a heavy rhythm plays.

The door behind me opens, and a wave of hot air and loud music pours out. The two people have already passed me on the stairs when I realize I know their voices. I look up.

Dylan—and Henry.

"Almost there, almost there," Henry repeats to Dylan. He's practically carrying him to his car, which (unfortunately for me) is parked way closer than Rylee did to the building. They're in earshot, and I don't need this pang of jealousy on top of the dizzying buzz of alcohol and my guilt for making Emma come get me.

"Thank youuu," Dylan says, as Henry opens the backseat door of his car.

"Yeah, yeah, get in."

Before he falls onto the seat, Dylan plants a kiss right on Henry's mouth. "You're the best. Why did we break up?"

This night couldn't get worse.

Henry shakes his head and closes the door. Even though Dylan can't hear him, he says, "You broke up with me, remember?"

Their car drives off long before Emma's pulls up thirty minutes or so later. More people walk up and down the stairs past me, arms wrapped around themselves and teeth chattering as the temperature drops, but the October chill doesn't reach my bones. Either from the alcohol or the jealousy. Maybe both.

Emma rolls down a window and calls my name.

"You are the freaking best," I say, buckling my seatbelt.

"Thanks for getting me."

Emma wipes her eyes with a sniffle and a frown. "You're drunk."

"I just smell like beer. I swear, I'm not even tipsy." Except the world spins as she pulls out of the bumpy gravel driveway onto the main road. "So don't judge me. Don't be a bad friend."

"Bad girlfriend *and* a bad friend. Great."

Her face is funny. I can't help but laugh at her wrinkled chin. It looks like a raisin.

"Sorry, you're not a bad friend. I love you!"

Emma doesn't respond.

Instead, she drives the full forty-five minutes back to Borns in silence, though I fall asleep halfway through. At least the world's a bit more stable when I open my eyes.

"I'll pay you for gas," I say, shutting the car door. "Promise."

"Don't worry about it."

Emma locks her car and walks away without a second look.

She's actually mad at me? I wrap my arms around my torso, alone in the parking lot.

No brunch tomorrow, then.

After grabbing my duffle bag from Rylee's room and leaving her key on her desk, I wander through campus. I pass a couple dorms to the quad, where the most lampposts line the sidewalk, and then the library and a few academic buildings. My feet lead me to the music building. Since I can't sleep on a mattress tonight —air mattress or otherwise—I'll have to settle for the next best thing: a practice room couch.

I tiptoe through the basement to the practice rooms, using my phone as a flashlight. Though I could and should brush my teeth, I stash my duffle bag in my original empty violin locker, since Dylan still has Violin. God, I hope he fixes it soon.

How the bag manages to fit, I have no idea. Maybe Kathryn's bag is more like the pants in *Sisterhood of the Traveling Pants* than I knew, though I'm not writing letters to Maddie and my other nonexistent friends about it anytime soon.

The practice room door seals shut behind me, and my shoulders relax. I kick off my shoes, flop onto the couch, and curl up into a fetal position on the loveseat.

A tear slides down my cheek and onto the cushion.

Crashing in Rylee's room had seemed like the perfect short escape from Harper. But most foster houses feel like an escape from the last house until they aren't. Why did I expect college would be better than foster care? I'm a foster kid, no matter where I am. My temporary triple was an escape from Foster House #11, Tom and Kathryn's house. Rylee's room was an escape from my temporary triple. Now a practice room is an escape from Rylee's room. Turns out each escape is another downward spin in my disappointing foster care cycle, foster house or no foster house.

Maybe Kathryn was right. If I'd stayed that weekend, confronted Harper, maybe Violin wouldn't be dead now. Maybe I'd still be sleeping on my top bunk.

I didn't hash it out with Harper. I didn't defend my right to our temporary triple. Instead, I left because that's what I do. Foster care taught me nothing about staying and only about moving, leaving, escaping.

I'm tired of escaping. Of not belonging.

Movement Twenty-Six

beat = "unit of measurement in music as indicated by the up and down movements, real or imagined, of a conductor's hand"

Sunday night, I sleep on the same practice room couch. At least it's more comfortable than Rylee's squeaky air mattress. Emma doesn't talk to me during First-Year Composition class on Monday, and although people have cut ties with me over far less, the silent treatment seems undeserved. I don't talk to Dylan as we cram together behind the semicircle of chairs for string orchestra. I can't look at him without hearing his question to Henry: "Why did we break up?"

But none of that matters today. Today's the moment of the truth. The day we find out our chair placements.

First chair waits for me at the front.

Professor Perry strides across the stage and steps onto the podium, holding a piece of paper. He lifts his head towards the stage lights. Some students fiddle their thumbs or play with their jewelry or yank on the hems of their shirts. I tap my fingertips into my palm for *Flight of the Bumblebee*, my go-to piece when I'm extremely nervous.

"I'll read the order of names within each instrument section from first to last chair. You may sit once I call your name." Professor Perry clears his throat and holds out the paper like he's the announcer at a fancy ball. "Let's start with the cellos."

He calls Henry first, then name after name until the last cellist, who wipes his eyes with the back of his arm on the way to his chair.

"Moving on to the violins…"

Every muscle in my body tightens. My extremities tremble like vibrating strings.

I cross my fingers.

"Dylan Mason."

My stomach drops to my feet like the brassy slide of a trombone.

Dylan. Not me.

I'm not first chair.

I'm not accepted into the music program, and I don't have a room in Harmony Hall.

"Corey Reed." Professor Perry peers down at me.

I bite my lip as pressure builds behind my eyes. I will myself to my chair, but my legs won't move. Professor Perry snaps my name for a second time, and I maze through the chairs to mine, as he calls Vicky, Dylan's friend, next. Dylan reaches around me to give her a high five, and I sink lower into my chair.

Yesterday, he had his lips all over Henry, who I can't help but look at, happy in his matching first chair. They're meant for each other. Two effing first-chair peas in a pod.

Jealousy curdles in my gut under the stage lights.

"You okay?" Dylan whispers, as Professor Perry moves on to the violas.

My bottom lip trembles. "Just leave me alone. I don't need you to rub it in."

"I'm not—"

"I said leave me alone. I don't want to talk to you."

Dylan's lips pucker as he slides his tongue over his front teeth. He nods, as if he's come to some hard conclusion, and turns away.

I stare ahead at our shared music stand, though I want to push it over and run offstage.

How could I ever think I'd be good enough to be a professional violinist? To go to Juilliard and join the Chicago Symphony Orchestra? How could I ever let myself compare my future to Stephanie Jeong? If I was good enough, I'd already be a music major living in Harmony. I'd be first chair.

Yet I'm second and stuck for another night on a practice room couch.

♪♫

I sleep unnoticed in the music building until Wednesday night, when a campus police officer shines a flashlight in my face.

"What do you think you're doing, miss?" His voice booms in the insulated practice room. "You having roommate troubles?"

I squint at the dark figure. "Something like that."

The officer drops the light to the floor. He leans side to side, switching his weight with his hands in enormous fists on his hips.

"I get it. I won't make you go back to your room tonight, but if I catch you sleeping in here again, I'm going to have to write you up."

I still don't know what "write you up" means. Is a fine involved? Do they call your guardians? Caseworker? Cause I don't need Drew, Kathryn, and Tom finding out about me not living in Harmony Hall/not getting into the music program because campus police caught me sleeping on a couch.

Whatever "write you up" means, it can't be good.

"Night, young lady," he says, though he hovers in the door frame for a moment with his back to me. "It gets better, I promise."

He closes the door, muffling the sound of his jingling keys as he heads back down the hallway.

My head flops back onto the couch.

At least college can't get worse. I'm already second chair; I'm not even a music major. Emma's not talking to me, and Dylan's still in love with Henry. And now I can't sleep here tomorrow night.

Will it get better?

And how long do I have to wait until then?

Thursday night, when the lights flick on and off in the library for closing time, I check back in my borrowed laptop but take a left before the doors into the stairwell. Though I've always studied with Emma on the first floor, the library has four floors, including a basement on the lowest level that I've seen once on my official campus tour.

I stop at the bottom of the stairs and adjust the straps of my book bag—which holds my pillow, not books. The ceiling seems lower than I remember. If I stood on a chair, I could brush it with my fingertips. The carpet, on the other hand, is exactly how I remember: it's the same gross shade of muted red as Foster House #9's signature meatloaf. Thick reference books continue to wait on condensed shelves, but no one's around.

Just as I hoped.

A ratty couch sticks out from behind one of the desks lining the back wall in the corner.

My bed for the night.

And my only option, at least the only option I can think of at 1 a.m., since the campus police officer found me last night.

Unlike the cushioned practice room couch, the stuffing has thinned in places, and the wooden frame digs into my hips. I unzip my book bag, pull out my pillow, and when the florescent lights blink one last time and remain off, I close my heavy eyes.

Tomorrow.

Friday.

I'd deal with everything tomorrow.

Movement Twenty-Seven

glissando = "to glide or slide the fingers along the
string, usually to create a special effect"

Luke:
Hey I'm not gonna be at the Brew tonight
It's time you do your shifts solo, but text me if you need me
Don't forget to put the lid on the fender
*blender

Me:
Sounds good
And it's too cold for frappuccinos anyway

Emma, Dylan, and now Luke. I blame all my relationship
fallouts on Dalefield Caverns.

The estate *did* remind me of *The Haunting of Bly Manner*.
Maybe it cursed me.

I miss them. Emma and Dylan more than Luke, but still. And not just because I eat all my meals alone now like I'm in elementary school timeout. Every time I think about saying something or texting them, though, I push the thought aside.

Foster Kid Rule #4
Don't count on second chances.

At the end of my Borns Brew shift, I pull the steel barrier from the ceiling to the counter, which encloses our work area with a thick lock. I yawn and lean against the nearest high-top table. I can't sleep in a practice room, and I *won't* sleep on a couch in the library again. I'd rather sleep on the floor. Or outside. At least I won't have bruises.

I sound like the damn princess in that pea story.

Where the hell am I supposed to sleep now? I just mopped the floor, so it's still wet, but I don't think I'll notice.

Still, the kink in my neck, my stiff back, my half-assed homework are all proof that not sleeping in a bed is catching up with me.

I glance around the Brew. We're closed, so the seating area is empty. No one would know if I slept here.

I drag myself to the nearest booth, plop onto the cushioned bench, and roll onto my back. I bend my knees so my legs don't hang over the side. My eyes burn for rest, but my mind won't relax.

How many butts sat here today?

Ew, think of something else.

Professor Perry said midterm grades would be posted by the end of the day, so I check if they're up yet on my student account. My palms turn clammy as I click on "Academic Profile" and wait for the screen to load.

First-Year Composition: C
Personal Development: B
Psychology: D+
String Orchestra: B+
Violin One-on-One Lesson: B+
World History: B-

My breath catches, and no matter how many times I refresh the page, my grades stay the same. I am *not* a B, C, and D student. I'm an A, B, and sometimes C student. How did I get a C in First-Year Composition with extra credit and all-nighters?

Oh god. Could I lose my scholarship for having a D?

Drew's going to be pissed. Tom and Kathryn are going to be so disappointed.

I have to do better, *be* better, than this.

Tears escape down my cheeks. My pulse slams into the back of my snot-lined throat.

First Violin's death, then second chair, and now this. My grades are dirt on top of my future's grave. RIP. Here lies Coralee Reed's career as a professional violinist.

I don't even have my own room to mourn my future in peace. At least in foster care, I had that much.

My sobs build to a crescendo.

"Corey?"

I peer over the table at Luke's blurry face, then flop back down on the booth. I groan internally. At least, I hope it's internal and not out loud.

"What are you doing here?" My voice sounds miles away through the congestion.

"I could ask you the same thing." Luke sits on the other side of the booth with a sigh when I don't respond. "I forgot my notebook under the counter. Really, though. What're you doing?"

I don't bother opening my eyes. "Sleeping."

Silence.

"Are you…okay?"

"No," I say with a sniffle, "I have nowhere else to sleep."

"Hold up. Aren't you Rylee's roommate?"

"Not really. She let me crash on her air mattress a couple nights." I prop myself up on my elbows. He's wearing sweats, and I'm not used to seeing him out of his Borns Brew apron. "Long story, but I'm supposed to live in a temporary triple. But I can't go back."

His back thuds against the booth. "I mean, I'm relieved you're not rooming with Rylee. I learned the hard way she's not trustworthy. But damn, Corey, you need a place to sleep."

"I know." I lay back down in defeat.

"Do you?"

I jerk to face him. "What do you mean?"

"You're looking like you've given up. Like you're about to go outside and pick a bush to sleep under for the rest of the semester."

"What am I supposed to do?"

"I don't know," he says. "*Something*."

"Well, I haven't slept outside yet."

"Don't sleep outside, Corey." Luke leans forward and sniffs. "Though you smell like you have already."

"Eff you."

"There are people who can help you. You just have to ask." Luke stands from the booth. "Hell, you can sleep on my couch if you want tonight. I don't know what went down with you and

Rylee, and I'm definitely not her biggest fan, but I know she wouldn't want you sleeping here. And there's that perky friend of yours. You know, with the unicorn shirts?" He takes a step forward, then takes one back. "Bottom line: you're not alone."

Aren't I alone, though?

Emma and Dylan aren't talking to me, and I haven't been keeping up with Kathryn and Tom. Or Drew. Not even Maddie, though that's probably for the best.

But I thought Luke hated me, and he offered to let me sleep on his couch.

"Thanks," I say, after a silent minute. "And are you sure? Cause a couch sounds a lot better than this sticky-ass booth."

"Come on." He gestures for me to get up, and after he grabs his notebook, he holds the door for me on our way out. "Find somewhere to sleep tomorrow night, though, okay? You need a bed."

We walk towards the nearby on-campus apartments for a minute or two before Luke says, "Wipe down the booths better. They shouldn't be sticky. That's disgusting."

I laugh. "You got it, boss."

He's right, and not just about cleaning the booths. I'm not alone.

Before we get to his building, I pull my phone out of my back pocket and text the two people that have always had my back, whether or not I realized it.

Me:

Can someone pick me up tomorrow morning?
I really need you both.

Tom, not two minutes later:
Of course *red heart emoji*
Be there first thing

Me:
Thanks. Miss you

Kathryn:
We miss you too.

Movement Twenty-Eight

grace note = "ornamental note printed small to indicate
that its time value is not counted in the rhythm of the
measure and must be subtracted from that of an
adjacent note"

Tom doesn't ask about my red, swollen eyes when he picks me
up from campus Saturday morning. (I did some more crying
on Luke's couch—which was a futon and not the three-seated
couch I had in mind.) He doesn't ask why I had him pick me up
in front of the on-campus apartment buildings. (Luke shares his
apartment with three roommates, one of which was Jackson, my
orientation leader. Gag. He waved at me with a mouthful of
Cocoa Puffs on my way out the door.) He doesn't ask about my
missing violin. He just taps the steering wheel and glances at me
every other minute during the entire drive. It's kind of nice.

The less he says, the more I know he's trying to make space
to listen—when I'm ready to talk. And it's time I did. I have to

tell them the truth about Harmony Hall. They might yell at me, they might end my extended foster care with them, but somehow, I know they won't. I hope they don't.

Inside the house, the sweet smell of butter wafts from the kitchen. I walk past the pile of shoes and navigate through the minefield of toys in the living room. Camila's dinosaur lays right in the middle of the carpet.

Kathryn stands in front of the stove, flipping pancakes on the griddle and looking over her shoulder every so often, as Camila sets silverware on the table.

"Look who's home," Tom says from behind me.

I give a rare grin to Kathryn. "Look who's making pancakes."

Camila runs to give me a hug. "We make pancakes together every Saturday." She beckons me closer like she's going to reveal a secret.

"Kathryn doesn't make them as good as you, though," she whispers.

I can't help myself. I lift Camila up and spin her around in a circle, and her high-pitched laugh warms my chest.

"I've missed you, little fish."

I've missed them all.

After I set her back down, she skips back to the table. Kathryn turns off the griddle and slides the last pancake onto the stack. Tom carries the plate of golden-brown pancakes from the stove, and we convene at the table.

Except Steven doesn't come bounding down the stairs.

Kathryn must read my facial expression. "He and his mom swing by sometimes. He seems really happy, Corey."

I smile. And then my heartbeat quickens. "Wait. Where's Zeke?"

"Upstairs in his room." Kathryn sets a plate and the syrup bottle down in front of me. "He's grounded, actually. Not that he has much of a problem with that."

"Why's he grounded?"

Tom shakes his head. "Why don't you ask him. We could use your help. Sometimes you're the only one who gets through to him."

With a nod, I slide off my chair. "Mind if we eat upstairs? I'll take him pancakes."

Kathryn agrees, so I fill two plates with pancakes. I drizzle syrup on mine and pour a pond of syrup on Zeke's like he prefers. As I dodge plastic obstacles through the living room on my way to Zeke's room, I can't help but notice how normal this feels. How *right*.

College may not have turned out like I hoped, but this house deserves more credit. I've never had a home, but for once, it feels like I do.

I knock on Zeke's door with my foot. "It's me."

Silence.

I kick again. "I have pancakes."

The door cracks open.

Zeke reaches out with his palm up, like I'm going to hand him a plate and leave.

"Let me in first."

He delivers a dramatic sigh and opens the door.

Either he really wants pancakes, or he's in a darker, more desperate place than Kathryn and Tom let on. He has never once let me in his room.

Now I know why.

My mouth hangs open as I pass him a plate. "Oh my god."

Sheets of sketch paper and charcoal pencils are strewn

across the floor. Drawings of people, buildings, shoes, dumpsters fill the pages. Ordinary and seemingly mundane objects that I overlook. The detailed drawings have an eerie style. The people wear misgiving expressions; the buildings crumble; the shoes have holes; the dumpsters stretch toward the cloudy sky in an intimidating posture. Right out of a zombie apocalypse, his subjects look on the brink of destruction. The strokes of charcoal reveal an intimate understanding of the grimmer parts of the world and empathy for people that have seen too much.

They're incredible.

Zeke is incredible.

"They're not done," Zeke says through a mouthful of pancake. His voice sounds higher than usual.

Intricate lines compose a feather on a bird's wing, and a rubbed area adds shading to a wrinkly hand.

"They look done to me."

"It's a waste, anyway. I'm not going anywhere with my art. Not after what I did."

I drop beside him on the navy carpet and take a bite of buttery pancake. I don't speak, so he knows I'm here to listen. Like Tom did for me on the drive here. For a long moment, we sit, eating our pancakes.

After he finishes his pancakes, he finally says, "I spray painted the bathroom and got suspended."

Against all odds, I don't spit my pancake across the room.

"Why would you do that?"

"I don't know." He shrugs his broad shoulders. They seem broader than the last time I saw him. "I'm suspended and have community service hours. Trust me, I wish I hadn't done it."

I squint at him. My curiosity overpowers my shock. "What did you draw?"

He pulls out his phone and scrolls through a few photos before handing it to me. A line of houses drawn in spray-paint drips down the cinderblock walls of his school bathroom. The words "foster care cares for no one" are scrawled beneath the row.

"I feel that," I say, handing the phone back to him. "But we're in a good spot with Tom and Kathryn."

"We are. But it's everything before them, you know?"

I do know. I know too well.

He stares at his hands. One side of his palm is smudged with charcoal. "My parents died a few years ago. That's why I'm in foster care."

"I'm— I'm so sorry, Zeke."

"I lived with my grandparents for a while, but they stopped being able to take care of themselves. I tried to take care of the three of us, but I just couldn't. It was too much. They went to a nursing home." His eyes shine as he rubs the smudge with his opposite thumb. "I haven't visited them in a while. I know it's not their fault, but I'm scared and lonely and, even though it's not logical, I feel abandoned by them. And by my parents."

He transfers all the charcoal to the lighter brown skin on the tip of his thumb, then asks, "What do I do?"

"You do your community service hours," I say. "See your therapist, take a damn art class, and apply to colleges. And you figure out how to heal, Zeke."

"I got suspended, though. I don't know if I can come back from this. Tom and Kathryn might even kick me out."

They wouldn't. They're the first fosters I know, without any doubt, that wouldn't kick out a vulnerable kid.

"You'll come back from this," I say. I squeeze his shoulder, remembering what Luke said. "You're not alone."

He picks up a drawing on the floor. An elderly man and woman sit together on a porch swing. They aren't smiling, but you would think they were from the warmth in their eyes. The viewer looks on from behind them, unnoticed and unimportant in the moment; the moment surges with their love yet leaves the impression of being left behind. Forgotten.

He thumbs the edge of the paper. "I guess I owe it to them to try."

♪♫

Later, I find Tom and Kathryn sitting on the living room couch. Tom reads a romance, and Kathryn flips through a running magazine. My heartbeat quickens as I freeze in the middle of the room and press an icy hand to the back of my hot neck.

It's time. I have to tell them.

"I need to talk to you both about something," I say.

Their eyes snap from their reading to mine.

"Okay." Tom reaches for Kathryn's hand after setting down his book. "Why don't you have a seat?"

I can't bring myself to sit. I can't bring myself to meet their eyes. "This is hard to say."

Kathryn tosses her magazine aside, but it slides onto the floor. "Is it about Zeke? Did your talk go okay?"

"Yeah, Zeke is fine. I, um, wanted to talk about…me."

Kathryn glances at Tom with a tight frown.

"We're here for you," she says. "You can trust us."

My heart beats in double time. I sit across from them on the loveseat, not because I want to, but because my legs start shaking.

"Can I?" The question tumbles out of my mouth. "I want to, but it's not like you all trust me. To be honest," I take a breath —I'm not usually honest, "we're not close."

They've kept me out of the loop about Camila and Nicole. Something's going on, and I wish they'd tell me. Whether or not they do, though, I have to tell them about Harmony Hall. But it'd be easier if they were vulnerable first.

Kathryn rubs her lips together as if she's evening out lip gloss, but she hasn't put any on. "How about this? I'll tell you something, and then you tell me something. Deal?"

She lets go of Tom's hand and extends hers to me.

I wipe my clammy hand on my thrift store jeans before grasping hers. "Deal."

"I'm sorry we haven't had a closer relationship," Kathryn says. "But have you considered that maybe I've been trying to give you what you asked for? Space?"

I tuck my knees and wrap my arms around them as I consider her words. The memory of my first night here floods back, after my horrific five-months-too-long experience at Foster House #10.

"All I want is to be left alone," I said then.

"Corey," Tom says. "We want a relationship with you. A more permanent relationship beyond extended foster care."

What does he mean, a more permanent relationship? They're already stuck with me until I turn twenty-one.

"You've taught us there's a line we cannot cross. I've tried so hard to respect your boundaries." She rubs her lips together again. "The truth is, I wanted space too. I didn't want foster kids at first. Tom did."

Ouch. The betrayal burns into my skin.

"Why become foster parents if you didn't want foster kids?"

Kathryn's eyes shine with tears. She never cries.

Tom pats her leg with a furrowed expression, as if to say, "You don't have to tell her."

Her lips become a straight, determined line. "I want to tell you this, so you'll have no doubt about whether you can trust us." She scoots forward on the edge of the couch, holding Tom's hand. "We found out a few years ago that we, well, *I* couldn't have kids."

Oh god.

I can't believe she's telling me this.

"I was really depressed." She takes a gulp from her nearby 40 ounce water bottle. "So I started running. A lot. But when I started having knee problems, I knew I had to take better care of myself. My body and my mind."

Tom's hand tightens around hers.

"Then Tom had the idea, if not our own—" Her voice breaks. She wipes a finger across her eyes and takes a breath. "If not bio kids, we could take care of other people's kids. But I couldn't stop thinking, 'This isn't fair. These people don't care about their kids, but I'd care for mine.'" She shakes her head, and her ponytail swishes back and forth. "I know that's untrue now. Steven's mom, Camila's mom, Zeke's grandparents. Even your parents."

I stiffen at the mention of my parents. I try not to hypothesize why they gave me up for adoption or why my might-have-been adoptive parents gave me over to the foster system. My parents couldn't have known the closed adoption would fall through. And my adoptive parents must've had a good reason, since they would've had to legally prove giving me back was in my best interest. Still, after eleven foster houses, I'm the control to their independent variables. I can't help but think that, as the consistent factor, I'm the problem.

"There are reasons," Kathryn continues, "systems inundating the foster system, that hurt and tear apart families."

"Anyway," she says, "I'm sorry if I haven't given you what you deserve. I'm sorry if I gave you too much space."

An unexpected chill slides along my arms. It's like I'm meeting Kathryn, the *real* Kathryn under the running tank tops, for the first time. Maybe the spandex hasn't cut off the blood to her heart.

I haven't given her enough credit. When Drew couldn't find another foster family to take me in, she and Tom did. They worked with Drew so I could get extended foster care. They gave me what my own parents hadn't: a place to come back to when my life goes to shit.

"I thought you wanted to be alone, but I want you to know that you and I..." a tear rolls down her face, "we don't have to be."

My lip quivers.

"You are a talented, thoughtful person, and we're lucky to know you. Despite the circumstances handed to us, we can find the family we've longed for, if it's not quite what we planned. We love you, Corey."

Love.

I've given her every imperfect part of me to reject. I've been short and detached. I've been rude. Coming here from my worst-ever foster house, even if theirs is the best, didn't make me some lovable teenager. Yet she's given me grace to be human. She loves me, despite the times I've been the worst version of myself.

Telling by his violent blows into his handkerchief, Tom loves me too. If they love me after all that, maybe they can love me after this.

I stand from the loveseat and sit between them on the couch. "Thanks for telling me."

Kathryn pulls me into a hug, and Tom wraps his arms around the both of us.

When we let go, I scoot backward into the couch. "I guess it's my turn."

"That was the deal," Tom says.

"Okay then." I roll my shoulders. Take a breath. Press my hands between my thighs. "I'm not a music major. The music department didn't accept me, so I couldn't live in Harmony Hall, and Reslife put me into a temporary triple. But I still don't have a permanent room. I've actually been sleeping on a couch in the music building and the library. Before that, an air mattress, and I slept on my boss's couch last night. Oh, and I might lose my scholarship."

They tense. Kathryn presses her lips together, and Tom's face reddens. The silence hurts, but I know they don't want to react and upset me.

"I wish you would've told us sooner, Corey," Kathryn finally says.

"Start from the beginning." Tom reaches around to rest a hand on Kathryn's back. "What happened?"

I tell them everything—about Dylan getting accepted *and* getting first chair instead of me, about Emma and Harper, about crashing on Rylee's air mattress and couch surfing across campus.

"Thank you for trusting us." The corners of Tom's mouth tremble.

"It's going to be okay," Kathryn says, wrapping an arm around me. "We'll help you get through this."

"When's the last time you talked with the housing director?" Tom asks.

"Not since my first day on campus, I guess, but I've left her messages. And I met with my RA a couple times."

"You should set up another meeting, first thing Monday morning," Kathryn says. "And try to make up with your friend Emma, okay?"

"Meeting with Ms. Birr won't make a difference, though. Reslife doesn't do freshmen swap rooms."

"You can't just sleep random places to avoid your room," Tom says.

"Nothing I say is going to change her mind."

"Do you honestly think that?" Kathryn asks.

"Yeah."

"Why?"

I know this is a problem. But the worst problem is being a problem. Being a burden. Being someone people wished would go away, disappear, move somewhere else.

I don't want to be a squeaky wheel. I'd rather end up in the junk yard.

"Because I'm not worth the exception. There are rules. And I don't want to be a problem."

"Think about that," Kathryn says. "You're struggling, but it's not because you're not smart. It's because you aren't safe. Your needs aren't being met. How can you do well if *you're* not well?"

"I didn't think about it like that. I'm just…tired."

Tom laughs a low, humorless laugh. "Well, no wonder."

Kathryn rubs my back. "Don't downplay your problems to make other people comfortable, okay?"

I nod. My throat's too tight for words.

"You know you're always welcome here, right?" Kathryn's eyes narrow with seriousness. "Not just on the weekends. We're just fifteen minutes away."

"I would pick you up every day if you wanted," Tom says.

"I—" I blink up at the ceiling light. "Thanks."

Kathryn pulls us into another group hug. "We love you."

Now that she's said it, she can't seem to stop.

"And we're sorry this happened to you." Tom smooths the back of my hair. "I didn't even know this could happen."

"Ms. Birr said it happens a lot. Most colleges overbook on purpose because students drop out and transfer."

"Parents and alumni wouldn't be too happy about students sleeping on air mattresses, though," Kathryn says.

"The local community either," Tom adds.

Oh my god.

I launch from the couch.

"I just got an idea." Their concerned eyes trail me as I pace in front of the couch. I stop. "I'm gonna take a nap."

"You got an idea for a nap?" Tom asks.

"No," I shake my head, "but I could use one."

Kathryn calls, "Sweet dreams," as I race up the stairs to my ex-room. Except it's mine.

My room hasn't changed since I left. Not the bed, the dresser, the nightstand. Right where I left them, though the bed has two new pillows, new sheets, and a new comforter. All a deep purple, my favorite color. I belly flop onto the bed and roll around on the velvety soft material. I pull the sheets to my chin and unlock my phone.

Me:

I know you hate me right now, but I'm sorry for everything.

Emma:

That's all I needed to hear *smiling emoji*

And I don't hate you. I could never hate you.

Me:

Thanks Emma. Really.

And I also need your help. Are you still on the

college newspaper?

Emma:

Yes??

Me:

Meet me in the library tomorrow? Usual spot and time

Emma:

Sure *sparkling heart emoji* I really miss you

Me:

Same *purple heart emoji*

After a week of the silent treatment, talking to Emma feels too easy. But I talked to Luke when I thought he'd written me off, and Kathryn and Tom listened after months of me hiding the truth from them. Maybe people give second chances—third and fourth and fifth chances—more than foster care had me believe.

I leave a voicemail for Ms. Birr next. Her career depends on meeting with me first-thing in her office Monday. She might've not taken me seriously or cared about finding me a permanent room before, but she will now. With Emma's help.

With my plans set, I rest my phone on my nightstand and have the best sleep of my life.

$\begin{smallmatrix} & \\ \mathcal{G} \\ & \end{smallmatrix}$

Movement Twenty-Nine

scroll = "the decorative 'head' of the violin"

Emma offers a timid wave as I near our first-floor table in the library Sunday afternoon. I set down two grande lattes from Borns Brew as a peace offering, one for her and one for me, and take my usual seat across from her.

"Sorry," I say, at the same time Emma says, "I'm sorry."

We smile at each other, and I know we'll get through the hurt and awkwardness of our first fight.

"No, I'm sorry." I look down at my Chucks. "For saying you're a bad friend."

Maddie and all my past friends have drifted out of my life—the last time I talked to Maddie was before my audition. (Not that I'm going to text her anytime soon. Our forced friendship should stay in high school.) I've been a bad friend. Because I hadn't known I could mend a relationship. I hadn't known pushing people away, isolating myself, made the fallout worse. I hadn't known people still might want me in their life after the first sign of imperfection. Tom and Kathryn were the first adults to model forgiveness to me, after lying and keeping secrets from them. The unbelievable thing is, I think our relationship is stronger for it.

Maybe my and Emma's friendship will be too.

"I didn't mean it," I say. "Especially when you're the best friend I've ever had. From day one."

"Oh my goodness." Emma throws out her arms and wraps me in a hug. "You're forgiven."

"Just like that?" I ask.

"Just like that."

My chest lightens. In eighth grade orchestra, one of the bass players, Sawyer, switched to the violin. He went from a ten-pound-plus instrument with a giant, bulky case to a much more portable 1.5 pounds. His shoulders must have felt how mine do now—weightless.

"In case you didn't know, you're my best friend too," Emma says, as we sit at the table we've gotten to know so well. "And I really am sorry. I shouldn't have taken my fight with Owen out on you. I knew you were drunk, and normally I wouldn't have taken an offhand remark so personally." Her smile drops to a frown, wrinkling her chin. "Also, I broke up with Owen."

Good thing I didn't just take a sip, or latte would've come out my nose.

"What?"

Nearby students shush me rather than Emma, their usual target.

"That night, the night of the party, he was so mad. Mad that I almost went and pissed when I left to pick you up. I felt ashamed, though I shouldn't have. I realized on the drive that

I've been trying so hard to make things work, when we're becoming more and more different. I mean, I was too scared to tell him about my doubts with Christianity." Tears well in her eyes. "I know I made the right decision, but it's still hard, you know? Two years gone."

I think about my long line of foster parents. Tom and Kathryn. All the foster kids I've known. Steven, Zeke, and Camila. Some I've known for less than two years, some less than two months. But they've left their mark on me like the scratches on my too-big violin case.

I reach to rest my hand on her forearm with a reassuring touch. "Your relationship's over, but it wasn't a waste. He made you happy. You made him happy. And now you'll find happiness apart."

Emma wipes her face with the back of her hand. "Thanks, Corey." She glances around the table, noticing for the first time I have nothing with me other than my phone and latte. "Aren't you going to check out a laptop?"

"Not today." Her chin wrinkles with confusion, but I smile. "I need you to write something for me. If you're still up for it."

Emma smiles back. "What are best friends for?"

Movement Thirty

luthier = "maker of a stringed instrument such as a violin, viola, cello, bass or guitar"

First thing Monday morning, I knock on Ms. Birr's office door. Her sour voice says, "Come in." She waves to the empty chair in front of her desk, which is no longer tidy like it was at the start of the semester. It's now covered in scattered papers.

She laces her fingers on the last clear spot. "Tell me what's on your mind."

"Like I said in my voicemail, I need a place to live. I don't feel safe in my temporary triple, and my one roommate broke my violin. I need you to assign me a new dorm room."

She presses her thin rose-pink lips together. "Every resident deserves to feel safe, but I still can't assign you a new room just yet."

I unzip my book bag and pull out a crisp piece of paper. I

slide it across the desk to her. "Maybe this will change your mind."

Her frown deepens the longer she skims. "What is this?"

"The feature story of this week's college newspaper. *If* you don't find me a new place to live." I zip up my book bag. "You can keep that copy."

The opening of Emma's article* for the newspaper:

"Every family sends their student off to college with the expectation they'll receive a superb education and proper guidance from faculty and staff, least of all a place to live. At Borns College, though, students can't count on living in a safe environment or sleeping a bed."

Since she wrote it only yesterday, Emma's editor hasn't read or approved the article yet. Ms. Birr doesn't need to know that, though.

Ms. Birr's tongue scrapes the back of her mouth. "Are you, a freshman student, trying to blackmail me right now?"

"No." I shake my head with an innocent frown. "It's not blackmail if you're the vulnerable party."

Kathryn helped me with that line.

Ms. Birr actually laughs. "Well, this is a first."

She looks up at the ceiling as if for godly strength to make it through the rest of our conversation. "Do you know Julia Hill?"

I nod. Julia, the lacrosse player. Julia, Harper's ex-friend.

"Her roommate, Ana, just transferred as of last week. I was going to let Julia decide," Ms. Birr continues, "then let you and a few others swap rooms in a couple weeks. But this makes it easier for me and your RA. The room is yours."

I gasp.

I did it. I actually did it.

Ms. Birr turns to her computer with a shake of her brown-blonde hair.

In a few seconds, my college room and roommate problems will be over. I'll have a normal, two-person dorm room. I'll be down the hall from my best friend. I'll be able to sleep enough to function, to make good grades, to maybe one day beat Dylan out of first chair.

I'll be in a new room. With someone I don't really know. In another bed. After a cycle of beds that are mine then not mine.

"Wait."

Ms. Birr releases her mouse and spins her chair back to me.

"I don't want to live with Julia."

Her slender nostrils flare. "Then where do you want to live, Corey? I don't have any other options for you on campus."

"Not on campus," I say. "I want to live off campus. But I want a refund for my room and board, like you said I could before."

Ms. Birr rubs her temples. "Fine. As long as the school newspaper doesn't print that article, fine. Registrar will process your refund in the next week or so."

"Thank you, Ms. Birr." I stand and push in my chair. "I appreciate your time."

"I have to ask," she says, before I step into the hallway. "Are you sure you want to live off campus? You're not going to come back in a week and demand to live with Julia or somebody else?"

"I'm sure."

I close the door behind me with a smile. I've never been more sure about where I'm going to live. For the first time, I have

a room and a bed that *feel* like mine.
A house that feels like home.

Movement Thirty-One

flautando: "a 'sul tasto' (over-the-fingerboard) bow stroke that creates a flute-like sound"

My steps are more of an allegro skip the rest of the day until string orchestra. As I grab my borrowed violin from my locker before class, Dylan leans against the wall behind me.

"Am I supposed to leave you alone still or what?"

I turn and leave the locker door open. Though the back of my neck warms and static buzzes in my brain, I manage to say, "Oh, come on, you were doing so well."

Dylan shoves his hands into the front pockets of his black, ripped skinny jeans and pushes off from the wall. "I'll just be going then."

"Kidding. I'm kidding. Don't go." I catch his arm, and he gives me a lopsided smile.

"I'm sorry about the other day," I say. "I was in my head, and I didn't want a repeat of high school orchestra. Cause you were way harsh back then, if you don't remember. But I should've been happy for you even though I was sad for me."

"I remember." He watches my hand leave his arm like he wishes it wouldn't. "I also remember you dishing it right back. But it's a good you apologized."

"Yeah?" I cross my arms. "How come?"

"Come with me. Leave the violin."

I close the door and lock the borrowed violin inside, then follow Dylan to the somewhat empty stage. He reaches for my hand, and we weave through the chairs and music stands to our chairs. First chair and second chair, at the front of the stage, to the left of the podium.

On my chair is a black, polished, unscratched and unstickered violin case.

"Is that—?"

"New case, same violin," Dylan says. "I can get you a new sticker, though. One with a curse word, if you like."

"You… You fixed my violin."

I let go of his hand to run mine over the smooth case.

I missed you.

My violin doesn't respond. I don't think it's a bad thing, though. I think it might be a good thing.

"I'm talented," Dylan says with a shrug. "What can I say?"

"Thank you. Thank you so much."

He wriggles his hand out of his pocket and takes mine again. "No problem. You owe me a bet, anyway."

"Ugh, I forgot about that." I roll my eyes with a grin. "You did get first chair. Winner's choice, like you said. Know what I owe you yet?"

"Not yet." He takes my other hand. We're almost as close to each other as we were in the human knot—chest to chest, my

Chucks to his Vans. He presses both his soft and calloused fingertips onto my skin. "But I will."

A wavy strand falls into his playful yet thoughtful eyes.

I brush it to the side of his forehead. No use. The strand and a few more fall back in place.

"I'm glad we're not adversaries anymore."

"Oh yeah?" His lips pull into a wide grin. Why's that?"

I step closer to his broad yet lean frame. Either the stage lights or his body heat burn me from the inside out. He leans down an inch and then an inch more, until I press my lips to his.

He tastes like strawberry chapstick. His lip ring sends an electric chill down my spine.

Someone whistles, but we kiss a second longer before finding our seats.

"I've been wanting to do that since high school," Dylan whispers as he lays sheet music on our shared stand.

"Don't lie to me, Dylan Mason." I stare down at my violin on my lap and try to keep my voice steady. "Up until just now, I thought you were still in love with Henry."

A page of our sheet music goes flying, and Dylan has to get out of his chair to snatch it. "You can't be serious. I broke up with *him* before coming to college."

I sigh. "I saw you kiss him at Dalefield Caverns. Which is probably why I was even meaner, and really immature, about getting second chair."

"I wish you didn't see that. It meant nothing. Really." His dark eyes widen. "Henry and I are friends at best. Do you want to know why we broke up?"

"Only if you want to tell me."

"Because he makes me feel like crap for being bi sometimes." Dylan's tongue fiddles with his lip ring. "He acts as if I'm allowed to have my bi flag and my bi friends, but I'm not as much a part of the queer community as him. That's actually why I didn't want to label how I felt—feel—about you. I've only been with Henry, and I know this might sound ridiculous, but I'm hesitant about being in a straight-passing relationship. Because I'm not straight, no matter who I'm with, and I don't want people to assume I am. I'm proud and happy to be bi. I mean, my parents threw me a coming out party in middle school with pink, blue, and purple balloons."

"Your parents sound really cool."

Dylan nods and looks behind me, as Professor Perry walks onstage and more of our classmates take their seats. Class is going to start soon. "Yeah, they're the best."

"I like you." My voice shakes, but I take a breath and continue. "Labels or no labels. And I know you're bi, regardless of the gender of the person who's lucky enough to be with you."

Dylan smiles his perfect half smile. "I like you too."

All through class, our hands brush as we turn our sheet music to the next page. We look at each other out the corner of our eyes.

I play the best I've played all semester that even Professor Perry glances at me with the hint of a delighted smile.

Dylan's cute, and I might want labels with him, but he better watch out.

I'm coming for his chair.

And maybe his heart too.

Movement Thirty-Two

a tempo = "return to the preceding tempo"

After orchestra, I move back into my room at Tom and Kathryn's house, and now mine. I'm pulling out clothes, refolding them, and putting them in my dresser when they knock on my door.

"Welcome back," Kathryn says, as she and Tom sit on the end of my bed. "Can we talk to you for a minute?"

I close my dresser drawer. "Sure."

They glance at one another until Tom's impatience wins out.

"You mean so much to us, Corey." He takes Kathryn's hand with a shaky breath. "We're so happy you're back."

"You're in our band," Kathryn says. "You're a part of this family."

I rock my weight between my heels and my toes, unsure of what to say. I've never thought of being in their family, but then again, I've never had one.

"Zeke too," Kathryn adds. "We don't want either of you to age out of foster care or extended foster care. *We* want you."

"What—" My bottom lip trembles. "What are you saying?"

"We've talked about this for a long time. We aren't sure if this is something you want, but we want to ask you nonetheless." Kathryn gives Tom's hand a squeeze, and they both break out into smiles. "Would you be interested in adult adoption?"

My arms shake, so I cross them and hug myself tight. I'd given up on getting adopted years ago, after the Fitzgerald's of Foster House #4 and then the Phillips's of Foster House #6 sent me packing.

I cross my fingers behind my back. *Please let this be real.*

"Can I think about it?" I ask.

Though I plan to say yes, I need to process this alone. This is the most important thing that's ever happened to me, after all. Even more important than getting accepted to Borns.

They look at each other. Their eyes cloud, but hope remains in their smiles.

"Of course," Tom says. "Take as long as you need."

A tear slides down my cheek. I wipe it away with the back of my hand, hoping they don't see.

"Dinner's almost ready," Kathryn says, pulling me into a hug on their way out. "I made stuffed peppers in the Crock-Pot. I'll call you down in a bit."

When they're halfway down the stairs, I close my door. My vision blurs, though I don't stop the tears this time. I dump the rest of the contents from my borrowed duffle bag onto the bed, and an envelope flutters onto the purple comforter.

The card everyone signed before I left for Borns.

I still haven't read it. I've been saving it—for this moment.

The envelope's edges have crinkled between my clothes, but at least it hasn't torn. I smile at "WE'LL MISS YOU" in Tom's handwriting across the front. I open it and read.

You are pretty and you find me when I run away.
Camila

You're like a sister to me. I'll miss Saturday pancakes, but I'll mostly miss you.
Love, Steven

Thanks for looking out for me. It's cool you're going to college.
Zeke

We see your potential, and I know Borns sees it too. You're talented and capable, and I'm proud you're pursuing your dream. Study hard!
Tom

Just because you won't be living here doesn't mean you're not welcome back anytime and that we aren't here for you. The house won't be the same without you. You'll always be a member of our band.
Remember we're a call away.
You are loved.
Kathryn

By the time I finish reading, I'm sobbed out. I place the card on the nightstand so my tears won't stain it. It comes in at a close second to my violin for my most cherished possession.

I can't believe I had it at the bottom of my duffle bag this whole time. I should've read it when they gave it to me. Maybe I would've realized then that Foster House #11 isn't just another foster house.

It's home.

Because Kathryn and Tom, even Zeke—the people who love me unconditionally—live here. *I* live here. No more sleeping around random couches and campus buildings.

From now on, I'm sleeping in my own bed.

Movement Thirty-Three

virtuoso = "highly skilled performer"

The crowded auditorium makes music of its own in the minutes before our Borns String Orchestra's end-of-the-semester concert. Whispers resound from the occupied chairs. Program pages ruffle as audience members read through tonight's pieces and our names. My name.

Second Chair Violinist and Soloist: Coralee Reed

I asked Professor Perry to include my full name.

We had another round of auditions for the solo piece, and since I got that, Professor Perry promised me a room in Harmony Hall next semester. I'm officially accepted into the music program, thank god.

Though I can't see through the bright stage lights into the darkened auditorium, I picture Tom and Kathryn—my official adoptive parents, my family—sitting in one of the darkened rows beside Drew, with Camila and Nicole between them.

Nicole lives with us now, in Steven's old room, much to my and the entire neighborhood's relief. No one's happier than Camila, though. Tom and Kathryn had been working with Nicole's case manager for weeks before they told us the good news. They said they wanted to tell us sooner but didn't want to get our hopes up if it wasn't a done deal.

I shouldn't have doubted them. But ten other foster parents didn't set a great track record for dependability.

Steven and his mom sit in a row near theirs. They both come by the house every Saturday for pancakes, though Steven swears they come to see me.

Zeke's texting his new art class friends or using his phone as a flashlight to sketch on the back of a program. He's applied to a handful of colleges for art, Borns included. I'm keeping my fingers crossed for him, but he doesn't need luck. He has talent.

And my, Kathryn, and Tom's unconditional support.

A few weeks ago, Tom and Kathryn asked how I felt about them adopting Zeke too, since he doesn't have any family to return to either. They didn't scold me when I said, "Hell yes."

Emma, my best friend and first-ever friend to spend the night in my bedroom at a foster house, sits in one of the dark rows. She's family too.

I smile out into the audience at them. Tom, Kathryn, Drew, Camila, Nicole, Steven, Zeke, and Emma. Before coming to Borns, I just had me and my violin. Now I have all these people who love me, despite my mistakes and miscommunications. Despite my imperfections. People who've proven I deserve second chances.

Dylan fidgets beside me—as he should. We have auditions

for spring semester chair placements next week, and he doesn't stand a chance. I swear on the grave of my old violin case, I'm getting that first chair.

The intensity of the stage lights increases, and Professor Perry walks onto the podium. He bows to the audience, and when he turns back, the orchestra readies their instruments.

The orchestra minus me.

My right hand grips the neck of my violin as I come to the front of the stage. When Professor Perry lifts his arms, I raise my violin to my shoulder. His hands flick down, out, in, up. One, two, three, four.

I tap the tempo with my toes.

On the next downbeat, my agile bow dances across and my racing fingers press into the strings. My violin resonates out into the auditorium and to the people I care about most in the world.

When the rest of the orchestra joins me, a wave of majestic sound washes over the audience. Professor Perry's face turns red with effort, as his arms exaggerate the emotion we're in turn supposed to portray.

I don't have any trouble with that.

At the end of the concert, after walking off and back on stage three times to recognize the audience's standing ovation, I hurry to put my violin in its locker and join my family in the auditorium.

They wait for me near the edge of the stage.

"Corey!"

Steven pulls me into a hug first, followed by Tom and Kathryn. He's a foot taller than he was when I started college.

Not as rail-thin either. Soon, I'll have to reach up to hug him.

"Wasn't she so good, Mom?"

I melt at Steven's voice. Squeeze Tom and Kathryn tighter.

"The band's all here," Kathryn says into my hair. "We're all so proud of you."

I know she doesn't just mean about the concert. She's proud of me as a person too. When they stop hugging me, Tom hands me a bouquet of crocuses and a purple envelope.

I turn over the envelope. "What's this?"

Kathryn grins. "A very, very early birthday gift. Or a late adoption gift, whichever you prefer."

I rip open the envelope and unfold a piece of paper.

> *You're going to summer violin camp! We'll cover all travel, room, and board expenses for you to go to the Juilliard Starling-DeLay Symposium on Violin Studies this summer in New York.*
>
> *You deserve it.*
>
> *Love,*
> *Kathryn and Tom*

No matter how many times I blink at the cursive words, they don't change. "Is this for real?"

Tom hands me a tissue from the pack he had in his pocket, always prepared for the waterworks. Telling by his red eyes, he must've cried during the concert. "You bet."

"You have to apply online and get in, but we researched everything. You'll need two letters of recommendation, from your faculty here, and a video audition." Kathryn gives my shoulder an affirming squeeze. "There are other violin camps too. No matter what, you're going to camp this summer."

Black mascara smears across my white tissue. (I should really invest in the waterproof kind.) I won't be the only college musician who hasn't gone to a music camp anymore.

"Thanks," I say, shoving the used tissue inside the pocket of my black slacks. "For everything."

They pull me into another hug, this time with Camila and Nicole smushed in the middle. Soon, Steven joins the group hug, pulling along a groaning Zeke.

"Coralee!"

I only let one person call me by my full name now.

Dylan weaves through the crowd with his parents and little sister in tow. He's the spitting image of his dad, who has the same lean build and messy hair. Dylan doesn't look much like his mom, though, apart from her fair complexion and bold nail polish choice. Her nails are a bright, electric blue.

Most moms I've known stick to shades of pink, and I've known a lot of moms. I may be a little biased, but Kathryn's the best. She never wears nail polish, but she paints Camila's toes— and Nicole's now too.

"We've heard so much about you," Dylan's mom, Lisa, says. She wraps her arms around me for my fourth hug of the evening. "Nice to finally meet Dylan's girlfriend. Though, I guess we've seen you before, years ago."

Dylan laces his left hand with mine. He gives a squeeze as if to say, "Did you hear that? Girlfriend. You're my girlfriend."

"Nice to see you both too. Again?" I say with a laugh.

Adam, Dylan's dad, nods in greeting. "Exquisite solo performance."

"Thanks to you and Dylan." Now I give Dylan's hand a

squeeze. His calloused left fingertips tickle the back of my hand. "For fixing my violin."

Adam shrugs off my thanks, reminding me again of Dylan. "Oh, that's all Dylan. He could run the shop already."

Tom and Kathryn come over, and Dylan and I introduce our parents. His sister, Holly, who hid behind her parents during our exchange, steps out from behind them to show me the embroidered violin on her dress.

"I'll do one for you, if you want," she says.

"I'd love that."

With Holly's help, Dylan and I convince our parents to all go out for ice cream, and as Kathryn rounds up the kids, someone touches my shoulder.

"That was beautiful." Emma's eyes beam like stage lights. "Do you have a sec? I need to tell you something."

"Of course."

Emma leads the way to some empty chairs in the front row.

"I wanted to tell you as soon as I knew for sure, so we don't repeat when I decided my major."

I smile, thinking of our hall event, How Well Do You Know Your Roommate? But my smile vanishes when Emma says, "I'm transferring sophomore year. Next year."

My stomach drops. I lean over my legs and exhale.

What I think: *Nooo!*

What I say: "I'm happy for you. If that's what you want."

"Oh my gosh, it is." Emma grabs my hand. "St. Bonaventure University, where I'm transferring, has an award-winning student newspaper. *The Bona Venture.*"

"Isn't that school in New York?"

Three states away.

One less from Maddie, though, who I now only keep in

touch with through Instagram comments and DMs.

"We'll text and call and FaceTime. And I'll be home on holidays. Maybe we could drive halfway to meet one another." Emma gives my hand a squeeze. "Still friends?"

This time, I initiate the hug.

Guess I'll have to take Tom up on his offer to give me driving lessons.

"The best."

"At least we'll have one more semester together before next year," Emma says, as we join my family to head out for ice cream —which she never passes up.

Next year.

If spring semester goes as fast as this one, Emma will leave Borns before I know it. At least I'll have Dylan. But who will go to the Brew with me on the off hours? Or make me eat dessert as a meal? Or study with me in the library?

Next year can't be that bad, though. No way it could possibly be worse.

Right?

Before I can think up worst-case scenarios, Kathryn hugs me to her side as we walk out of Bewley Hall and to the car. No matter what happens next year, I have her and Tom and a bed at Foster House #11.

My home.

Corey's Music Definitions

Clark, Mary Elizabeth. *The Clark New Pocket Music Dictionary: A Compact, Comprehensive Guide to Music*. Edward Schuberth & Co., Inc., 1979.

Niles, Laurie. "The Violinist.com Glossary of Violin-Related Terms." Violinist.com, 2012.

Corey's Playlist

1. "Flight of the Bumblebee" by Nikolai Rimsky-Korsakov, Isaac Stern, Milton Katims, Columbia Symphony Orchestra
2. "The Lark Ascending" by Ralph Vaughan Williams, Hilary Hahn, London Symphony Orchestra, Sir Colin Davis
3. *The Planets, Op. 32: 2. Venus, The Bringer of Peace* by Gustav Holst, Chicago Symphony Orchestra, James Levine
4. *Sonata for Violin Solos No. 1 in G Minor* by Johann Sebastian Bach, Hilary Hahn
5. *Water Music, Suite 1 in F, HWV 348: 5. Air* by George Frideric Handel, The English Concert, Trevor Pinnock
6. *Serenade for Strings in C Major, Op. 48: II. Walzer: Moderato, tempo di valse* by Pyotr Ilyich Tchaikovsky, Moscow Soloists, Yuri Bashmet
7. *Holberg Suite for String Orchestra, Op. 40; V Rigaudon* by Edvard Grieg, Jan Bjøranger, 1B1
8. "House of Bach" by Ezinma
9. "Alone" by Marshmello, Bond
10. "Dreamer" by Black Violin
11. "positions" by Vitamin String Quartet

Corey's Essay "Foster Care's Broken but Not Me"

Works Cited

Johnson, Lisa; Slayter, Elspeth; and Livingstone, Allyson. "Locating the Intersections of Disability, Race and Ethnicity in Adoption Rates among Foster Children Introduction." *Adoption Quarterly*, 2020.

O'Neale, Shalita. "Foster Care and Homelessness." *Foster Focus*, 2015.

Wiltz, Teresa. "For Foster Care Kids, College Degrees Are Elusive." The Pew Charitable Trusts, 2017.

Thank you to the many foster care organizations for their education and advocacy—including the National Foster Youth Institute, Music Is Unity, and my local nonprofits HumanKind and People Places, Inc.

Acknowledgements

First, eternal gratitude to the boy who shared his iPod with me on the school bus junior year and the man who starts dance parties in our car. The love of my life, my best friend, my biggest fan—Kelvin. You fill my life with music. (And thanks for making sure I eat when I'm writing.)

I couldn't have finished this novel without my writing companions, Osito and Piñita. Thanks for keeping my feet warm and licking my face when I cry.

Mom, Dad, Susan, and Allison: I cherish my childhood memories with you on our hill. Thank you for encouraging my imagination back then and today.

Thank you, Mrs. Deeds, my third grade teacher, for telling me I could write a book. You were right! Fingers crossed this one's better than the one I wrote and read to our class.

Many thanks to the people who helped shape this story: my sensitivity readers; my beta readers—especially Adrienne, Allison, Brooke, Courtney, Gillian, Jamie, and Madison; my writing group (shoutout to fellow indie author Tamara Shoemaker who went to NYC with me for the Writer's Digest Conference, where I first pitched *Sleeping Around*); my beyond supportive and talented launch team— Ally, Aspasia, Becky, Cecilia, Jasmine, Mandy, Mika, and Xee; my advanced readers; and my editor Kate Sederstorm, who made this book better in every way.

Last (and best of all, haha), thank you to me. For researching into the night, for not giving up after rewriting the story three times. Oh, Sunflower, you've worked so hard for this. Don't forget to enjoy it.

About the Author

Morgan Vega earned her BA in English from Bridgewater College and MA in Writing, Rhetoric & Technical Communication from James Madison University. She worked in higher education for seven years before transitioning into the publishing industry. Morgan interned at Kore Press, worked as an editor at Scarsdale Publishing, and now does marketing for No Starch Press.

Morgan grew up and lives in the Shenandoah Valley in Virginia. When she's not writing, Morgan's freelance editing and talking about books on social media. *Sleeping Around* is her debut novel.

Visit her website morganvega.com, subscribe to her YouTube channel Morgan Vega, and follow her on social media at @MorganVegaWrite.

CPSIA information can be obtained
at www.ICGtesting.com
Printed in the USA
LVHW021528250721
693626LV00013B/1470